Stella Duffy was born in Londo[...] Zealand. She has written three [...] Saz Martin: *Calendar Girl, Wave[...] [...] Blonde*, also published by Serpent's Tail. She has written two other novels, *Singling Out The Couples* and *Eating Cake*, many short stories, several articles, two one-woman shows and, most recently, a stage play for Steam Industry, *crocodiles and bears*.

She is also an actor, improvisor, comedian, and occasional radio presenter. She now lives in London.

FRESH
FLESH

Stella Duffy

Library of Congress Catalog Card Number: 99–63374

A complete catalogue record for this book can be
obtained from the British Library on request

First published in 1999 by Serpent's Tail,
4 Blackstock Mews, London N4 2BT
website: www.serpentstail.com

Set in Century Book by Intype London Ltd
Printed in Great Britain by Mackays of Chatham plc,
Chatham, Kent

10 9 8 7 6 5 4 3 2 1

for Yvonne Baker
with love

Thanks to:
the mothering advisory service – Maki, Sarah, Janet, Esther and Jo; Duffy sisters/in-law; Shelley and Yvonne; and Laurence for sunny cordiality, arguably.

ONE

Sara was screaming. Screaming in her head, screaming through every bone and muscle in her body, screaming out loud, dry mouth ripping at the corners of her broken and chapped lips, harsh other voice, not her own voice, pushing through her body, through the pain and into the cold nothing on the other side of her skin. Screaming beyond what she thought she could even bear to hear herself, into her own eardrums, blood pulsing and scratching against the tiny bones, beating a non-stop rhythm. Except the people kept telling her not to make a noise, lined up against her pain, denying the distress. Telling her to concentrate. To breathe. To shut up and just do it. You're not special. Stop it. Stop it right now. It's far too late for that kind of thing. Screaming won't help you now.

They were right. The screaming didn't help. Didn't make the pain go away. Didn't make them go away. But then she couldn't help herself either. Couldn't stop the noise of the great pain, welling up and forcing its way through her. Pushing against them, against the moment, wanting them all away. Not able to believe this was still happening to her, not knowing how it could ever stop. And from far inside the pain and the harsh noise and the searing white light, not wanting it to stop either. Not wanting to move on to the next moment. Pushing against and holding in anyway. And then, despite herself, the last abrasive lament and over and all finished and all done.

They were not used to screaming, wanted their quiet again. They brought the rubber mask back to her face, clamped the sickly gas to her mouth, her nose, no choice but to breathe it in, to take it into her. Arms too weak to push them away, no fight left. Breathe in deep, breathe it all in, there we are, that's it, hush now, good girl, good girl. But she didn't know who the good girl was. It certainly wasn't Sara. Trying not to breathe it in, not to sink back down, but she couldn't scream with the thick black mask over her face, couldn't make it go away either, arms, legs growing limp, drifting away from her, body and head almost held together by a thin ether thread, almost set free. Hush now, that's enough, it's done. Go to sleep, it's nearly over, you'll feel better when it's over. But Sara didn't want to sleep, didn't want to be put away, didn't want it to be over.

And then it was dark and Sara woke with pins and needles stabbing half-sleeping feet and arms, twisted sweating in thin sheets, lumpen pillow bunched under one shoulder. She came to in the sterile night, back in bed, quiet room, five others deep sleeping around her, breathing slowly through the aching dark, the three o'clock Town Hall chimed atonal in the distance. She lay still, empty and hurting, body beaten and bruised, vomit retching through her scream-ripped throat, up and into the plastic bowl by her head, bloody vomit, bloody bed. She wiped her face on the rough sleeve of the regulation nightdress, laid her aching body out in the silence and cried herself back to sleep, dry tears smothering her pillow.

TWO

Saz Martin ran through a summer shower, short breaths of cool morning air stabbing the back of her throat. She crossed the road from the Heath, turned the last painful half mile uphill, took another left turn and slowed to a jogging walk around the corner of the big old house, three ugly wheelie bins lined up as testimony to the London tradition of house conversion. She walked up the last four stairs to the flat, fumbled in her zipped pocket for her house keys, managed to drop them almost immediately, bent down to pick them up again, ripped the wailing Neil Young from her ears and heard the phone ringing from inside.

"Shit, fuck, shit, damn it, fuck."

Her agitated fingers then dropped the walkman and it clattered down the concrete stairs behind her. She chose to ignore the sound of splintering plastic. Eventually she twisted all three keys into each of the correct locks and flew into the flat, slammed open the kitchen door and reached for the phone past two dirty coffee mugs and a barely touched bowl of soggy muesli. "Hello?"

"Any news?"

"Oh fuck, Carrie, it's you."

"Great reception, thanks. Now if I were you and I had been given this opportunity to realize that my oldest and dearest was so concerned for your future and your welfare, not to mention that of your charming girlfriend . . ."

Saz interrupted her ex-girlfriend before she had a chance to get into her stride, "Carrie, I've just got in from my run—"

"Late for you, Richard and Judy are already halfway through their second bottle. I thought you usually ran first thing in the morn—"

"Carrie! Enough. I wanted to be with Molly this morning. I waited to go for my run until she'd left."

"I thought you were going to go to the hospital with her?"

"I thought so too. I was until this morning. Then Molly woke up even more nervous than she was last night and decided she needed to be alone. That's also why I went running so late, we had a huge fight about it this morning. She didn't want me to go with her, wanted to get the news by herself."

"Are you OK?"

"Yes, no, I don't know. I mean, I understand that in many ways this is much harder for her than it is for me . . ."

"It does involve both of you."

"Yes, but fuck, Carrie, it doesn't matter right now. And I don't want to talk about it, not with you."

"Thanks."

"This is between the two of us. And it's passed now too. It's irrelevant. Molly's doing what she wants to do." Saz looked at the kitchen clock, "And she should be on her way home by now, so that means she's done what she wants to do."

"You shouldn't let her take control like this, Saz."

"Carrie, I don't want you slagging off Molly."

"I wasn't slagging her off. I was bolstering you."

"I don't need bolstering thank you. You're not my therapist, you're my ex-lover."

"And tenant."

"More's the pity."

"Illegal tenant."

"And another month overdue with the rent."

Carrie was uncharacteristically silent for a moment.

"That shut you up."

"I'm only trying to help."

"I know."

"Any advance on Chris's parents?"

"No news, Carrie, and no gossip either. Now piss off. I want to check my messages, I want to lock the back door, I want to retrieve my walkman which I dropped while rushing to answer your phone call and which is now either lying in a crumpled minor technological heap at the bottom of the stairs or has no doubt been stolen by any one of the evil local urchins lurking in my back garden."

"They don't do evil urchins in your part of the world, Saz, they do designer babes, accessory children. You should know."

"Carrie, will you please get off the fucking phone? I'll tell you as soon as I hear anything. OK?"

"Fine, whatever, but make sure you call me first. Bye!"

Carrie hung up as cheerfully as she had called and Saz went outside to pick up the detritus of her morning's run. She collected her walkman, bruised and slightly battered, but not broken, from the bottom of the steps leading up to their flat, locked the door behind her and went into the lounge. There were three messages on the answerphone, one from her mother and one from her sister, Cassie, both urgently asking if there was any news.

The third was from Molly, "Hi babe. I'm sorry about this morning. I know you wanted to come with me. I just . . . oh whatever, of course I know what you want and you know I wanted to be by myself to do this. Anyway, I'm on my way home now. I'm OK, but I want to talk to you in the flesh, not leave a message, I don't want to do this on the phone. I'll be home soon."

Saz's stomach turned, tight intestinal coil pushing out against the worked-on torso, old burn scars covering clearly delineated muscles, body flinching, preparing itself for whatever blow was about to land on her. She slammed off the machine, furious with Molly for not leaving her a full message, dying to see her girlfriend and hating the fact that she had no choice but to wait.

For the next forty minutes Saz paced the big, airy flat. She washed the barely used breakfast dishes from a meal that had been more argument than nourishment and then made herself a pot of too strong coffee she couldn't drink. She tidied up the clothes that had made their scrambled way all over their bedroom floor and then returned to the kitchen where she took a bite from a fat danish she couldn't even chew, let alone swallow. She made their bed, opened curtains and windows, moved flowers around from one vase to another and ran a foaming oils bath she would leave to go cold. She glanced at three different newspapers, turning two pages at once and not reading any of them, and flicked through half a dozen cable TV channels. All the while she was checking clocks, her watch, and calling Molly's number every five minutes. Molly's mobile remained resolutely switched off. Finally she heard a key in the door, ran to the hall holding her breath.

"Moll?"

She ran up to her lover, scanned her face, every muscle in her body aching with the tension of needing to know.

Molly stood a foot from her and nodded, arms out to hold her girlfriend, "Yes. It's yes, Saz."

Saz burst into tears.

THREE

Saz pulled Molly into the flat, slammed the heavy wooden door behind them, held her lover tight to make the new words real, to make the new truth felt as well as known. Held her as tight as she could while also suddenly feeling that the woman she was holding was now made of translucent fine bone china, "Oh God."

Molly nodded, "I know, it's bloody terrifying."

"It's fucking fantastic."

"That too."

The two women stood rooted to the spot in the sunny hallway, the enormity of the news hitting them both, planting their feet on the smooth wooden floor. They stared at each other for a moment and then Saz spoke aloud what neither had been brave enough to even whisper for the past couple of months, except for dark minutes in the quiet of the night, except alone to herself in the bath, in the empty flat – with loud music in the background drowning out the fear, "Oh my God, Moll. You're going to be a mother."

Molly shook her head. "We're going to be mothers Saz."

"Christ, we must be grownups."

The two women slowly moved through to the lounge, the morning showers gone, sun was now pouring through the long windows lining one wall of the room, twenty degree light burning off the damp London morning. Together they sank to the floor and sat for a while in silence, arms around each other, each one contemplating her new, radically changed future. Leaning against the sofa, Saz's head on Molly's shoulder, they looked out the balcony windows to the Heath beyond.

"So, Moll, they're sure that it, the baby, the foetus is – you know . . ."

"Viable?"

"Yeah, viable."

Molly shrugged her shoulders and launched into circumspect doctor speak, "By three months, as long as it has implanted properly—"

"And this has."

"Yeah, it would seem that this one has, and as long as that's all OK, then the rest of the pregnancy should be as per usual. You know, nothing's really certain until the baby is born, we can't take anything for granted until then, but at this stage, from now on, everything ought to just be like any other pregnancy. Normal."

Saz laughed, "Bloody expensive kind of normal, babe."

"Yeah, but worth it."

"Oh yes, very worth it," Saz sat up, the better to kiss Molly, then she drew back to look at her, shook her head in utter astonishment, "God, Moll, we're actually doing it, all that planning, and the clinic and treatments and everything. We're doing it. You're having my baby."

Molly nodded, "Just don't sing me any crap '70s songs. I've made an appointment for the scan next week."

"Brilliant."

"Do you want to call Chris?"

"Don't you?"

Molly shook her head, "No. I don't actually. I thought I would, but now I think you should tell him. As one gene pool to another. And make me a cup of tea while you're at it."

Saz went to put the kettle on and call Chris from the kitchen and Molly stretched herself out on the floor. The morning's fear and nerves and excitement and elation had worn her out, not to mention the nausea she'd woken with. Or the tedious argument they'd been through before she left, determined to do this alone, nervous enough for herself but even more concerned for Saz. Saz's huge desire for this baby, what would inevitably be her major depression if this attempt had also failed like the last one, like the one before that. Molly knew that if there had been bad news to break, she wanted to be the one to tell Saz. A doctor herself, she didn't want to leave it to yet another insensitive white coat. She also knew that if things worked out well she wanted the opportunity to deliver that great news in person.

When Saz came back into the room twenty minutes later she saw Molly sleeping soundly on the floor. She sat beside her and drank the tea herself, watching her girlfriend's rising and falling breath, each exhalation of air clearly delineating the tiny stomach that had grown on the tall, slim woman in the past three months, a stomach that no one else would ever have noticed, a tiny belly that Saz and Molly had laid all their hopes on. For ten minutes Saz was completely lost in the incredible nature of the feat they appeared to have achieved. After a while Molly woke, too uncomfortable on the floor to do more than half sleep in the sunshine.

"What did Chris say?"

Saz laughed, "His exact words were – I would be grateful if the donor of the egg would convey to the keeper of the child the warmest wishes from the donor of the sperm."

"Idiot."

"That's what I said."

"Idiot?"

"No. I called him a fucking tosser. He also invited us over for drinks."

"Good."

"Champagne for him and Marc and me, water for you."

"Great. Can't wait."

"And he asked when we wanted the documentary film crew to come round."

"You told him to piss off?"

"I told him there was nothing to document. What's so unusual about one woman carrying another woman's foetus?"

"Perfectly normal."

"Exactly."

Molly paused a moment and then added, "He didn't really ask that, did he?"

"Whoops, hormones taking over the sense of humour already. No, of course not," Saz hesitated for a minute. "But he did ask if you'd decided about Marc videoing you, though."

"That sounds more likely. Well, I think it's OK, I mean, I don't know about the actual birth, I saw enough of that sort of thing in training to know I think it's a bit naff at the very least and pretty gross at the worst. But the progression of the growing bump, that ought to be fine. I just didn't want to make a decision until we knew how successful this had been."

"They know that."

"I suppose when you do find his birth parents it'll be nice for him to be able to show them the whole story."

"Don't get too excited – if it was that easy, I'd have got it all sussed by now."

"You've barely started. But at least you're not going to be taking world trips and dashing off from me in the middle of the night to hunt his mother down."

"She might have moved away from England."

"I don't care if she has. That's what e-mails are for."

"I'll stick to letters and phone calls thanks."

"Traditionalist."

"Happily."

Molly leaned her weight heavier onto Saz, "You, my little Luddite, are not going anywhere. I want you here with me. We want you here with me."

Saz nodded, aware of the seriousness under Molly's light tone, "I know you do. Don't worry, I'm not going anywhere."

Saz was well aware that Molly had never been easy with her choice of career and worried for her safety. Worries which had good grounding in a basis of unpleasant past events.

Molly smiled, a smile which quickly turned to a smirk, "Well, I don't think you should consider yourself completely tied to me. Right now, for instance, you might just want to pop out and pick me up some ice cream."

"There's some in the freezer."

"No. I finished it in the middle of the night."

Saz groaned, wrenched herself up from Molly's side, "If I'd have known that being pregnant was going to become an excuse for you to turn yourself into a sitcom cliché, I'd never have agreed that you should carry the baby."

"Too late now, babe."

Saz tried another tack to get her out of having to leave the comfort zone, "You'll get fat."

Molly stretched her long lean body in the sunshine on the floor, "That, my darling, is, I believe, the whole point of me being pregnant. No one would notice. Off you go." She waved a regal hand, "A tub each of pistachio, coconut cream, coffee walnut and chocolate chip. And none of that low fat rubbish either."

"Hell no," Saz muttered as she backed out of the door.

"It's hard enough that this kid's going to have four queers for parents, we wouldn't want it growing up to be anorexic as well."

FOUR

Molly first met Chris four years ago at her hospital. Like her, he specialised in child medicine, like her he had often expressed the desire to be a parent, but unlike her he had never felt mature or settled down enough to take that desire seriously. Until he met Marc. Marc worked in the City, was out, was fairly well-off, and was incredibly normal. All the things Chris – mixed-race, adopted at birth into an extremely wealthy family, intensely gay-political from his early teens – was not. It was love at first argument. Two months later Chris moved in with Marc, eighteen months after that they suggested to Saz and Molly that perhaps it was time to start thinking about propagating the species. Not that this was a new thought for Molly and Saz. For some time now they had wanted to do the next thing – the baby making – that couples had done quite naturally and with no need for societal prompting since long before the bible writers got around to deciding God insisted they go forth and multiply. However, unlike the more fortunate women of the biblical myths, Saz and Molly were aware they needed an actual father. In body as well as in spirit – which made things slightly more difficult.

Saz and Molly talked about the suggestion. Molly talked to Chris. Saz talked to Marc. All four talked endlessly about the obstacles, the problems, the difficulties. Put off making a decision until more information could be garnered. Thought long and hard about what they were planning to do until they'd thought it out so much it seemed an impossible leap. Too difficult, too complicated and just something they might have to turn away from – great idea, too bloody hard to enact. Until Saz's cousin, still living in a hostel with their two year old, announced her second pregnancy at nineteen, and both Saz and Molly finally realized that if the kids could make babies with so little thought, then surely they could at least attempt the same with four adults, four incomes, two homes and, not to put too twee a point on it, a whole lot of love. They invited the boys over for dinner and spent the evening discussing how and when and who and, not least by any means, all the legal implications involved. Three months later everything had been agreed and the long technical process of creating life could begin.

After all, as Chris so delicately put it, "Face it, girls, your eggs aren't getting any younger."

Molly was to give birth to Saz's baby. It was an expensive and invasive process, but by carrying Saz's egg fertilized with Chris's sperm, all three would be intimately involved in the process. Because of the extensive burn scarring Saz had suffered some years earlier, it would be safer and healthier for Molly to carry the baby anyway. Also, Molly, with a proper job in a real hospital, was able to claim great care from her own system and extensive maternity benefits. Saz had no such benefits in her self-employed status. With Molly carrying Saz's baby, both women would to a degree be biological mothers, though only one had provided the necessary genes. Molly liaised through medical colleagues and eventually found a clinic willing to take them on – for an exorbitant fee, of course. Chris and Marc offered to pay but both Saz and Molly felt that was asking far too much, so the two women pooled all the resources they had ever had, came up with the necessary funds and prayed the treatment would work first time. Meanwhile they found a very co-operative lawyer and drew up an incredibly complicated contract. And, as they knew the contract would not be legally binding should either of the birth parents ever change their minds, all four of them signed their copies with copious promises to never fall out. And silent prayers that they were doing the right thing.

Saz went through the difficult egg extraction process, Chris and Marc took care of the somewhat less difficult sperm extraction themselves, and the first fertilized embryo was implanted. All four held their breath in hope. Molly miscarried at five and a half weeks. Though it was such a short time and though they had been prepared for this possibility, there was still a feeling of great sadness, especially horrible for Molly and also strangely difficult for Saz who, though she was not experiencing the same hormonal changes as Molly, was nevertheless undergoing a very real vicarious process of becoming-mother. The second attempt also ended in disappointment.

After another awful night of tears and disillusionment, Molly and Saz agreed they would try only two more times. It meant they were half way through the possible. At one month it looked like everything was fine, but it would take until the third month, first place of safety for any pregnancy, but so much more so for this one, until they would begin to speak of the foetus as a baby and Molly's obstetrician would allow them to hope in earnest.

Meanwhile Chris asked to speak to Saz.
"It's about business. About my mother."

"She's making a fuss about the baby?"

"Hell no, she couldn't be happier. Like us, she's just waiting until we all know it's OK. No, I meant my birth mother, I think I'd like to try and find her."

Chris had always known he was adopted, growing up mixed-race with white parents, he could hardly have missed it, and anyway, his parents had always been very open about the fact they'd adopted him when the youngest of their own children was ten and they missed having a small person about the house. Chris, though, had always maintained a complete lack of interest in his blood parentage, so Saz was stunned to hear he'd changed his mind.

"I thought you didn't want to know."

"I didn't. And now I do. Maybe it's thinking about being a father myself. Or just that we've been talking about all the implications of parenting for so bloody long that it's sparked my interest. I can't really say. I just know I feel different now."

"I don't know if I'm the best person to do this for you, it's not something I know much about – and I am sort of personally involved. Shouldn't you contact an agency or something?"

Chris shook his head. "I've thought about that. But I don't want my real mum – I mean my adoptive mother – to know I'm looking. Much as she's always been really honest with me, I still think it might hurt her if I told her I was starting to look. And I suppose an agency might want to contact her, find out what she remembers, what my dad knew."

"They couldn't if you told them not to."

"Maybe, but it's also I'd just rather it was you. Because you're personally involved. You and Molly have become our best friends. I trust you. I never cared about my birth parents before and now this wanting to know has kind of thrown me. I guess I think you'll be more delicate, more careful."

Saz laughed, "I'll try, but I wouldn't go round saying how delicate I am in front of Molly, that's about the last thing she thinks of me as."

Six weeks later Molly came home alone from the hospital and announced the great news and Saz realized that, like Chris, she too had become a little interested in the genetic history of her baby. It was time she launched herself into more direct action on the birth-parent front.

FIVE

Chris's father had died three years previously and his mother, wanting to be nearer to Chris and Marc with whom she got on brilliantly, and slightly further away from her oldest daughter Anna, with whom she had a somewhat less enviable relationship, had sold their massive family home in Surrey and relocated to a more manageable house in Wimbledon. Saz took the opportunity of Mrs Marquand's annual summer holiday with her middle son in Edinburgh to spend a day going through the family archives. According to Chris, his mother was the tidiest woman in England and the move from country to town had simply enabled her to be even more so.

"I love the woman dearly, Saz, but she's an order fanatic. I grew up in a nine bedroom house and we never once had a cleaner. God knows, they could have afforded half a dozen, but she never wanted one. My mother actually likes all that dusting and polishing stuff. More than that though, she likes filing things away. Absolutely fucking loves it."

Chris wasn't wrong. The entire attic of the Wimbledon house, originally converted into a spacious study by the previous owners, was now the repository of four six-drawer filing cabinets, one each for Chris and his three older siblings. Each drawer was stuffed with files, every one of them labelled by both date and category. It took Saz less than five minutes to locate all thirteen of Chris's school reports.

"God, this is amazing. A bit bloody weird, but it's fantastic as well. And she's always been like this?"

"Yeah, it was bloody useful when I was little. Other kids had to tidy their own rooms and their mothers were always yelling at them to pick up their toys, that sort of thing."

"Not you?"

"Nope. Mummy did it. She said it made her happy."

"Spoilt little brat. I hope you learnt to look after yourself eventually."

Chris grinned, "I think I have. Mind you, I'm not sure Marc agrees."

Saz pointed to a pile of boxes stacked against the far wall, "What's that lot?"

"My dad's things. She hasn't sorted his stuff yet. I'm not sure she wants to, it would be too much like admitting he was gone."

"How long were they married?"

"Forty-eight years."

"Bloody hell!"

"Yeah, and every single one of them happy."

"Really?"

"Afraid so. Perfect marriage."

"No such thing."

Chris shrugged, "Whatever. They always looked pretty bloody happy to me. Anyway, everything was kept in boxes at the old house and she used to get so pissed off whenever we came round and wanted something, left it in a mess or whatever, that she devised this new filing system when she moved everything to London."

"Didn't any of you want to keep your own stuff?"

"And deprive our mother of hours of pleasurable activity? You are a hard hearted bitch at times, Saz."

Saz ignored him and carried on, "And the filing cabinets work better than boxes?"

"They certainly stop Anna tipping everything upside down to get at her baby photos and then just throwing it all back in any old how."

"Maybe she does it to keep your mother busy. Perhaps she thinks she's being nice."

"Not Anna. She does actually do things to piss Mum off."

"Thought you said you were a perfect family?"

"No. I said my parents were the perfect couple. Not quite the same thing. Actually, I don't think Anna's ever forgiven them for getting me."

"Your parents?"

"Mmm. When I came along, it meant she wasn't the baby any more."

"So doesn't she get on with you either?"

"Hell no, Anna adores me, she's ten years older than I am, it was like having her own personal doll. No, it's my mother Anna has the problem with. Anna didn't mind getting me as a toy, she just also wanted to be the most special at the same time. Always has."

Saz shrugged, thinking that perhaps the ten-year-old Anna probably had a point. She then made a beeline for the as yet un-filed boxes. Not only was a conversation on best child-rearing practices not going to shed any new light on Chris's parentage, but it also left her feeling woefully unprepared as a mother-to-be. She resolved to buy some parenting books as soon as possible. That or watch *The Waltons* more often. Chris left her alone in the attic while he returned to the hospital and Saz worked on through the long, hot afternoon.

When Chris returned to pick her up several hours later, Saz had a selection of papers to go through with him. They went downstairs to the wide south-facing garden and over a couple of very strong gin and tonics, Saz explained her findings to Chris.

"OK, there's half a dozen letters from your father's solicitor – Richard Leyton. Do you know him?"

"Why?"

Saz put the letter to one side, "I'm not sure. But you were born in '63, weren't you?"

"Yeah, March."

"Right, well it's not as if there were loads of lawyer stuff but, given that I only found about twelve letters from Leyton in total, and of that lot four of them were dated early '63, and they are the most circuitous, non-specific legal-speak letters I've ever come across—"

"You think he might have helped arrange the adoption?"

"Yeah, maybe. He was your father's solicitor, no reason for him not to, I guess. And obviously, it's not a lot to go on, but in two of these letters he makes references to 'the acquisition', and in one of the others he refers to 'the arrangement'. Could be you, it's not as if they were pretending you were theirs in the first place."

"Christ, it sounds like a bloody purchase."

"That's just the terms they use. Of course, it could just be crap legal speak, but given they've got the right date, I think it's worth looking into. Do you think I could get to speak to him?"

Chris shook his head, "Dead and buried, I'm afraid. His daughter took over the practice a couple of years ago."

"OK. Well, maybe I'll check her out. Leyton must have kept some record of what he did for your father and she can't have been completely ignorant about his business if she knew enough to take it over. Maybe she'll be able to tell us something."

"You'll be pushing it to get any secrets."

"Yeah, but we're a damn sight more likely to get something out of a younger woman than an old bloke."

"Fair enough. You're welcome to try. I think I've got a number for her somewhere. So what else did you find?"

"Not a whole lot really. Some letters from your dad to your mum, which certainly refer to the new baby – you, that is – but they don't give anything away about the birth parents."

"They may not have known anything."

Saz nodded, started to speak, briefly thought better of it, and then opened her mouth anyway, "You could ask her, you know, Chris."

Chris looked away, "No, I couldn't."

"Yes, but it would really help even if we only find out that your mother knows nothing. At least we'll know where we're starting from."

Chris kept his gaze firmly on the blackbird digging worms from the lawn, "No, Saz."

Saz waited a moment, realized she wasn't going to get any further just yet and then carried on, "Whatever you want. There's a letter to Leyton about changing your father's will to accommodate you as well. And there's this. Do you know who the people are?"

Saz handed Chris an old black and white ten by eight.

He looked at the photo and smiled, "This is my christening."

"Is that your mother holding you?"

"Yeah. My dad behind her. These three on his left are the other kids. That's Anna, glaring at my mum for hogging me. My father's brother and his wife, my mother's mother. Oh, and this must be a young Richard Leyton. Well, fairly young. I only ever met him a couple of times in my teens and he always seemed old as fuck, very serious. And that's it. I've got no idea who these two are, or the other kid."

Chris was pointing at a couple on the far right of the group, a small boy of maybe three or four hanging on to the woman's arm.

"Not relatives?"

"Not ones I recognize."

"Good. All we need to do is find out who they are then."

"Ah, Saz, I hate to say this. But I don't think either of them are going to turn out to be birth mummy or daddy."

"You don't know that."

"They're white, Saz."

"Yes, Chris, I noticed. And white people fuck black people and make black babies. Or brown babies. Not white babies anyway. It's why the neo-Nazi fuckwits are not only complete morons, but they're also shit out of luck. That's just the way the world's going anyway."

"Good point."

"But I wasn't actually thinking either of them might be your parents. It would have taken a great deal of enlightenment to invite your birth parents to your christening and I doubt if even your mum and dad were that groovy. But as these people were there, and you can't have been more than a couple of months old, maybe they know something. They certainly would have known you were adopted."

"So how do we find them?"

"I don't know. Tell your mum I was getting broody and wanted to see some old family photos."

Chris glared at her.

"OK. Don't talk to your mother. Tell Anna you remember playing with this little boy when you were a bit older, but you can't remember his name now. Take it to this Leyton woman and see if she knows who it is, say you can't remember your dad's mate's name but wanted to get in contact now he's died. Ask a picture researcher to help you locate your mother's long-lost ex-boyfriend for her seventieth birthday present. Whatever, just make it up as you go along. That's what I always do."

"I think you mean lie, Saz."

"Yes, Chris, I think I probably do."

SIX

Chris and Saz left his mother's house and travelled north against the traffic to meet up with their partners for dinner. Molly was already waiting when they arrived, her feet up on the seat opposite, one bowl of olive pips in front of her, the waiter just bringing another bowl, this time with extra bread.

Saz kissed her girlfriend as she sat down, "Bit peckish?"

"Bit pregnant. Any news?"

Saz and Chris brought her up to date with the parent search and she in turn answered their pregnancy questions. Yes, she was well. Just as well as she had been that morning when she'd left for work. As well, in fact, as she had been when she'd last seen Chris at the hospital only three hours earlier. No, nothing exciting had happened in the intervening period. It still wasn't really moving yet. Nothing that couldn't more likely be attributed to normal digestion anyway. And finally, wasn't there something more exciting to talk about than the fact that she was three months' pregnant and nobody noticed anyway, certainly not the inconsiderate bastards who had no intention of giving up their seats to her on the tube?

"Moll, that's because you still look so tall and thin and gorgeous."

"That's very sweet of you, babe, and I'm delighted to say, probably true. Now get that bloody waiter over here so we can order. If Marc insists on working late, he's perfectly welcome to eat late too. I don't see why we have to suffer as well."

By the time Marc arrived from his office, managing to look penitent, harassed and beautiful at the same time, Molly had just about finished her first course and was waiting hungrily for her main, Saz and Chris were starting on their second bottle of wine and all three were studying the photo of the christening, hoping that their own baby might look quite so angelic at the same age. Marc picked up the photo, looked at it for a moment, smiled at the sight of his boyfriend as a baby and then, in the same breath as he asked for a rare tuna steak, inquired why Gerald Freeman had been at the christening.

Saz spluttered on her glass of wine, "Who?"

"Gerald Freeman. Big businessman."

Molly shook her head and grabbed a couple of chips from Saz's plate. "Dead businessman."

Saz grabbed the photo from Marc. "You know who this bloke is?"

"Yes, Saz. As would any other person in the whole of Britain who had even a passing acquaintance with the financial life of this country."

"Chris didn't recognize him either."

Chris smiled and poured the last of the wine for Marc, "I have a passing acquaintance with Marc. That's plenty of intimacy with the City for me, thank you."

Over their third bottle of wine, Marc filled them in on details about Gerald Freeman. Eventually only Saz was left listening, Chris and Molly deep in discussion about one of their colleagues whose new orthopaedic techniques were marginally more interesting than Marc's account of Gerald Freeman's rise to fame and fortune.

Finally Saz interrupted him, "Um, Marc? Freeman's great career in plastics is all very well, but what about the kid?"

"What about him?"

"Maybe the kid knows something about Chris's family."

"Why should he?"

"Why shouldn't he? I'm grasping at straws here, but it's all we've got. I might as well get in touch with him if I can, see if he does remember anything." She turned to Chris, "Your parents were white, you're black. Even to a four-year-old, it might have seemed a bit memorable – the early '60s were hardly a hotbed of racial integration."

Marc frowned, "Well, you could try. I doubt you'll find him easy to get anything out of though."

"Why?"

"God, Saz, do you really not read the Sunday newspapers?"

"No, Marc, I really don't read any of the rubbish they write about how well the offspring of the rich and famous are doing, thanks to Mummy and Daddy's connections. Who did this boy grow up to be? William Hague?"

"Patrick Sweeney."

"The chef? The shouting one?"

"The very same. Bloody good cook though."

"Why'd he change his name?"

"Perhaps he didn't want anyone to think he became rich and famous by trading on Mummy and Daddy's connections?"

"Yes, thank you. Right, well, you boys had better get the bill for tonight then, I've got a feeling my next dinner out is going to be a damn sight more expensive than this."

Patrick Sweeney was a forty-year-old success story. Only child to Sir Gerald Freeman, wealthy industrialist of the

sort often cited in Sunday supplements as the cream of
the crop. Patrick's mother had died when he was just eight
years old and since then his father had groomed him to
take over the family business. He bitterly disappointed the
dynastically ambitious Sir Gerald, however, when at
eighteen he turned his back on the planned business degree
and his great expectations in plastics, and started work
instead as a trainee chef in one of the capital's tackier hotel
kitchens. Patrick changed his name to avoid suggestions
he was trading on his father's fame and became a career
dishwasher. Eight years later, by dint of a brilliant left hand
with a pot scrubber, an enviable ability to imbibe vast quantities of hard alcohol and harder drugs to all hours and still
emerge chirpy enough to fight market traders at four-thirty
in the morning, he was running his own kitchen and featu-
ring rather more often in the Sunday supplements than his
own father. He cleverly eschewed the tumult of television
offers coming at him from all sides until he was finally
offered a vehicle with himself both as star and executive
producer – and therefore holder of absolute power – and
then the money really started rolling in. He bought his first
restaurant at thirty-two, all with his own hard-earned cash
and then, at thirty-four he finally agreed to discuss business
with his father. Three months later the second generation
Freeman industry was born.

Thanks to Marc's intervention, Saz now knew all she
cared to know about Patrick Sweeney's brilliant career.
None of it, though, was likely to get her an interview with
the notoriously difficult chef. From what little she knew
about his personal myth, a request to help her look into a
friend's parentage, just because he happened to feature in
an old photo, was likely to get her nowhere. Fast. She'd
need to go to him with something juicier than that.

It was Molly who suggested an alternative. Her appetite finally sated, she eventually came to bed after devouring half a packet of fig rolls when they got home from the restaurant.

"You're not going to sleep tonight, are you, babe?"

"Not until I work out how to get to meet this Patrick, no."

"Are you going to ask Gary to check up on Chris?"

"Yeah, I was going to call him in the morning."

"Then ask him about the Freemans too."

"Why?"

"Oh, I don't know, bribery, corruption, any of those things you're so good at."

"Thank you."

"You're welcome. I mean, come on, there must be something odd about them. Marc seems to think they're this amazing dynasty of successes. And quite frankly, there's nothing that makes me more suspicious than a big success. Got to be something bad in there somewhere."

"You, my darling, are a wicked cynic."

"But I'm probably right."

"Probably. So what do I do once I have this bribe-worthy information?"

"Give Patrick a call, have a little chat, threaten to reveal his mother was once a man—"

"Very likely."

"Shut up, I'm telling you how to do your job. Then Patrick says of course he remembers every detail of Chris's christening and yes, his father did happen to leave Chris's birth parents' names and addresses on his death bed, you get the info and Bob's your uncle."

"And Janet and John are Chris's parents."

"Something like that, yes. And now that's sorted, do you think you can relax enough to allow me to get to sleep?"

"I'll give it a go."

"Good. We mothers need our rest, you know."

Saz lay still, listening as Molly's breathing slowed to sleep rate. She would call Gary in the morning, but it was more a gesture than anything else, she didn't expect any major revelations from her friend at St Catherine's House. She was pinning those hopes on the visit to Richard Leyton's daughter she had planned for the afternoon. She lay in the quiet dark and tried very hard not to fidget and disturb Molly, waiting for the night's alcohol intake to do its work and calm her racing brain enough to allow welcome sleep. Tired overtook tension at two in the morning. Four hours later she got up for her run.

SEVEN

Gary was Saz's sister's ex-boyfriend. So ex, in fact, that Cassie couldn't remember the last time she had seen him, let alone why they had broken up, though if pushed she might have dredged up an image of someone never content with almost happy if abjectly depressed would do. A fairly unsuccessful actor for the past ten years, Gary had recently expanded his repertoire of angry young men to include a few slightly less angry older men. Not enough of an expansion though, to guarantee him any more than the maximum one episode of *The Bill* and two fringe plays a year. Following his last blistering *Time Out* review – "Perfectly adequate if you really want to go all the way to Battersea for a very dull production of one of Harvey's early plays" – he was now back to his regular job at St Catherine's House. Though Gary had worked on and off for years registering deaths, he also knew a little about births. That and rather a lot more about illegal data retrieval. Though not without some persuasion.

"Saz, it would be a very bad thing for me to look up Patrick Freeman."

"No, it wouldn't. It's not really wicked. I could even do it myself, you just have faster access."

"And further access, you know that."

"I know, but I'm only asking you to check birth certificates – though of course if anything else does turn up—"

"You'd like to know?"

"Well, there'd be no point in you keeping it to yourself, would there? You know, his parents' names, addresses and National Insurance numbers aren't exactly going to be of huge interest to you."

"Saz, the birth certificate doesn't necessarily tell you anything."

"Tells you who the parents are."

"Not always. If he was adopted like your friend, in that case the parents could always lie."

"What?"

"The kid could be registered in London by the mother on one day, taken away and registered in Liverpool by completely different people the next."

"Really?"

"Really."

Saz was not impressed, she'd been hoping for something slightly more concrete, "OK, well then . . . I don't know. But I guess if anyone who's registering a birth might be lying, then it doesn't really matter what information you get for me, does it?"

"You're not going to be put off, are you?"

"Look, Gary, I'm honestly only really interested in anything you can get me on Chris, he's my job, and I do have his permission. This Patrick Freeman idea is just a wild card."

Gary laughed, "Are you trying to tell me you've got a hunch, Saz?"

"Fuck no, you know I'm nowhere near that clever. I just figured I might as well try to get what I can while I've got you on the phone. And remember, I did go all the way to Battersea to see you in that play."

"True. In that case I do owe you. I'll see what I can do. Give me a call tomorrow morning and maybe I'll have something for you."

"Gary, you're an angel."

"No, Saz, for you, I'm a criminal."

"So you are. And I'm very grateful."

Saz hung up, delighted her wheedling skills were so successful. Now for Georgina Leyton.

Saz only knew one solicitor personally – her pisshead friend Claire, who had become a lawyer rather more by accident than intent, and still didn't know how to behave in front of her own mother, let alone an important client. Other than Claire though, Saz imagined all other solicitors to be anal retentive paranoids living in dark, cramped offices surrounded by boxes of mouldy files that hadn't been touched for years, sad obsessives who'd be delighted to have the chance to rifle through their old papers for anything that might be of use, welcoming the breath of fresh air that a young, new face brought into their otherwise dusty lives.

Not this one. Georgina Leyton worked in a mid-sky oasis of big money and fine design, on the tenth floor of a new building at the south edge of Regent's Park. The view from the reception area was of smooth green, the hot and sticky city kept safe behind floor to ceiling windows. The office was silently air-conditioned to a temperature just below that which was comfortable on Saz's bare arms. Clearly Georgina Leyton's clients didn't wander summertime London in thin T-shirts. The whole floor was taken up with just one large central reception area and six individual offices leading from it in a semi-circular, no doubt feng shui'd, arrangement. Far from dusty and dank, this particular shrine to wealth was cool, airy and calm. Although not exactly welcoming. Not without an appointment, anyway.

The receptionist was polite enough when she walked in, but he evidently didn't appreciate unexpected visitors arriving, messing up his perfect appointments schedule. After a whispered telephone conversation, he looked at Saz, over-arched eyebrows indicating his surprise that she'd even been let into the building, let alone that his boss had agreed to see her.

"Ms Leyton wasn't expecting you?"

"No. I just popped in. Thought it might be easier this way."

Actually Saz had thought it might be easier to surprise Georgina Leyton, rather than call ahead and ask for the privileged information she knew wasn't likely to be forth-coming. At least this way Georgina Leyton might have to fob her off in person as opposed to getting her receptionist to do so.

Adam, the non-smiling receptionist, wasn't impressed, "Yes, of course. Anyway, as this is evidently such an important issue . . ." He left the rest of the sentence hanging in mid-air just long enough to indicate how much she was pissing him off, and then he directed her down the short corridor to a large office on the left. It was clear Saz hadn't made a new friend.

The woman who greeted her at the office door was small, thin and depressingly perfect. Though an inch or two shorter than Saz, her four-inch heels and designer suit contrived to give the appearance of legs that seemed to make it all the way up to somewhere past Saz's shoulders. Her sleek hair was cut into a classic symmetrical bob, dyed darkest blue-black, her chiselled cheek-bones and sheer brows fighting against the shining hair for supremacy in the severe-but-bloody-gorgeous stakes. Georgina Leyton was wearing a black linen suit that emphasized every fine inch of her miniature catwalk body and managed to look perfectly respectable while at the same time suggesting more than a hint of eminent shaggability. Her french-manicured nails were long and flawless, her jewellery understated but elegant, and the scent of Thierry Mugler's "Angel" wafting from her body was still as clean, clear – and expensive – as it must have been when she put it on at seven that morning. Georgina was beautiful, relaxed and in control. Saz was not. She tried to put her innate distrust of the rich to one side, tried hard to take Georgina Leyton at face value and not judge the woman by her accent and clothes, by the ease with which she clearly inhabited her own wealth. But her attempts at fairness were impossible. Saz loathed the woman on sight. Not the best of attitudes with which to start a begging interview.

And not the best of begging interviews either. Maybe Georgina Leyton really and truly did care about the binding requirements that meant her father's papers had to remain totally confidential. Maybe it was Saz's fault for making a snap judgement and deciding Georgina was going to be difficult the minute she set eyes on her, thereby setting herself up for a hard time. Whatever the cause, Georgina Leyton wasn't giving anything away.

"I'm sorry, Ms Martin, I do understand your client's predicament, but there really isn't anything I can do."

"Don't you know anything about it?"

"About my father's practice when I was a newborn baby? No, Ms Martin, I don't."

Saz checked her itchy slapping hand and forced a smile, "No. Sorry. I didn't mean that, of course you wouldn't know about Chris's adoption. I meant, maybe you've looked through your father's stuff?"

"Not in total by any means and only where absolutely relevant to current clients."

"Well, couldn't you check? Your father must have known about the adoption, there's papers from him to Chris's

father, there must be originals, correspondence that
prompted the other letters?"

Georgina half smiled, clearly amused by Saz's evident
stupidity, "Yes, there probably are. But, you must understand, my father was in this business for almost fifty years.
Even if I had the right to do so – which I don't – it would
take forever. And anyway, I simply don't have the time. So
I am sorry to disappoint you, but I really must get on."

Saz stopped at the door. "What if we demanded to see
the papers, could we do that?"

Georgina Leyton's smile stayed fixed on her face, "Well,
of course you could try. Anyone can attempt to get a court
order to do so. It might take some time though."

Five minutes later, Saz was out on the muggy street again,
no more informed about Chris's parentage, but rather more
certain that Georgina Leyton had something to hide.

As she said later to Molly over dinner, "Bitch was lying
through her back teeth. And front ones, though they looked
capped anyway."

"Saz, that's a bit much from one meeting. Are you sure
you weren't just pissed off with her for being richer and
more successful than you?"

"And more gorgeous and better dressed?"

Molly grabbed a couple of prawns from Saz's plate, "Nah,
she couldn't be more gorgeous."

"I thank you. Well, naturally I felt a minuscule twinge of
something vaguely resembling envy, but it wasn't just that.
I mean, I went to her with a perfectly reasonable request."

"And no appointment."

"Strategy."

"But irritating if you're her."

"Maybe. Anyway, what's the big deal? Yes, she'd have to

bend the rules a bit, but it's not like I was asking her to perjure herself or anything. Richard Leyton's dead, Chris's dad is dead, we can't get the information any other way. Of course, if Chris's mum gave permission, we'd be able to get at the stuff immediately, he just has this thing that he doesn't want to upset her."

"Fair enough."

"Exactly. And you'd think anyone would understand that. But no, it's all got to be by the book or not at all."

"She was just doing her job, Saz."

"And it's because of that I don't trust her. If she's so hot on doing it all so properly, then she'd already have informed herself about her father's work, she'd have made it her business to know everything when she took over from him. And I think she probably does."

"Why do you think she was lying to you?"

"Don't know, but it makes her a damn sight more interesting than she seemed this time yesterday."

EIGHT

The next morning, Gary had disappointing news about Chris.

"Sorry, Saz, nothing at all."

"What, no Chris Marquand ever?"

"None that I could find."

"Well that's impossible, there must be something, he is alive, for God's sake."

"Of course there's something, but it's like I tried to explain yesterday, he could have been registered in any number of ways. The only name you've given me is that of his adoptive parents."

"So that means Chris must have been registered under his birth mother's name?"

"Very likely."

"But he must have needed a birth certificate at some point in his life?"

"No, not really, when did you last use yours? And anyway, his parents probably have other documentation about the adoption. Why doesn't he ask them about that? They may even have the original birth certificate, that'll give the birth mother's name."

Saz sighed and explained Chris's reasoning again. As both she and Gary agreed, it wasn't as if they didn't understand Chris's motives, it just made things a damn sight more complicated. Either she would have to have another go at Mrs Marquand's attic files or she was going to have to try to get more on Richard Leyton's life work from his under-eager daughter.

"And what about Patrick Freeman? How far did your squeaky clean conscience let you get with him?"

"It's interesting you should ask."

Saz stopped scribbling grumpy faces on the phone book and paid attention, "Why? What about him?"

"Don't get too enthused, in fact it isn't anything really, but—"

"But what?"

"Well, nothing definite."

"Oh for God's sake, Gary, get on with it."

"It's just a discrepancy with the dates."

"How do you mean?"

"We are talking about the same Patrick Freeman, also known as Patrick Sweeney, the chef?"

"You know we are."

"OK, well, Patrick Sweeney/Freeman lists his birthdate in *Who's Who* – and a couple of other articles I checked up on – as 30th August, 1959."

"You have been taking this research seriously."

"I try to help."

"So what's the confusion?"

"The birth certificate signed by Gerald and Eva Freeman, his parents, lists his birthdate as 3rd September, 1959."

"You're sure that's not just the date of the certificate?"

Gary sighed, "Give me a break, Saz, it is my fucking job. I do know the difference between the date of birth and date of registration. On the copy I've seen, Eva and Gerald's baby son Patrick was born on 3rd September, 1959, registered on the 5th. Now we all know people who lie about their age, and this guy is a bit of a media whore, so maybe he has more excuse than most, but while your average bloke might say he was three years younger than he really is, there doesn't seem a hell of a lot of reason for lying about three days."

"So you're saying the Freemans did that thing of re-registering him after someone else had already done so?"

"I'm not jumping to any excessive conclusions. What I am saying is that for some reason Patrick Sweeney, famous chef, real name Patrick Freeman, has stated quite categorically, on several occasions, that his birthday is August 30th when his parents told the state it was September 3rd"

"Could be there was a better horoscope for people born in September that year."

"Yeah, Saz, big businessmen take a lot of notice of horoscopes in my experience."

"Or could be someone's lying."

"That option had crossed my mind. But look, take it easy, all right?"

"Take what easy?"

"Just don't go rushing in. Maybe his parents have been lying. Maybe he doesn't even know there's a discrepancy. Just be careful."

"For God's sake, Gary, I'm hardly going to go and confront him with it just when he's serving up the main course. Of course, I'll be discreet. I'll be careful of his feelings."

Gary laughed out loud. "It didn't even occur to me to think about his feelings. I meant be careful of yourself. The guy's got a ferocious reputation."

Saz hung up wondering just how dangerous could a bloke be while wearing a silly hat and checked trousers?

The minute she got off the phone, Saz started another round of calls. After ten minutes with directory enquiries she started with Patrick Sweeney's agent. Two different secretaries later she eventually got through and asked if there was any chance she might meet up with the great man himself to discuss the possibility of her writing the Sweeney/ Freeman biography. Saz figured that as everyone seemed to think they knew all about him and as almost anyone she mentioned his name to spoke of Patrick as a media starlet, then the people who looked after him might well go for the idea of an authorised biography. It would give him a chance to show off still more and, at the same time, correct any myths about himself. Any myths he wanted to correct, that is.

After the third phone call to his agent, and then a second with his business manager, and a third – albeit briefly – with his wife, Patrick himself called back and asked her to lunch. That same day. With half an hour to spare Saz washed, dressed, left a note for Molly and grabbed a cab into town. Patrick's restaurant in Soho was closed, but he'd offered to make her lunch there himself, it would be quiet and private. She was ten minutes late, he – though only coming from the kitchen – arrived half an hour later. And brought lunch with him. He then proceeded to tell Saz in which order she should eat her meal. Saz would have complained if the food itself hadn't been quite outstanding. It was, she didn't.

Contrary to expectations, Patrick Sweeney didn't wear a silly hat. Or checked trousers. He greeted Saz in old faded jeans, trainers with holes in each big toe, a perfectly white T-shirt and a rumpled leather jacket over the back of his chair. His long fringe was kept out of his eyes with his youngest daughter's fuzzy rainbow hairclip, which by some feat of natural grace that Saz couldn't quite fathom, miraculously didn't leave him looking like a tosser. He also wore a very sweet lopsided grin, and a locket with pictures of his kids inside. Saz was completely charmed.

When they had finished eating, Patrick sat back and smiled at Saz, "So, this is how it's going to work. You ask the questions. If I think they're interesting enough, then you can show me some of your writing. What do you do?"

"Oh, you know, feature journalism, opinion pieces, *Guardian* Women's Page, that sort of thing."

"OK. So if I like what you have to ask, and if you're still interested once I've answered, maybe we'll talk further after today."

"Right, well I really appreciate you seeing me, I mean, not knowing anything about me."

"I was cooking, I wanted a guinea pig to try the meal out on. And you did like it, didn't you?"

"Hell yeah."

"Fine, you've done me a favour, now I'm doing you one. Anyway, John's checking you out this afternoon. If you're crap I just won't see you again. OK?"

"Yes. Sure. Great. Thank you."

Saz racked her brain for an interesting question that wasn't "Why do you tell people your birthday is different from your birth certificate?", something that might make her sound like the great journo she'd purported to be when she'd spoken to John the manager earlier. Sadly the best she could come up with was "How long have you been married?"

Fortunately it wasn't a boring question to Patrick. Katy Betterton was clearly the love of his life. "I met her here, she actually came into the kitchen to complain the lamb was too rare."

"What did you do?"

"Told her to fuck off. And not to bring her baby into my kitchen – she was breastfeeding at the time."

"Breastfeeding while you were arguing?"

"Yeah. She's always liked to make people notice her.

Having half a dozen screaming kids in tow tends to help. Anyway, I kicked her out, she went, then came back at midnight just as we were getting rid of the last of the punters."

"With the kids?"

"No, they were at home with the nanny. She apologized about the lamb and asked if I'd make her breakfast."

"Did you?"

"Devilled kidneys. Cheese sandwich for lunch. And then I moved in. We got married a month later."

While Saz hadn't known quite enough about big business to link Patrick with Gerald Freeman, she did have a slightly more meaningful acquaintance with tabloid gossip than she was prepared to let on to Marc. She hadn't known much about Patrick other than that he was a famous chef with an infamous temper but as a teenager she'd avidly scanned column inches for the lives of interesting girls who were having more fun than she was – Katy Betterton chief among them. A rock chick with a CV of ex-boyfriends that read like the cast list for Band Aid, Katy had lived through the '80s and early '90s in a haze of delicious excess, usually with a Premier League footballer lolling somewhere in a coke-fed background. When she and Patrick first met she already had three children from her first two high-profile relationships and very soon afterwards she was pregnant with the first of her three other children with Patrick. And from the look on his face as Patrick told the story, marriage and fatherhood were all they were cracked up to be – and more.

They talked for a while longer, Saz asking obligatory questions about the nature of his business, his relationship with the media, his ambitions for the future. Things were going fairly easily and she was about to slip in a question about how Patrick's parents had known Chris's family, when it occurred to her that she could soften up the doting father even more by first asking a few specifics about the children. Not the right move. The smile disappeared, his hands held fast to the edge of the table and the pretty little clip in his hair didn't look quite so cute.

Patrick shook his head, "No. We don't talk about the kids. Katy's middle daughter Marina died a year after our first baby was born. It took forever and it was really fucking horrible. She had leukaemia, we were splattered over all the papers, we did all the right charity things we were supposed to and . . ." Patrick faltered, fiddled with the linen tablecloth. "And nothing made it any better. It was all bloody awful. Still is. It doesn't go away. And over time, Katy and I have found that talking about it doesn't help either. I mean talking about it to strangers. So, we'll leave that bit out for now, all right?"

The smile was back, but Saz knew she'd been clearly warned. And while anyone else might have chosen to back off then, following up with a few innocuous questions about his cooking style, she decided to push on anyway, "Then I wonder if I could just ask, before we finish, why is it you tell people your birthday is the 30th of August when on your birth certificate it says you were born on the 3rd of September?"

Patrick Sweeney didn't answer. He picked up Saz's bag and then he picked up Saz, carried them both to the door and dropped them into the street. He locked the door behind him. Saz had just found out where too far was.

NINE

Three hours later, as Saz was gingerly applying half a tube of Arnica to her bruised knees, the doorbell rang. And rang again. And again. Then the whole flat resounded to the clamour of furious knocking. By the time she'd made it down the hall she was expecting the wood to be broken through any minute.

Patrick Sweeney stood on her doorstep, red-faced and practically foaming at the mouth, "So who the fuck are you?"

"I'm sorry?"

"I said, who are you?" Patrick pushed past her into the flat, looking into each of the rooms, presumably to check if anyone else was around.

Saz raced after him, "Look, you can't just come barging in here like this. What do you want?"

Patrick rounded on her, "I want to know who the fuck you are. You're not a journo, you can't be. You wouldn't have made such a twat of yourself today if you were. That lot know how to lie a fuck of a lot better than you do."

"Obviously."

"So I want to know why you've been checking up on me. And John couldn't find anything about you. Did Briony put you up to this? Are you working for her?"

"I don't even know who Briony is."

"Ex-wife."

"I'm not working for anybody. Well no, actually I am, but not in the way you think."

"Right, so what were you doing this afternoon?" Patrick stood in the middle of the lounge, dwarfing the space with his anger. Saz figured honesty was the most sane policy. At least it might get him safely sitting down.

She told Patrick about Chris, adding just a little of her own baby story but not too much, she didn't want to overdo it on their first real conversation. Or test any latent homophobia he might be harbouring. Not while he was in her own home, anyway. Then she told him about her findings in Mrs Marquand's attic and showed him the christening photo.

"How did you know this kid was me?"

"I didn't. Chris's boyfriend recognized your father and we assumed the child was probably you."

"Well, these are my parents and that's me. These two certainly weren't my mother and father's closest friends or anything like that. At least not from when I was old enough to know. I don't recognize them at all. And I certainly don't remember the photo being taken."

Saz was disappointed, she had hoped Patrick might have been able to tell her more about why his parents had been there that day.

Patrick was still more concerned with what she knew about him, "OK, you found this photo, but the thing about my birth certificate – where did you get that?"

Saz really didn't want to give Gary away, but at the same time she realized her knowledge of the discrepancy was what had made Patrick assume the worst about her. She explained a little of her source, not naming Gary and making it sound as much as possible as if she had forced the information out of him. His face fell when she explained what Gary assumed was the reasoning behind the discrepancy.

"I assumed a similar thing myself. The problem is that I only found out last month."

"About the birth dates?"

"Yeah. That's why I was so fucking angry with you. Since my father died there have been a few journalists wanting to do life pieces on him, and I was prepared to go along with it at first, but once I started going through it all, letters from the solicitor, that sort of thing – well, that's when I found out about the dates."

"So you knew you were adopted?"

"Always. But it was supposed to be a big secret. The only people who knew were me and my parents."

"You never told anyone?"

"Just the two wives. No one else."

"That's a big thing to keep to yourself."

"Well, I also knew they never wanted me to do anything about it, so there really wasn't any point in telling anyone. My parents told me the truth, but that was it. We didn't talk about it. Ever. And my father made it very plain that he'd be fucking pissed off if I ever tried to find out the rest of the story. Emotional blackmail at its strongest."

"And very successful?"

"I didn't make a move until my father died. Anyway, the point is, once I did start looking into it, I realized there was more to it than I'd expected. And I really want to find out the truth myself before any of the fucking journos do. And God knows someone probably will."

"So why did you agree to speak to me this morning?"

"I didn't. At least not in the way you thought. I assumed you were lying about something, I just didn't know what it was. I agreed to talk to you so I could find out. But because your angle was the biography, I assumed it was me you wanted to know about. That's why I was so furious when you brought my parents into it. You touched on something very raw. Very new."

Having exposed himself that much, Patrick decided he might as well tell Saz the whole story. As he explained though, the whole story was still a very incomplete one. After Gerald Freeman died, Patrick finally felt free to uncover the truth of his past. As he explained to Saz, he'd already started going through the usual, lengthy channels. So far there had been no developments.

"But if you're doing it for your friend, maybe I should get you on my case too?"

"I don't think so."

"Why not?"

Saz frowned, "It's not that I don't want to help, Patrick. I'm just not sure I'm the best person to get to do the job."

"I've contacted Social Services. I've got an adoption counsellor, but the whole bloody thing takes forever."

"There are loads of private agencies who do this sort of thing too. Who specialize in it."

"Yeah, and they're all full of strangers who have more to gain from knowing my secrets than from passing those secrets on to me."

"You could say the same about me."

"I could. But you're doing this to help your friend. Who you're having a baby with. Some poof and his boyfriend that you and your girlfriend are having a baby with. Now, correct me if I'm wrong, but there's a good chance you know a little more about the necessity for discretion than most?"

"Yeah."

"And I'll pay well."

"Yeah?"

"And believe me, babies are bloody expensive."

"So I've heard. Look, can I just ask something?"

"What?"

"You said you were looking through things from your father's solicitor, right?"

Patrick nodded confirmation.

"What was the solicitor's name?"

"Richard Leyton."

"Fantastic!"

"What?"

"Leyton was the Marquands' solicitor. He's in this photo."

Patrick shook his head. "Damn sight younger there."

"Well, anyway, maybe your parents weren't great mates with them, but they shared a solicitor, who had something to do with Chris's adoption. Perhaps Richard Leyton had something to do with yours too."

"I know he did. That's how I found out about the different birth dates. In with my father's things, there was a letter from Leyton. I didn't really understand what he was on about, but he gave a different birth date for me than the one I'd grown up believing. I'd been meaning to check it against my birth certificate, but I hadn't got round to it yet. And now you've done it for me."

"God, it must be weird to think you don't know for definite when your birthday is."

"It gets worse. The main part of the letter is actually an invoice to my father demanding payment."

"For arranging the adoption?"

"No. That was a different fee, the one Leyton put through his company's books. I'd already found that bit. This other letter was on Leyton's private notepaper. This was about the actual fee for buying the baby."

"I'm sorry Patrick, I don't understand."

"My parents paid for me. Gave Leyton money, not merely for arranging the adoption, but also to actually buy me."

"Bloody hell."

"Yeah. Really."

T E N

Patrick left Saz's flat only after she had agreed to travel down to his father's house in Sussex with him the following day. She then called both Chris and Molly to give them an update of her news. Molly was delighted she'd met Patrick Sweeney, furious when she heard that he'd physically removed her from his restaurant, and intrigued when Saz told her about the solicitor connection. She was also more than a little miffed that not only had Saz had her lunch made for her today, but also that she would most likely be getting dinner tomorrow and breakfast the day after.

"Bring me back a doggy bag. Or better still, make best friends with him and get him to cook for us."

Saz, knowing Molly wouldn't have been quite so impressed by the celebrity had she been at home when he was beating down their back door, suggested they leave the best friend thing for a bit – "At least until I've spent a night with him, babe."

Chris was equally excited about Saz's day, though not at all concerned about the state of her bruised knees. He was rather more upset that Saz had almost blown her chances with her too blatant questioning.

"Yeah, I know, Chris, I took a chance. But it was all right in the end, I am going to get to take a look at his father's things."

"Right, and at least he trusts you now and there must be some connection, with the photo and now the same solicitor."

Saz had decided not to tell Chris about Patrick's revelation of baby-buying, at least not until she'd seen Leyton's letters herself. While Chris had a very good relationship with his mother, she wasn't sure it would withstand that sort of allegation.

"Yeah, maybe. Just don't get too excited yet. We've still got a long way to go. I'll call you as soon as I get back."

"Or if you find anything juicy."

"Of course."

They hung up, Chris hopeful and Saz worried.

Saz left home the next afternoon both excited and nervous. While she was pleased to be getting on with the job – both jobs – she was also a little uncertain about spending the next twenty-four hours in the company of a man she barely knew, who only a day before had bodily removed her from his presence. This was a client she'd need to be especially careful with. Patrick filled in the first part of their journey with a detailed account of what was happening with the investigation through the traditional channels. What was happening was almost nothing.

"The thing is, they don't really have anything to go on. Apparently it's really unusual to get to my age and not know. Or rather to be my age and never to have been encouraged to find out by your parents. Keeping it all a big secret is what they did in the bad old days. Not in the enlightened '60s."

"Your parents were hardly children of the '60s."

"Clearly not."

Patrick's disapproval of his parents' actions translated

itself to a tighter grip on the steering wheel and his right foot pushed down ten miles an hour faster on the accelerator.

Saz tried another question to distract him. "So if you didn't know there was a different date on your birth certificate, how have you managed without it so far?"

"My father sorted out my first passport when I was sixteen, that's the only thing I would ever have needed it for. And however he did it, money and connections no doubt, it does give the date I'd always believed, the 30th of August. They opened my bank accounts for me when I was little, put various things in my name that I took over when I was sixteen, or eighteen, whatever – just like most kids, I guess."

"Most rich kids."

"That's what I am," Patrick retorted. "I'm not prepared to go into the story of being a self-made man again. I get enough of that sort of shit from the press."

"I'm sorry. Taking the piss out of the rich is a reflex reaction." It was only half an apology, but it was the best Saz could manage.

"Well, anyway, it meant that by the time I needed to do anything for myself, I already had a whole selection of other legal documents to prove the birth date I believed in. And there's really not an awful lot you need your birth certificate for. Not having it to look at wasn't something I questioned. It may be that rich kids get more things done for them, but I don't imagine even you knew all the finer points of your legal details when you were sixteen."

Saz shook her head. "I knew nothing when I was sixteen, except that I hated my parents, hated my sister, would die if I didn't move to London within the next week. And that no one was ever going to understand me. Or love me."

"What changed?"

"I moved to London. But no, you're right, the legal stuff only begins to matter later. So what about your wedding?"

"Las Vegas. Passport."

"No, I meant your first wedding."

"Las Vegas. Passport."

"Both weddings were in Las Vegas?"

"It's quick and easy. And kind of romantic."

"And you didn't need your birth certificate."

"As luck would have it."

"Or fate."

"Same thing, aren't they?"

"Only if you're naturally lucky."

Saz imagined that until just recently, naturally lucky was exactly how Patrick had seen himself.

"And you didn't need your birth certificate when you changed your name?"

"It's not a legal thing. I'm just known as Patrick Sweeney. Patrick Freeman trading as Patrick Sweeney. I didn't change it by deed poll or anything. It's just for business." Patrick shook his head, "Shame really, if I'd have made it a legal change, I probably would have had to prove who I was, I would have needed to check the records ages ago, when my father was still alive. I could have asked him about it."

"Yeah. It is a pity. Tell me again about the letters."

"I'll show you when we get to the house. The first one is just a legal letter from Leyton confirming the adoption had gone through, and asking for the arranging fee. It doesn't say who I was adopted from or where or anything else. Adds that I would now be the son and heir to the Freeman family empire. Or I would once I was old enough. And that's it. All I have to go on. Other than the second letter which tells me they paid the vast sum of five grand for me."

"Not cheap then."

"No. Not cheap."

Patrick heaved a sigh of relief as the irritatingly slow old-man driver in front of him finally turned off and he was able to drive once again at his preferred speed of just under a hundred miles an hour. In a car that made the speed feel like gliding across just-cleaned ice, even on a winding country road. He continued with his story and Saz quietly checked that her seatbelt was securely fastened.

"Leyton dealt with all of my father's matters – family, business, the lot – none of that modern delegating rubbish for him. His daughter Georgina was one of the partners and she sent everything on to my father when her father died. Which is why all those papers are in such a mess, he just never got round to sorting it himself."

Saz wondered how well Patrick knew Georgina and decided that for the moment she would keep quiet about their unhelpful meeting.

"Why didn't your father take her on as his solicitor?"

"He didn't want to. My father was bloody old-fashioned too."

"Didn't want a girl?"

"Well, that is what I used to believe, but now I think that maybe it was actually more than that. Perhaps he didn't want Georgina looking through this lot, finding out that her father was involved in selling a baby, and the only way he could make sure she wouldn't be able to was to get the papers back himself. Very considerate of him."

"How well do you know her?"

"Our fathers did business together, our families occasionally met, you know the sort of thing."

Saz didn't, but didn't want to tempt Patrick's temper with another explanation of their difference in upbringing. "So all the private papers were sent on to your father's house?"

"I think so. But I honestly couldn't say anything for definite. Once I'd found that letter about the money I was a bit gobsmacked really. Katy made me call Social Services, I got myself landed with an adoption counsellor – which was absolutely not what I wanted – and they started on what would appear to be their very slow and inept process of getting to the truth."

"It's only been a month, Patrick."

"I know that, and well-meaning Lucy, the irritating social worker girlie who's supposedly helping me through this awful trauma, was at great pains to tell me it may take years."

"Have you told her about the baby buying?"

"Hell no. I've told her as little as possible."

"You don't like her?"

"I don't like being patronised by a twenty-two-year-old just out of college, who's done a couple of modules on dealing with something like this, and wouldn't yet know a real emotion if it hit her over the head."

"Just because she's young?"

Patrick snarled, "No. Just because she's stupid. I don't need counselling, I need action. And I'm not prepared for it to take years. I want to know now. I kept quiet for thirty-nine years, to please my parents. Now I want to please me. I need to know who else I am as well as Patrick Freeman. Sweeney. Whatever. And I'm fucked if I'm going to wait another forty years to find out the rest of the story."

"I don't imagine it'll take that long," Saz said with more certainty than she really felt. "We'll see what we find when we look through everything else. There's bound to be something."

They sat in silence for the next ten minutes, Saz craning her neck over hedgerows to the fields beyond, until Patrick announced they had arrived. He slowed the car and turned on to the steep driveway leading up to his family home. Saz looked at the long, squat stone and glass building ahead, hoping for Patrick's sake that the rest of the truth was something his father had not yet managed to tidy away. And that just maybe she'd find something for Chris – and therefore herself – at the same time.

ELEVEN

Saz was stunned when Patrick ushered her into his father's office.

"Good God! What is this? You've been burgled recently?"

Patrick shook his head and had the decency to look slightly embarrassed, "No burglary. I got a bit annoyed when I found the letter about the money."

"Yeah well, between this and the state of my knees, remind me never to get you a lot annoyed."

Saz surveyed the damage before her. Piles of papers lay across the tops of the cabinets, their shades of clean white to brittle yellow indicating the timespan they covered. Some of the file drawers were fully open, musty papers spilling out of the old dark wood, other drawers were half closed, old files jammed haphazardly back in. The floor too was covered in a late autumn scattering of Sir Gerald Freeman's life.

Saz grimaced and kicked over a few pages, "No stone unturned, then?"

"I found the letter and I kind of just . . ."

"Went off your face? Trashed the room?" Saz was clearly unimpressed.

Patrick offered an alternative to further explanation, "How about I go and make us some supper?"

Saz turned her frown from the papers on the floor to his would-be innocent face, "And leave me to sort this lot by myself?"

"Well, I left a few provisions down here on my last visit. And there's a fresh salmon in the boot. So if you'd rather whip us up a quick salmon on puy lentils, fresh basil mayonnaise for the couscous and roast pepper starter . . . perhaps a dessert of early raspberries and a little salted butter shortcake . . .?"

"You've got all that in the car?"

"No. I've got the fish in the car. Most of that little lot grows quite happily in the garden and the rest lives in the pantry. It's what we call ingredients in my trade."

"It's what we call showing off in mine."

"Well, if you want to get on with supper and leave me to tackle this, I'm perfectly happy to swap jobs for a bit?"

Saz, whose idea of a gourmet meal was anything cooked by Molly and rarely enhanced by the touch of her own fair hands, shook her head, "No really, it's fine. Puy lentils are hardly my forte. And anyway, I'd much rather stay here. Honest. Bastard."

Patrick held back on his smug grin until he'd closed the door behind him.

Saz settled down to work, reminding herself that calling the client a bastard possibly wasn't the best of business practice. Within ten minutes she decided she'd let him off lightly. Gerald Freeman may well have considered his self-designed home the cutting edge of British architecture in 1972, but it was sadly clear he hadn't bothered to apply any modernist criteria to his office. Not only had Patrick's father failed to use anything as prosaic as either a chronological or an alphabetical filing system for the huge wooden cabinets housing his records, what little order there was had been comprehensively destroyed on Patrick's first foray into his dead father's realm.

Two hours later dinner was nearly ready and Saz was feeling slightly happier than when she'd first walked into the office. All of the files that had not been thrown to the floor in Patrick's rage were now put away as tidily as possible in the cabinets, if not in alphabetical and chronological order, then at least facing front and right way up. With the drawers closed, Saz had eventually been able to start sifting through the papers on the floor without smashing her head on an elegant walnut corner every time she raised an eyebrow. The papers that had swamped the intricacies of the purple and red carpet were now laid out in four piles on Sir Gerald's writing table. The first and by far the largest was the selection dating from as early as 1895 (the deeds to Sir Gerald's grandfather's home in Scotland), up to and including 1954. Saz figured she was fairly safe to assume there would be little reference to Patrick over five years before his birth. The next pile covered that four-year period until January 1959. The smallest of the four piles were the six pages from 1959, and then the second largest sheaf of papers dated from 1960 until Sir Gerald's death.

She explained her method to Patrick. "Of course I haven't started on the cabinets yet, so there's probably loads more for the year or so we're really interested in, but at least now we can walk to the files instead of skating over a sea of your family history."

Patrick nodded absently, his attention taken by the papers from his birth year. "Yeah, good job, and this stuff? Anything here?"

"Sorry. But it is early days. There's a whole Amazonian rainforest of drawers to go through yet. You are looking at a mere six sheets of paper."

"What do they say?"

"Well, this one says that your father sold twenty-five acres of the Scottish property in late 1958. Or rather, he tried to get the deal done in '58, it finally went through in February '59."

"That'll be the golf course."

"Good. We can put that in the sorted pile. Then in May 1959, your father tried to buy a property in France."

"They didn't get it?"

"Not from what I can see so far. Your father was supposed to visit the place in June, and then again in July. He never made it. Apparently your mother was 'indisposed' and he stayed in England all year."

"Indisposed?"

"Well, either she really was ill or perhaps it was a euphemism."

"For what?"

"Maybe it was their way of perpetuating the story that she was pregnant. Your father writes to his property bloke that he can't go away because your mother can't travel, can't be left, implying what he hopes would be believed . . . it's a good way of getting other people to corroborate the story."

"Maybe my mother really was sick."

"Maybe. We can probably find some way of checking out her medical records, but that's not actually the most relevant part. What we do know is that something was going on which meant that your father didn't feel able to leave the country in the months closest to your birth."

"My assumed birth. It's not as if there's a photo of baby me next to a copy of *The Times* from August 30th, 1959, umbilical cord still attached. Or September 3rd. For fuck's sake!" Patrick spun around, smacked his fist into the table, narrowly avoiding spilling another pile of papers on to the floor. "I don't even know how old I am any more. Not just by days, for all I know they could have been lying about whole years."

Saz lunged for the papers and placed a few other things out of the reach of his anger.

"Patrick, calm down. Even if we don't really know the exact date, they're not going to have been lying by much. You do have tiny baby photos of yourself, don't you?"

"And my family photo albums tell us what?"

"Well, though you can lie about your age when you're as old as we are, it's a damn sight harder to do the same with a newborn baby. They might have got away with those couple of days, but people would get bloody suspicious if they'd taken it any further than that. And I would have thought the last thing your parents wanted to do was arouse any sort of suspicions at all."

"Then why would they lie about it at all?"

"So they could register you under their name. As theirs. It's very likely your birthday is August 30th and maybe you were registered for that day by your birth parents, then when the Freemans got you a day or so later they re-registered you in September."

"So why tell me the August date in the first place?"

"I don't know. I mean, in a way, if they were lying on the birth certificate they had filled out, it's quite nice that they told you the other date."

"Nice? What the fuck are you on about?"

Saz shook her head, "I just mean that, even though they were prepared to lie to the authorities about your birth date so they could corroborate their story, maybe they wanted you to know your real birth date after all. That's why they told you August 30th all along. Maybe they didn't want to lie to you about something as important as that."

Patrick wasn't prepared to be appeased, "Yeah, well, if they'd adopted me properly and not fucking well bought me in the first place, they wouldn't have had to lie at all. Seems like they had an odd idea about what matters and what doesn't."

"Yeah, but obviously they really wanted to make other people believe you were theirs. It's not rational, but then I don't imagine taking on a new baby – particularly under those circumstances – is going to lead to constant sensible and rational thought."

He shrugged, "You could be right."

Saz smiled, "And the night is young, there's a whole lot more drawers and files still to attack, and didn't you mention something about eating?"

Patrick looked at his watch, half an hour since he'd left it, the salmon was probably close to perfect now and the wine would be acceptably chilled. He nodded, "All in good time, there's a rather tempting couscous to start with, diced tomato and pepper salad, soda bread . . ." Saz, her appetite wiping all thoughts of client protocol from her mind, pushed him out of the room and down the hallway, "Patrick Sweeney, you've waited forty years for this truth, another half hour isn't going to hurt."

Patrick rounded on Saz, "How dare you? Half an hour? Good God, woman, this meal needs savouring, time. Charm."

"Yeah, whatever, you're the boss."

"No. I'm the chef. And the client."

Saz followed him down the hall, more aware of her place than ever.

TWELVE

The meal took precisely two hours and thirty-nine minutes. Saz timed it. She also ate one and a half servings of couscous with sweet pumpkin confit, a massive chunk of the salmon and an excessive portion of dessert. Saz forced Patrick to give her a second helping of the starter despite his protestations that it would ruin her appetite for the main course. It didn't.

As she explained to Patrick, relations between them now markedly warmer after a meal and a couple of bottles of wine, "What's the point of torturing my body with an excess of exercise every day if I don't then abuse it mercilessly to make up for it?"

"Just wait. You'll pay in the end."

Saz looked at Patrick's full glass, his long lean body, finely sculpted face with barely an unnecessary wrinkle in sight, "Yeah, right. Just like you and Katy have."

"We take very good care of ourselves!"

"Sure you do. Now. But if I'd spent my twenties in a haze of drugs and drink and shagging around like Katy did—"

"I didn't do too badly myself."

"My point exactly. If I'd done all that in my younger years—"

"Careful!"

Saz ignored his protest and continued, scraping up the last of the shortcake from the serving dish, "And if I still managed to look as fantastic as she does now, you wouldn't find me advocating a quiet lifestyle of yoga and country walks."

"Not even to clear out the rage and bitterness?"

"Nah. Long runs and chocolate. Double the endorphins. And sex, of course. Works every time. Now, are we going to sit here chatting all bloody night or get on with the job?"

Patrick looked at his watch, "You can't be serious, it's half-past eleven! I'm not even sober!"

Saz waited while he took another great slurp of his wine, "I had noticed. But we've got to get through it and you have to be at work tomorrow afternoon – so we do need to put in at least another couple of hours tonight."

"You could have mentioned it sooner."

"I did. You told me to stop being so bloody boring, pointed out yet again that you were employing me, and went on to rave about the fantastic Australian wine you were opening. How we could drink it all night and not notice any adverse effects. Remember?"

"Mmm. Sorry."

"Never mind," Saz looked closely at Patrick, "Would it be pushing things too much if I suggested you might have a little coke somewhere about your person?"

Patrick laughed out loud, "There's half a gram in my wallet."

"Good. That ought to wake you up for a bit and it'll certainly keep me going for another hour or so."

Patrick shook his head sadly and reached into his coat pocket, "I'm shocked that's the kind of person you assume I am."

"Oh, I don't know. I would have thought it might be a compliment – for a bloke of your age."

For the next ninety minutes they went methodically through

the files. Saz had Patrick start on the earliest ones, while she tackled those starting in the year or so before his birth. She figured that while the early files were unlikely to shed any great light on the matter of Patrick's adoption, it was still necessary to go through them just in case something had been hidden away. She guessed too that it might be safer if she went through the likely files herself and left the more innocuous ones to him – she didn't want their whole evening's hard work ruined if Patrick came across something else that wasn't to his liking and decided to trash the place again.

They worked in silence for awhile, every now and then Patrick exclaiming over something from his parents' past, old photos of his mother as a débutante, a watercolour painted by his father when he first went to university, a stern letter from his paternal grandfather to a lost little boy sent away from home at the tender age of seven and apparently not certain when he'd be allowed back again.

"God, he was a bastard."

"Your grandfather?"

"Pompous old tosser."

"Was he horrible when you were a kid?"

"No, not at all. He was wonderful with me. And yet, this—"

Saz shuffled some blameless papers and filed them away. "Yeah?"

"Well, in this letter, he just doesn't get it. My father's obviously upset about something – he was only seven, it was his first time away from home, and yet all the old git can say in response is 'It'll be good for you, son'. Good for him? Christ!"

"When's the letter dated?"

"1929."

"Well, exactly. You can't judge your grandfather by your

standards. Everyone sent their kids away to school then. It was normal for your lot."

"It can never have been normal to send a seven-year-old off by himself."

"Didn't your parents send you away?"

"No. At least, not until I was fourteen and even then I asked to go."

"You asked to go to boarding school?"

"I didn't want to leave home when my mother first died. Didn't want to leave my father by himself. I felt responsible for him. I think he was really shocked when I eventually asked to go away."

"What changed your mind?"

"Tom Dunsford went to Charterhouse. It sounded good."

"You fancied him?"

"Maybe a little. But that wasn't really the point."

"What was?"

"He could get hold of grass a damn sight easier than I could. So off I went. Of course, once I was there I realized I hated being away from home, but by then it was too late, I couldn't go back having made such a fuss to get there. That's the problem with making big decisions at fourteen, you've got no way of knowing if they're sensible or not."

"Nah, that's the problem with making big decisions at any age."

They worked on in silence for a few more minutes, then Saz added, "I'm glad your father didn't want you to go away to school."

Patrick looked up from a sheaf of papers from his father's university years. "Why?"

"Well, after all the trouble they took to get you."

"We don't know it was trouble."

"Patrick, big secrets always involve some kind of trouble – it's just kind of nice that having got you, they wanted to keep you around. They didn't do what all their peers did, didn't shove you off to be brought up by strangers."

"Yeah. Nice."

Patrick stopped, looked around the room and then looked at his watch. "I'm sorry Saz, I'm just too tired. And to tell the truth, I'm finding it a bit hard dealing with all this. I don't feel up to going through these things. It's been good to remember that they did want me, cared for me. Trouble is, it's . . ." Here Patrick stuttered a bit, then faltered. Saz nodded for him to continue when he could. "It's just a bit much. I've been able to ignore his being dead for the past month or so. It's been easier to just be bloody angry with my father since I discovered the letter from Leyton, and now, looking at all this has reminded me. The old bastard's dead." Patrick shook his head, "In the past few years, once he'd accepted what I wanted to do with my life, we became good friends. I miss him."

"Yeah. Of course you do."

While Saz wasn't sure Patrick would be willing to accept comfort from her, she didn't know how to stop herself offering it. She clambered across several piles of papers to hold Patrick, and was relieved he accepted her touch, his lean body shaking slightly with held-back emotion.

"I'm sorry, Patrick, I ought to have been more aware of how this would affect you. You go to bed."

"No, we do need to go through all this."

"Yeah, but not half-pissed at two in the morning. Go on, I'll just finish the drawer I'm at and then get to bed myself. I've pretty much had enough of paper cuts for one night."

Patrick didn't need much persuading. He headed for the door, turning to Saz as he left the room, "Thank you, I do appreciate the support. Goodnight."

Saz nodded and then kicked herself once he'd left the

room, guiltily acknowledging that until he'd actually broken
down, the thought of his grief hadn't once crossed her mind.
She worked on, resolving to be a bit more sensitive to
Patrick's loss in future.

An hour later Saz took herself off to the over-pink guest
room, more than a little confused, but also gloating happily,
all thoughts of insensitive behaviour relegated to the back
of her mind. She'd been right to push them to get on with
the search, she'd been right to start when they did, and
she'd also been right to suggest she be the one to go through
the papers from the year of Patrick's birth. The long night
had been worthwhile. At the back of a file she'd nearly put
away because it just looked too boring to even think about
opening, she'd found another letter from Richard Leyton.
Who was very unhappy with the Freemans. He didn't like
their attitude and he didn't want to comply with their latest
batch of insistent requests but, purely because Patrick's
doctor was demanding to know his full medical history,
he was prepared to enclose the briefest account regarding
Patrick's birth mother's state of health.

Saz flipped over to the attached page. The letterhead gave
a private address in St Ives. Doctor Samuel Lees stated that
to the best of his knowledge Lillian Hope had not in the
past, nor was she in the present, suffering from any form
of congenital arthritic condition. If young Patrick had been
diagnosed as such by his current medical practitioner,
Doctor Lees strongly recommended that the Freemans
obtain a second opinion. Given the mother's history, it was
highly unlikely that Patrick had been correctly diagnosed.
On an attached sheet of paper, Richard Leyton further
recommended that should they ever make such excessive
demands again, the Freemans would do well to consider

engaging the services of a new solicitor. He did not sign off the letter with his warmest regards.

THIRTEEN

Patrick rubbed his eyes again, twisting hard-balled fists into each dry socket, trying to rub through exhaustion and into comprehension. It didn't work. He raised his hands to his eyes for the sixteenth time, the sound of flesh grating across the rapidly decreasing supply of eyeball lubricant had Saz wincing. Gross body noises had always been far more unpleasant to her than the longest of fingernails on a dusty blackboard.

"Will you please stop that?"

"It helps me concentrate."

"Yeah, well it helps me throw up. Patrick, your eyes are blood red and now you've made them puffy as hell. You look like you're allergic to yourself. How can that possibly help you concentrate?"

Patrick grinned, "Yeah, it really pisses Katy off too."

They were back in the kitchen, huge windows letting in filtered light from the excessively well-protected grounds outside. Saz had gone to bed with the letter placed carefully on the bedside table, weighted down with the now-empty whisky bottle. She was prompted to hang onto the letter by an irrational concern that, having found a clue for Patrick, it might slip away before light came again – despite the famed security in the grounds. She slept a solid four and a half hours, then rose bemoaning the fact that she had no idea how to turn off said impressive security and so wasn't able to get into the beautiful grounds for her morning run.

Saz was agitated from lack of sleep and lack of exercise. Patrick had a too-much-coke comedown, a mother of a hangover and a father he now couldn't place anywhere. They were hardly the most cheery of breakfast companions.

"But Patrick, this could be brilliant. We've got a name for your birth mother."

"Yes, from Leyton. A man who quite probably arranged for me to be bought as a baby, a man I've known most of my life, who clearly encouraged my parents to lie to me, so what makes you think we can trust the name he gives for her?"

Saz's voice whined upwards in exasperation. "We can't trust anything yet, but at least we've now got something to go on."

Patrick turned the letter over in his hand again, then threw it down and put on some more dark roast coffee, "It's all just so many fucking maybes."

"So we find out about your birth mother – and see where that leads us."

"Assuming what's written here is true."

"Yes, of course, assuming loads of things, that's how it works. We make assumptions and then have them proved or disproved. Kind of like real life."

"Kind of like no one's real life but mine."

Saz sighed. She was furious with herself for letting Patrick drink so much the night before and pissed off that every time she started to think she knew how to be with him, his temper – or her insensitivity – took them back to square one. Or worse. Now that they had a name, the actual search could begin. She would get Gary to work on the mother's identity. At the very least they could find out if a Lillian Hope had ever existed. The step-by-step method of uncovering the truth was pretty basic. Even Saz, tired as she was, couldn't fuck up on that one. What she didn't know was how to deal with Mr Grumpy. It was ten-thirty, they'd done nothing since she'd told Patrick about the letter an hour earlier, they had just three hours left before he needed to head back to London for work. She'd heard that the only way anyone got a response from Patrick when he was in one of his famed "moods" was to simply ignore the tantrum and get on with it. Mindful of what was soon coming her way, the years of breath holding and supermarket trolley terrors to come, Saz figured it was time to get in some mothering practice. She decided to give guilt a go.

"OK, Patrick. You do whatever you want. You can sit here and complain about how shit it is, and believe me, I agree with you, the position you find yourself in really is truly fucking distressing. But moaning won't help. Not today, and possibly not ever. God knows, I accept your grief is valid, but it doesn't actually have any bearing on what we're trying to do right now. We haven't got a lot of time today and though we can come back down here again if we have to, I'm sure that you, like me, would actually rather go back to London thinking we've made some progress, instead of wasting our time doing nothing except depress ourselves. I'm going back to the study to sort through some more papers. Hopefully we'll find something else that might take us a little bit further. Which gives you two options. You can sit there feeling sorry for yourself all morning, or you can come with me to do something about this mess. Which is it to be?"

Saz stopped at the door and turned back to look at him. Patrick stood up and lunged towards her. For a moment she wondered if he was going to smack her in the face. He grabbed her hand, hard. Then stopped, softened his grip, bent his head, kissed her hand and followed her meekly through to his father's office. He also whispered "patronizing cunt" beneath his breath.

By the time Patrick triple-locked the house and they set off back to London, another five cabinets had been methodically sorted and there was a solid selection of new possibilities for Saz to take home with her. They had a thin pile of Eva Freeman's medical records which might possibly throw some light on what Sir Gerald had referred to as her illness in the year Patrick was born. Saz was delighted to note that the doctor who had been treating her then was the same man Leyton had quoted as stating Lillian Hope was in perfect health. Clearly this Doctor Lees was some sort of link in the adoption chain – she made a mental note to find a way to check Chris's mother's medical records too. There was also another letter she decided to take back with her, a request from Richard Leyton for Gerald Freeman to speak with another of his clients. Saz's interpretation of the legal jargon was that Leyton seemed to be asking Patrick's father for a reference. Patrick didn't know the Jonathan Godwin referred to in the letter but, as he pointed out, he hadn't thought he knew the Marquands either. Leyton may well have been asking simply for an endorsement of his great conveyancing skills. Though Saz was hoping for more.

Along with a pile of papers dated around the time of Patrick's birth, Saz was also taking home a slightly more sensitive collection, basically anything marked "Private" or "Confidential". She had Patrick's permission to go through the lot, though he asked her to be careful. "I want to know about my parents. But if you open any of that and find it's a pile of love letters from my father's mistress—"

"He had one?"

"More than one if the gossip columns are to be believed. I'm not interested in any of that sort of thing."

"You're sure?"

"Definitely. I have a right to know about me, no matter what they wanted. But there are also things he should be allowed to keep private. If he'd have wanted me to know about lovers or any other secrets, he'd have told me."

Saz refrained from pointing out the same reasoning could be applied to the adoption in the first place – she didn't think it was especially appropriate while Patrick was driving at seventy miles an hour down a very narrow country lane. She was, however, glad she'd kept aside the two pale pink letters she found among some travel documents, intending to look through them without Patrick present. Just in case. Her reasoning, though, was less to do with Patrick or his father's delicate sensibilities, and rather more to do with her assumption that one personal secret might well know more about others.

She nodded and asked, "Anything else you're not interested in?"

"My father was a successful man, there's bound to be a few dodgy deals he didn't want known. Naturally, anything like that would have stayed with the personal files. Use your discretion."

Saz frowned, wondering where she was going to draw the line between what was safe to report to Patrick and what would send him into another towering rage, "And your reasons for not wanting to know?"

Patrick shrugged, braked suddenly and swerved into a side path to avoid an oncoming tractor travelling almost as fast as they were. "Stupid fucker!" he screamed into his rear-view mirror and then drove off again, not noticeably disturbed and certainly not choosing to slow his speed to a safer winding-road rate.

"I just don't want to know any more shit. If you find out things about my birth parents, then tell me. But as far as anything else goes ..." Patrick took the car up a slip road and onto the motorway, deftly crossing the two lanes of heavy traffic to plant himself in the fast lane and settle at just under ninety-five miles an hour, "I only just got my father back in the past few years. We were becoming real friends. I don't want to lose that entirely. Certainly now that I'm a father myself, I have a very different view of my childhood. I don't want to lose any more."

Saz nodded, understanding, if not completely agreeing, with his desire to hold onto some kind of rosy glow. "Yeah, fair enough. I'll do my best." She closed her eyes and settled down to listen to Pulp blaring from the perfectly placed speakers. Jarvis was singing about fathers and sons and Saz knew she was walking through alien territory.

FOURTEEN

Sara's dreams were of a huge redbrick building, windows facing out, but no light coming in. Long dark corridors of Edwardian prepossessing – pressing down and possessing her. Heavy shadows looming over, double-lit by the bright of harsh sun and the light of her closed eyes. Sara saw, eyes-closed, watching through her own skin, everything flesh-tinted, bloody not rosy. It was full summer outside, the world beyond the red brick was hazy and sweaty, it walked past her building in slow motion, labouring under a yoke of June into July into August and still the rain did not break. Waves of thick heat melted skyward from the pavement, then fell heavier still on the passing walkers. Strolling stumblers. Sara did not walk by in the street. Sara was far inside the thick walls. Inside there were white-washed paths, curtains moving in no-breeze. Inside she was frozen.

Sara was not alone. There were several of them in here, there may have been many, Sara did not keep her eyes open long enough to count those around her, feeling the closeness of their skin was enough. Misfits, anti-social, no-fit.

There was no satisfaction of darkness, no retreat, just the constant light that fed growing things, fed on growing things. A cold light of examination, blue and piercing. Sara kept her eyes shut tight. She would have slept if she could, sleeps whenever she can. She answered their questions and made the rounds and was again good girl, learnt to be quiet girl. But she could not make the face of the happy girl. The hot summer had stilled happiness, slowed it to a single pulse, mouth opened wide and head thrown back in silent laughter, image frozen in rictus of a scream.

Sara was sleepwalking, deep into winter.

FIFTEEN

Saz spent the afternoon on the telephone. She left a message
for Chris asking him if there was any way he could get hold
of his mother's medical records – specifically those from
around the time he was born. She left another message for
Carrie asking if she'd ever heard of Jonathan Godwin, and
then she was delighted when Gary actually answered his
telephone and she could speak to him rather than a
machine. She gave him the good news about Lillian Hope.
Gary was less enthusiastic than she might have hoped.

"It's not at all certain that this Doctor Lees is giving the
mother's real name, Saz."

"No, but there's not a hell of a lot of reason for him to
lie. This is a confidential letter sent to the only other person
who knew about the baby sale."

"Still doesn't mean anything."

Saz groaned down the phone line, "Gary, it's all we've
bloody got so far. There's no movement at all on Chris's
birth parents and this roundabout way is the closest I've
got yet. Maybe it's the birth mother's real name, maybe the
doctor isn't lying about her . . ."

"Maybe she's not dead and gone to heaven. It's a lot of
maybes."

"Yeah, but none of them are that far-fetched either. Just
get onto it, will you? Please? At least you know which part
of the country to look."

"She probably moved away long ago."

"You didn't. You only live five streets away from your parents' place."

"A good twenty minutes actually. A whole different town."

"My point being you could have moved to the big city, but you didn't. You just moved down the road. Maybe she still lives in the wilds as well."

"Gillingham is hardly wild."

"It was last time I looked."

"And what is it you want me to do about this Jonathan Godwin?"

"I don't know, run him through some database or something. Tell me what you find out."

"Run him through a database? Saz, you have a very strange idea of how I conduct my working life."

"I'm sure I do, Gary, but believe me, my limited knowledge of your office life is more than I want to have. I'm perfectly happy to drag myself across London to see you in every bloody fringe venue in town. And then talk for three hours afterwards about the complexities of your character. Or how you just have to get a better agent. And how hard it is trying to be an artist in this hard-bitten world. You know I'm willing to support that part of your work. You know I always have."

Gary grudgingly agreed with her analysis of his other career, "Yeah?"

"But really, far as your money job goes, I don't need to know how it happens, I don't care. I'm only interested in the results."

"Mercenary bitch."

"Through and through. Call me when you know something and I'll have a pressie for you. 'Bye."

Saz put on a fresh pot of coffee and ate her way through a

half a packet of dark chocolate Hobnobs while flicking through the phone book, her heart falling at the pages of J. Godwins. A strong cup of coffee in front of her, she was just about to get stuck into the pile of Gerald Freeman's papers when the phone rang. Hoping it was Gary back to her already with good news, she answered it rather than let the machine take the call. Big mistake. For the next forty minutes Saz listened as her old friend Judith slagged off her even older friend Helen – now Judith's ex-girlfriend. Of course the bitter rant that started about Helen's new lover ended with Judith bemoaning her inability to win Helen back and her heartbreak at the thought of the rest of their lives apart. Even if Helen was a two-timing, callous, deceitful bitch. Saz managed a few insignificant utterances and otherwise contented herself with shuffling through the pages in front of her as quietly as she could so Judith wouldn't hear. Not something she could do when, ten minutes after Judith finally got off the phone, Helen popped in "for a quick coffee". Coffee turned to whisky and tears, and she was still there when Molly got home from work at seven, stayed for dinner, drank two bottles of wine and three good-sized brandies. Apparently the new relationship wasn't going especially well.

At one in the morning when Helen eventually fell into a waiting cab and Molly staggered off to bed, Saz pulled out the love letters she'd started to look through while Judith was on the telephone. Both written in purple ink on pale pink paper, the paper so fine it was almost tissue paper, they were addressed to "Darlingest Gerry" and signed with a flurry of uneven kisses from "Dearest Sukie". Both letters were overflowing with soppy sentimentality interspersed with some unpleasantly coy sex references. Neither of the soft pink missives were dated, though one did mention Gerald's son, and as they were so obviously records of an affair, they must have been from before Patrick's mother's death. The second letter was a little more specific. At the bottom of the final page, most of it recalling their last "delicious cuddlings", Dearest Sukie revealed her true colours to Darlingest Gerry. And they didn't look especially pink and fluffy. A coda was scribbled in the bottom right hand corner: "I do so want you all to myself, dear Gerry. Sometimes I actually pray that her sickness comes back, properly. I want her all gone. Aren't I the naughty one?"

Saz put the letter back on top of the pile. Patrick's mother had first had cancer when he was nine, then she'd gone into remission until the second bout which killed her, slowly, in the two years before he turned fourteen. So Sukie must have been with Gerald Freeman somewhere between 1968 and 1973. Anyone who worked her lover as well as she did in those letters had to have uncovered some of the truth. And Patrick had said the gossip columns had often referred to Sir Gerald's mistresses, which meant all Saz had to do was check through the society pages for those years until she figured out who this Sukie was. Then she'd go and talk to her. A summer-of-love pink paper bimbo from the days of grass and roses shouldn't be too hard to find. Unless of course she'd remodelled herself and was now living happily in Kensington. Running a multi-national chain of shops. Or a posh brothel. Or the government.

When Saz climbed into bed just after two she wondered about the propriety of waking the pregnant one for middle-of-the-night sex. Or "kissy-and-stuff" as Sukie had called it. But the evening with Helen had exhausted them both and the added thought of this Sukie and Sir Gerald Freeman hard at "kissy-and-stuff" rather put her off. Instead she slid into bed, wormed her way across the king-size mattress to where Molly lay right on the edge. Always the possibility that she might fall to the floor during her night's sleep, never any proof that she had. Saz wrapped herself around Molly's warm back, slipped her arm under Molly's to stroke the barely rounded stomach and imagined she could feel inside, was holding the sleeping baby, curled inside its mother, curled inside its mother.

Saz woke with Molly at six-thirty when they were both surprised by a severe bout of morning sickness – which looked like it might stretch irritably into early afternoon sickness. Looking after an increasingly depressed Molly meant that not only was Saz's running routine knocked out for another morning, but she was also forced to leave her enquiries about Sukie and her requests for Gary until later in the day when Molly had finally sloughed off her nauseous daze and gone into work. Though not before Saz presented her girlfriend with the pages she had found of Patrick's mother's medical records.

"And you'd like me to decipher this lot for you?"

Saz was cautious, "I'd be really grateful."

"Medical school doesn't specialize in teaching you how to read the forty-year-old case notes of long dead strangers" – Molly peered at the pages – "in absolutely appalling handwriting."

"I know. But it would help to know if Patrick's mother was really ill at the time or if that was the cover story for her non-pregnancy."

"And I suppose it would help if we found out she couldn't get pregnant at all, wouldn't it?"

"Probably. It would add to the other confirmations of our suspicions, anyway."

"It's hardly ethical, babe."

"Mmm. Buying and then lying to your kid for the whole of his life isn't especially ideal behaviour either."

"That's true. All right, I'll have a look and see what I can do."

"And anything you can find on this Doctor Lees?"

"Him too."

Molly left for work and Saz watched her head down the road towards the tube, the tall, lean woman walking out in bright sunshine, nothing other than a stretch of her stiff shoulders to indicate her tiredness, her difference this summer from last. Saz and Molly were both concerned about the sickness. While at least two of their friends had been ill for the full terms of their pregnancies, and they had heard all the stories about how each pregnancy was bound to be different, Molly's illness that morning had thrown them both. What she was going through was already far from typical and anything even slightly unusual had them both worried. Worried but hiding it from the other so the fear didn't spread. Which simply meant the unspoken anxiety blossomed far too easily into unpleasant irritability. They were both treading very carefully.

By the time she finally got down to work it was too late to do anything much about Sukie, and Saz had to content herself with booking a library time to go through old press cuttings – at ten the next morning. Sleep looked like it would have to wait until the weekend. She had a little more luck with Gary, in that she was at least able to talk to him in person, but despite the excessive nature of the bribes Saz was offering, he'd not had enough time to manage anything yesterday afternoon and, further, declared himself far too busy to do anything other than real work for at least another day. Either he really did have too many dead people to file, or his disdain of "sell-out" theatre meant that Saz's offer of dress circle seats to the latest Hollywood-actor-in-West-End-triumph just wasn't quite as enticing as she'd hoped. Then again, perhaps he knew she was lying about the tickets.

Annoyed by her lack of progress, Saz made herself sit down and sort through a couple of boxes of papers. Hours later she knew rather more than she could ever have wanted to about land purchase options in France, Scotland and southern Spain. She knew that Gerald Freeman thought his world had collapsed when his wife died – and that for some time, especially in his business dealings, it seemed that it had. She knew he had rallied a few years later and taken his company into the aggressive '80s with extreme force. She knew he'd had several disagreements with various shareholders and advisors – chief among them was Richard Leyton – about the diversification of his business in the late '70s. Not everyone had been as aware as Sir Gerald of the boom potential of the plastics industry. Even, and Patrick had guessed right here, its potential in the burgeoning arms trade. Saz was glad that as yet she didn't have any definite deals to report. She did though, find something that Sir Gerald and his solicitor were in complete agreement about – the necessity of keeping Patrick's adoption entirely secret. Saz was starting to get the impression that Richard Leyton was more in control of the situation than Gerald Freeman. She found six different letters, dealing with a range of concerns from Patrick's initially slow development at school, to the arthritis-related condition he had suffered in his early teens. According to Gerald Freeman, Patrick's treatment would have been more successful if his doctors had had access to Patrick's complete medical history. The solicitor, however, was the one calling the shots about how much information could be passed on. And according to all the letters, how much was absolutely none at all. At least nothing more than Doctor Lees' initial assertion that Lillian Hope had been completely healthy at the time of her son's birth. Saz didn't know an awful lot more about Patrick's adoption, but she knew for definite that she intended to have a serious talk with Georgina Leyton at the earliest opportunity. No matter how suddenly her father had died, if she had sent all those papers back to Freeman she must have made some attempt to sort through his business first. And if she hadn't, then Saz would just have to ask her to give it a go. She wasn't prepared to be fobbed off a second time.

Saz was just thinking that perhaps a late afternoon run might make up for the lack of an early morning one, when the phone rang. It was Carrie, "You know that bloke you asked me about? Jonathan Godwin?"

"The man I told you about in confidence, Carrie, yes. In case you heard anything. Not for general public consumption."

"Well, I knew I recognized his name."

"You haven't said anything to him, have you?"

"Give me credit, Saz, I'm not quite as rash as you might like to think." Saz contented herself with a short laugh and asked Carrie what she wanted. Carrie wanted to take Saz dancing.

SIXTEEN

Carrie's reasoning was vague to say the least. She wanted Saz to go out with her that night because she thought that a bloke she sort of knew who ran a bar not far from her flat was called Godwin. Luke Godwin. And she thought that maybe he had a wealthy family. Not especially definite and, to Saz's mind, not very tempting either. So she called Helen.

"How's your head?"

"Bloody awful. Sorry about last night."

"That's fine, Hells, anything to help; you know Molly and I have been really concerned about you since the break-up. Honest, we didn't need a rest at all last night and I hadn't been up for hours and I didn't have loads of work I needed to get on with."

"Saz, you sound suspiciously like a woman in need of a favour."

"Helen, you sound suspiciously like a woman who owes me one."

Half an hour later Helen called back and told her that the owner of Bar Rage was one Luke Godwin. "He used to run a couple of gay venues in pubs in West London, then he bought up this old pub in Brixton and did it all up."

"So it's a gay club?"

"No, Saz, it's an incredibly groovy anybody's club. I take it you haven't been?"

"Why, have you?"

"Alex and I went there once when we were first getting together."

"When you were still with Judith?"

"Yeah, it was somewhere I knew she'd never go. It's very big. And very loud. And very young. Jude would hate it."

Saz hurriedly pulled them back to the subject in hand before Helen launched into another rave about Judith – whether it was to be negative ex-lover or the slightly more positive "I never knew what I had until I lost it" – Saz couldn't wait to find out, there was too much else to get on with. Not to mention her distinct lack of desire to be any more involved in her friend's ex-relationship.

"Yeah but, Helen, I can't waste my night at this club just because the guy who owns it has the same surname as someone mentioned in a letter to Gerald Freeman."

"No stupid, I wouldn't bother calling otherwise. I think he is his son. Or at least the Luke Godwin who owns this bar is the son of a Jonathan Godwin. Maybe yours, maybe not. Possible though. Luke Godwin's father put money into the bar and he must be pretty bloody well off, because it's a big step up from running a gig a couple of nights a week to actually owning your own place. I reckon he's worth a try, and Jonathan Godwin is more or less the same age as Chris's parents."

"I suppose so, just the thought of asking a complete stranger if he's adopted seems a little excessive."

"Get Carrie to do it for you. She's good at excessive."

"Yeah, right."

"Anyway, that's all I have for you. I'll get back to my real work now – oh, and Saz?"

Saz heard Helen's tone change to formal in the space of a few words, "Yes?"

"You will tell me if anything starts to get messy, won't you?"

"I'm only trying to find Chris's birth parents, Helen. It's not exactly illegal to adopt a baby."

"Yeah, but keep me informed, all right? Just in case?"

Saz crossed her fingers and agreed. She hung up, glad she'd chosen not to mention the matter of baby-buying. Helen and Judith had both proved extremely useful friends in the past, but there were also times when their dutiful attitudes clashed with Saz's work plans. She had no doubt that given the whole truth, this would have been one of those times. And while police-issue DM's tramping through Georgina Leyton's offices would probably kick up some interesting information, it would also bring Chris's search into the open, and she knew her first priority was to honour his desire to protect his mother. She was the only mother he had. So far.

Saz and Molly had intended to spend the evening with Marc and Chris. Rather than put them off, Molly agreed to go out with the boys while Saz went clubbing with Carrie. Molly was perfectly happy to miss out; an evening of loud music in smoke-filled rooms was the last thing she felt like doing, though she seemed just a little bit more interested once Marc and Chris knew where Saz was going and who she was hoping to meet.

Chris's first reaction was to burst out laughing, "You went all the way to Sussex, trawled through Patrick Freeman's stuff, only to come up with Luke Godwin?"

"Well, Jonathan Godwin actually. He's the man who Leyton talked about in the letter. Luke is his son. Or might be his son. At least he's the son of a Jonathan Godwin, whether or not he's the son of our Jonathan Godwin . . ."

"Yes, Saz, I know who Luke is. Or rather Marc does, don't you, darling?"

"You what?"

"Marc knows Mr Godwin quite well actually."

Three pairs of eyes turned to Marc who was looking resignedly out the window across to the Heath. "God you've got a big mouth, Chris."

"It's important. Saz needs to know for her research. Tell the girls about your first love, darling."

Marc shook his head, finished his beer. "He wasn't my first love, he wasn't love at all. Lot of sex though. For about two months, it was never going to be a relationship. I was twenty-six, he was just turned twenty, I met him at the first club he ever ran. He is Jonathan Godwin's son, he is adopted, his father went completely crazy when he came out at sixteen and refused to talk to him for about five years. Godwin senior gave Luke no help at all for ages but – and I only know this from mutual friends, not because I see him any more – apparently he helped him set up this new business, so I suppose they must be best of buddies again. Enough?"

Nowhere near enough for Saz and Molly who had never been able to get much out of Marc about his past and were astonished to find it thrown up at them like this. Saz pressed Marc for information about Luke's old clubs, the move from the smaller venues to actually owning the more successful one, and any other family background that might more clearly tie him to the Jonathan Godwin in Leyton's letter. Molly asked juicier questions about the relationship. Chris maintained that Luke had broken Marc's heart, Marc held to the view that his ex-lover's various drug habits and the dangerously violent streak he occasionally exhibited meant that Luke would be hard-pressed to find anyone who would be willing to give themselves to him totally.

"The guy can be very warm, quite lovely, but he's also completely fucking unpredictable. He can be fantastic to be with, even when pissed, especially when coked off his face. And the next minute, on the slightest provocation, he's threatening to smash your head in. And the way he says it, you think he actually might mean it. I couldn't fall in love with that. I liked it, fancied it, really fucking wanted it, but anyone with half a brain wouldn't fall in love with it."

Saz and Molly listened to him, each woman acutely aware that she had fallen just as dangerously more than once in her past.

Molly left for a movie and dinner and Saz stayed at home to get ready. Despite the potential leap forward in the job, she was not looking forward to her night ahead.

SEVENTEEN

Carrie had first met Luke three months earlier, talking her way past the girl guards at the door and directly into Luke's face as she fell over his out-stretched feet and landed in his lap on the sofa. He thought it was funny enough not to have her thrown out and they embarked on the first of their drinking binges. Since then, they'd welcomed the morning together a few times, aided by enough vodka to clear up the Russian national debt in a weekend and the odd line from Luke's constant coke supply. Carrie finally realized the value of drug-confiscating bouncers on club doors. In an early morning discussion the weekend earlier, they revealed they'd both run away from home at fourteen. Carrie because she came out to her mother who was horribly shocked that the flesh of her loins turned out to be a dyke. Baby Barbie-dyke, but gay all the same. Carrie and her mother had been best of friends for years now, but the age fourteen trauma still made a good pissed-at-the-bar story. Even easier to tell when the bar was a big fat sofa and Luke was ordering free drinks for the duration of the session.

Unlike Carrie, who had lived with friends, relatives and one very amicable ex-nun until her mother relented, Luke's was a rather different runaway experience. It was also not a story he was used to telling. Not a story he especially wanted to tell. Except that Carrie poured him another vodka, and another. Then she cut him another three lines of his own coke and rolled his own fifty-pound note for him. Carrie wasn't after any information in particular, had no especial desire to hear Luke's personal teenage tragedy. But Luke had both free alcohol and much better coke than she did, and the girl she had been eyeing up at the bar had now left in the arms of a twenty-year-old ski-bunny. It was just gone three in the morning and if Carrie didn't force Luke to keep talking, then she'd soon be going home too. Alone. And going home alone was bad enough, but going home alone before dawn was too awful to contemplate. The bar was practically empty, Luke was off his face, his mouth was starting to run away with him in a cocaine free-fall and Carrie thankfully sat back to enjoy the show. Luke Godwin began to stutter out the background to his fourteen-year-old departure and, as the story got juicier, Carrie slowly became aware that some of what she was hearing had a familiar ring to it.

Luke's impetus to depart the familial grasp came when his mother, in the throes of despair as her husband of twenty years left home, revealed that Luke was not really her son. Nor was he his father's son. Whatever it might say on his birth certificate. Luke went immediately to question his father, was told his mother's revelation was true and that his father now intended to start a new family with the young blonde who, unlike the old blonde, was actually capable of bearing him a child. Not the finest of partings. The old man and the young man didn't speak for five years and then met just once, a week before Luke's twentieth birthday. Luke came out, his father walked out. All this was explained to Carrie in a long and rambling drunken diatribe. What he hadn't explained, though, was how father and son came to be reunited in business – Carrie being far more interested in messy beginnings than happy endings.

Once Carrie explained what she knew, Saz agreed to go out with her. Saz was hoping the father and son partnership had developed to such an extent that Luke might now know – and would be willing to divulge – details of the adoption process. If Jonathan Godwin was linked to both Richard Leyton and Gerald Freeman, then it wasn't too much to hope there might be a further connection to Chris's parents.

However, just because she'd agreed to go out didn't mean she really wanted to. Four years of happy coupledom with Molly had removed any desire to experience the joys of early morning clubbing. On a Tuesday night. The idea of revisiting a land of early twenties' angst, peopled with flesh-hungry youth, and ending the night trying to decipher the incoherence of her own drunken babble filled her with a vomit-scented horror, underscored with seriously nostalgic ennui. She had never particularly enjoyed the dubious delights of an ill-lit room surrounded by a trade fair of sweaty flesh. Saz did not like clubbing. She didn't like pubs. She didn't like drinking cheap yet over-priced alcohol, and she had long ago worked out that coke sniffed from one's own clean hand mirror in the privacy of one's own sitting room was a damn sight more attractive than the same substance imbibed from the cigarette-burnt cistern of an overflowing toilet where there was no toilet paper left by midnight.

Saz did not want to go out. She wanted to stay in and pore over boxes of papers until she could pore no more. To sink to the floor beside her beloved and watch trash TV, eat hot bubbling gruyère glued to dark rye bread with extra strong mustard, followed by half a bar of gooey caramel chocolate, drink one or more bottles of well chosen, very chilled wine and then get a good night's sleep. Carrie, however, demanded otherwise. That she was probably right to do so didn't make Saz any more gracious. Her mood was not improved by a difficult journey to Carrie's flat, evening traffic squeezing down the Walworth Road at a rate of inches, ten minutes spent in a steamy bus outside the old Labour Party headquarters, wondering yet again about the People's Transport Policy. She spent the first half-hour with her ex-girlfriend moaning about all that she expected to loathe in the hours between midnight and dawn. She expected to loathe quite a lot.

"What do you mean this place charges fifteen quid entry?"

"Twenty."

"What?"

"After midnight. Doesn't matter, we're on the guest list."

"Bouncers looking us up and down when we try to get in—"

"I said we're on the guest list."

"I thought you barely knew this bloke?"

"It's not like he's a close mate or anything, but we've been pissed together a few times, talked a bit. I'd already asked if I could be on the guest list for tonight. And I mean, I don't know him well—"

"After all, you've only ever talked when you're both pissed."

"Yeah, but that can be a great bonding experience, Saz."

"I know, Carrie. I wasn't sober when I met you."

"Anyway, even if we weren't on the guest list, we'd have no trouble getting in, we're gorgeous."

Saz glared at Carrie in the mirror, the truth of the statement lost on her irritated mask, "What about the music?"

"What about it?"

"I don't think I like young people's music."

"Christ, Saz, you're not that old."

"I'm not old at all."

"Then stop bloody well acting like it. You'll probably like it. You might even have a good time. It's not going to be like the clubs you went to when you were a kid and nor is it some crappy venue given over to a bunch of dykes with no taste and even less money playing Tracey fucking Chapman all bloody night."

Saz bit her cheeks to hold back a grin. It wasn't often she managed to push Carrie enough to upset her; the reverse was far more common. Carrie riled might just cheer her up a bit.

"It's just a bar, Saz. With music. No one is going to look at what you're wearing, they don't care. It isn't about that, it's just a place to go. Anyway, you're going for work, not fun. It isn't a big deal."

Saz applied more mascara, disappointed. She'd hoped for a better fight-back than that. She swallowed down another large mouthful of cheap white, not nice enough and not cold enough, but easily the best she could expect from Carrie's fridge.

"Carrie, I would question your ability to stay sober long enough to notice what kind of a deal it is."

Carrie smiled, "Well, yes, there's always that." She handed Saz the mirror on which she'd laid out four short lines of coke, "Now shut up, cheer up, and get this in you."

Saz did.

In the past two years Carrie had been through four different lovers who, if they weren't quite in their late teens – Carrie met Justine at her twenty-first birthday party – certainly liked to behave as if they were. She had therefore become something of an expert on the new bars and clubs that had sprung from the ruins of badly-run corner pubs in the past few years. And, even without a partner by her side, going out alone was bliss to Carrie. She loved talking to strangers. It was why Carrie was useful to Saz – she so often knew someone who knew someone who might know something: in this case, the part-owner of the latest dingy old-man's-pub turned sex-scented lair of the sweet young things, a century of nicotine-stained afternoons remodelled for the price of eight cans of bright purple paint and a couple of dreadlocked Australian girlies installed behind the bar.

According to Carrie, Luke Godwin spent most nights at one of the three bars in his building and, while he'd drink solidly from midnight on, he always seemed sober enough to make sure the doors were firmly locked when he let himself and his manager out at five in the morning. Carrie knew Saz would want to talk to Luke – if only she could actually get her through the doors. First though, there was quite obviously some softening up to do. The coke would work its into-the-world magic soon enough, but Carrie understood Saz well enough to know she'd need more than just drugs and alcohol to get her really looking forward to the night ahead. She'd need food too.

The couple of lines had cheered Saz up considerably, as did the comfortable feeling of hot London night sticking to her skin. Even her irritation at walking from Camberwell to eat in Stockwell for a night out in Brixton didn't go too deep, and the extremely circuitous route was a good memories' walk for Saz.

They stopped outside a small Spanish café, "I figured that as you're being so brave tonight, we might as well push the boat out and do something really daring."

"Tapas is daring?"

"It is when every other café round here is Portuguese."

Saz, who'd had her mouth set on a small sweet custard tart and maybe a glass of chilled wine since they'd crossed Brixton Road, put aside her Lisbon fantasies and went in ahead of Carrie. An hour later and after several small plates of chorizo, spicy mushrooms and public-friendly garlic-free squid had disappeared from their table, Carrie was just about to order a second bottle of wine when Saz reminded her they weren't there for a girls' night out, but for work. Carrie took the cash from Saz's wallet to pay the excessively attractive waitress, leaving a large tip more for the young woman's long curly hair than for the service which had been efficient if uninterested. But pretty. Very pretty.

Saz refused to walk any further. Although she'd been softened up by the food and alcohol, and despite not having managed to get in a run that day, she didn't really see traipsing from one bar to another as the perfect form of exercise. They caught a bus to Brixton tube, jumping down into the street as an overflow of fast-moving and loud bodies spilled out from the Academy. Not loud enough, though, to drown out the familiar cries of the Jesus preacher, town crier of late-night doom, ensconced in his regular perch opposite the entrance to the tube. Carrie insisted on one more drink before they went to the bar, so they stopped at the Ritzy and drank another couple of glasses of wine and Saz enviously watched the people leaving the movies, rubbing their eyes against the bright bar lights – and heading home. Carrie met a couple of people she knew and Saz looked around, thinking how when she and Molly first got together they used to go to the movies all the time. Until life took over and they had no spare time any more. Spare time she knew she had given up willingly and wanted to do so even more now that the baby was on its way – but, all the same, lost time it didn't do to think about too closely.

She listened in on Carrie's conversation for a while and then rummaged in Carrie's bag and held out her wallet, "Can I take this?" Carrie turned from admiring her friend Beth's new tattoo and looked at Saz. "Of course. I thought you'd never ask. Might I enquire why?"

"Yeah. I'm starting to get maudlin and as we've got a

while to go yet, I thought I'd do something about it, rather than pissing you off even more. If that's OK with you?"

Carrie waved her in the direction of the girls' toilets, "Help yourself. That's what it's there for."

"Only because I'm tired and we've got a long night ahead."

Carrie smirked, "Naturally. Why ever else?"

Saz went into the toilets, found an empty cubicle and was grateful that the Ritzy had seen fit to renovate so nicely and install such smooth cistern covers. Carrie still owed her last month's rent so Saz didn't feel too greedy helping herself. And as she sniffed up the second long line, she reminded herself not to enjoy the evening too much, it wouldn't do to get to like going out. She couldn't quite see Molly happily sanctioning late-night working parties once the baby arrived.

Ten minutes later Carrie led Saz down a maze of short back streets, round a few dark corners and up to the front door. They walked the length of the queue, ignoring the disdainful stares of those who'd been waiting for half an hour or more, past the vast bouncer who kissed Carrie on both cheeks, and then through the glittering silver doors into the warm dark.

EIGHTEEN

Teeth numb, tongue buzzing, sharp sting at the back of her throat – with four lines of cumulative coke and most of a bottle of wine inside her, Saz was surprisingly unfazed by the raucous heat that slammed her face as Carrie took her hand and led her though the mess of bodies to the bar. The music was loud, noisy enough for the few people who were dancing not to feel stupid, but not so bad that the shouted conversations all around were completely pointless. Carrie bought two strong sea breezes and shepherded Saz to a safe corner, three tables on a slightly raised dais giving a good view of the room.

It was a basic layout, corner doors, the traditionally small windows now replaced with huge single glass panes facing directly on to the street, clearly delineating the new pub ethos – this place was not about getting away from it all for a quiet half, it was about getting into it all, any of it. And ideally having the whole world know you were there at the same time. Where once there had been a central bar, serving two or three different sections of the room in rotation, the new bar had been pushed back and stretched into a stainless steel barricade right along the far wall, leaving a central space for tables and chairs, some of them pushed together to make more room for the dancers. There were two long wooden tables with a few large groups around them, the other smaller tables were occupied with couples and the would-be couples who hoped this might be their lucky night.

Once she'd drawn her eyes from the clientele, Saz's attention was gripped by the image-overload of cartoons and features being screened directly onto silver painted walls. The colour wasn't ideal for picture clarity, but with the pounding techno forebeat the aim was hardly to give undivided attention to the silent celluloid. They were mobile art, sometimes obscured by the clump of dancers moving as one, occasionally keyed into perfect relief when the image seemed made for a literally silver screen. Bette Davis slinking down the stairs in *All About Eve* was the perfect black and white bitch foil, jostling for space with a washed out Captain Scarlet: '50s glamour and '60s aqua swimming on the unevenly plastered walls. Elsewhere Saz glimpsed Judy Garland deep sleeping in a field of poppies, Top Cat grimacing behind Officer Dibble's back, while on the back wall Steamboat Willie waited to grow shorter and fatter into his more famous baby-mouse body.

Beneath the fake pictures were the real fantasy images. There were some suits, obviously locals who'd come in on their way home from work and never quite managed to find the ruby slippers at the bottom of their pint glass. There were a few very over-made-up little ones. Easily too young to be buying the alco-pops they were drinking by the bucketful, but scraping past the guys on the door with a lurid mix of eyeliner and exposed flesh. There were a few groups of loud laughing blokes, a wide selection of couples, drinking and kissing but not engaging in conversation with each other – physically close rather than emotionally connected.

Carrie pointed out a couple of young women to Saz, "Over there, straight as fuck, acting dyke flirt for the boys at the bar."

Saz followed Carrie's index finger to the women, one attractive, one very pretty, neither yet old enough to have made it to beautiful, dancing in a way that could have earned them a more than adequate living in the Soho basements still to be pinked-up. They didn't look any sexuality in particular and Saz thought they were being a bit damn kissy for straight girls. "How can you tell?"

"Every time the blonde touches her friend, she looks over at that tall thin bloke by the bar. She's showing off for him. Wouldn't be surprised if her mate didn't fancy her, though. She's just that bit more interested in the act than she is in the lads."

Saz watched as the tall blonde stroked her smaller friend's arm and shoulder with a slow hand and then looked up from beneath her fringe to the grinning guy at the bar. He couldn't take his bloodshot eyes off the blonde and the little brunette appeared sadly unaware of the meaningful looks taking place over her head. Saz whispered "Shame" and Carrie burst out laughing, "Yep, she's shit out of luck tonight. Poor thing."

Saz recognized the tone of Carrie's voice and looked back from the doomed girlie to Carrie. Sure enough, her ex had a gleeful leer on her face. Saz reminded herself that, despite the mandatory coke and alcohol rations, they were actually supposed to be working and she had better keep a tight rein on Carrie's lusts. While the sight of straight women acting dyke pissed her off immensely, Saz didn't think the pretty little brunette deserved anything quite as dangerous as Carrie in payment for her deception. Saz managed to divert Carrie's attention to the five blokes dancing apart from the main party of moving limbs. They were bliss-smiling and waving themselves in front of the fat speakers, each one pretty much dancing to his own rhythm, and each rhythm nothing like that of the music. Which, given that it had now mutated into an insistent four-four drone, would have seemed almost impossible if Saz hadn't been there to see it herself. It was happening though and, in their gently spaced-out way, the five men were providing their own syncopated anti-rhythm. And they were certainly happy.

After an hour of viewing and two more sea breezes each, Carrie figured Luke should have made it through the back door for his nightly shift as chief executive and she led Saz upstairs to the other rooms. They went past a bouncer, surprisingly small compared to those at the front door, but with a range of facial scars that indicated his nastiness more than made up for any lack of stature. He opened the door for them, shepherding Carrie through first with a low bow and a big smile. He saved his malevolent glare for Saz.

"Cheery chap. Doesn't like your friends?"

"Victor – short for Victory – doesn't like my girlfriends. Wants me all to himself."

"Carrie, you haven't?"

"No. But it pays to let him think he's on a promise."

Saz shook her head and forced down the big sister lecture she felt rising at the back of her throat. It wasn't the fucking a bloke she objected to, or even the idea of fucking for a purpose. Neither of those activities were especially unusual for Carrie, nor had they once been for Saz, though her sexual activity had long been limited to a one-woman arena. Primarily. She just thought it wasn't especially nice behaviour to encourage someone who had no hope whatsoever.

They went up one flight of steps and Carrie poked her head round a scarlet door, a wave of fierce laughter turning Saz's head.

"What's that?"

"Comedy club."

"At this time of night?"

"Extremely late night stand-up. Very groovy. Sharon's on the door, she'll let us in."

"I don't think . . ."

"She says Luke's watching too, so we can corner him at the interval."

Saz snarled, stand-up comedy was about her least favourite form of entertainment, but at least she would be closer to this Luke whom Carrie was promising so much from. She shrugged and followed Carrie past the woman on the door, taking a seat at the back of the room with an ungracious, "Yeah, fuck, whatever."

Twenty minutes later the tall, red-headed comedian bounded off the small stage that had been struggling to contain her energy and Saz found herself grinning painfully, cheek muscles hurting from trying not to laugh out loud and win a sniggering "I told you so" from Carrie – who wasn't fooled. "I said she was good, didn't I?"

Saz refused to give in, "No. You said it would be good. If you'd told me this woman was actually funny I might have been more eager. Possibly."

Carrie sneered, "Admit it Saz, you liked her."

Saz stood up, "Yeah, but that's not why we're here, is it? It's nearly three in the morning, for fuck's sake. Are we ever going to talk to this Luke Godwin or what?"

The build up of post-set chat that accompanied the rush to the bar chose just that moment to fall into an unpredict-able lull and Saz's tone, perfectly defensible in a room crowded with boisterous, semi-pissed punters, stretched sharp above their heads, loud words falling into a sudden quiet moment.

Luke Godwin, seated twenty feet away at the side of the stage, in earnest conversation with a couple of young women, looked up from the two of them, directly at Saz. "And who the fuck's asking?"

NINETEEN

After the hasty apologies, Luke's hard stare softened a little. Having blown a kiss to each of the pretty little things still holding out pointless hopes for him, he took Carrie and Saz upstairs to the third bar. This was still a public room, but it was even harder to get into than the rest of the building – unofficially reserved for those who were rated markedly cooler than merely chilled. The two women guarding the door had strict instructions regarding the dress code and sobriety of those they allowed to enter. More than that, though, they were required to use their discretion in the trickier matter of style. Nothing quite so simple as admission only for the young or the beautiful. Here entry was reserved for the purely interesting.

The small bar had several old armchairs, two uncomfortable modern sofas and a few low tables loaded down with a strangely eclectic selection of magazines. Saz looked in vain for evidence of irony on the face of the pretty boy reading aloud to his girlfriend from the *Woman's Realm* problem page. In fact there were remarkably few raised eyebrows in the entire room, despite the fact that most of the furniture consisted of twelve huge cushions, lighting was provided by waist-high candles and the background music was a loop of Petula Clark singing "Don't Sleep In The Subway". When Luke handed them a walnut whip each from a tray on the bar Saz figured that even if he didn't have anything to offer, her night wouldn't have been wasted after all. All that excess and cheap chocolate too.

Luke sampled and rejected four different wines before settling on a bottle of Chenin Blanc. He directed Saz and Carrie to a very low, overstuffed sofa, brought glasses from the bar and, once he'd poured a glass for each of them, placed himself on a straight-backed chair at a right angle to the sofa, sitting a good foot above either of them. Saz was perfectly happy to accord him all the respect due to the venue owner, but she didn't see why he found it necessary to rub in their status discrepancy quite so clearly.

Having made the introductions, finished her wine and explained that Saz knew Marc – which drew a raised eyebrow and a "no comment" from Luke – Carrie wandered off downstairs in search of the little brunette and left Saz and Luke to talk – which had seemed great as a concept when Carrie introduced them, but didn't seem to work in practice once Saz explained what she was after. "Right, well – I'll get straight to the point. I'm trying to help a friend locate his birth parents and I have reason to believe that the solicitor who helped your family adopt you might have helped his family adopt him."

"Richard Leyton was my father's solicitor. He's dead."

"Yes, I know. I've tried to talk to his daughter but didn't get much help there actually."

"Well, Georgina can't give out confidential information to just anyone, can she?"

"You know her?"

Luke smiled, "Business."

"Right. And I do appreciate she's in a difficult position if she helps my client. It's just that, because she wasn't able to help me, I'm having to go about this indirectly. And I found a letter from Leyton suggesting that another client might want to contact your adoptive father when your parents were thinking of adopting you."

"Who was that letter to?"

Saz shook her head, "I'm sorry, I don't really think I can say. My client is sort of well known and I'd rather . . ."

"You'd rather I gave you personal information about me and my parents, but you don't intend to trade in kind, is that it? Doesn't seem very fair really, does it?"

Sadly, while Luke may have been willing to tell his life story to Carrie with half a gram of coke inside him, he wasn't quite as willing to do so semi-sober. Saz had been expecting someone much more willing to talk. Perhaps he had a potential Marc waiting at home; whatever the reason, it was clear that Luke didn't fancy wasting his warm and charming side on Saz.

She tried placatory tactics, "I'm sorry, I guess I shouldn't have come to you about this while you were at work. I realize this is a very personal issue for you."

"No, it's not, everyone knows I'm adopted. It's one of my party pieces. The big discovery at fourteen. Poor boy, family heartbreak. It's always worked fantastically well for the sympathy fuck."

"Oh, right. So then you must understand how my client felt when he discovered he was adopted?"

"Yeah, I suppose so, but it's not really my problem, is it?" Luke took another sip of his wine, sat back in his chair and smiled at Saz, "I mean, you're saying Richard Leyton asked your client's father to talk to my father. Or not. It's not really that much of a link, is it? Why don't you go direct to my father?"

"I could. I probably will. I just thought . . ."

"I'd be a more convenient start? Easier to talk to? Poor little wounded soldier wanting to confess all, eager to help a fellow searcher caught in the parent trap?"

"Um – yes, no . . . I don't know really." Saz didn't know what to say, clearly something she'd said or done had upset Luke, but she couldn't imagine what it was. He said he didn't mind talking about being adopted and yet he was being no help at all, "I just thought from what Carrie told me, you might want to help someone else who's found themselves in your position."

"Not a bad thought, but wrong. I don't mind people knowing I'm adopted, but I don't particularly want to talk about all the legal and technical details. Not with a complete stranger and not in the middle of the night anyway. So, if you'll excuse me?"

Saz wasn't being asked to excuse Luke, she was being asked to leave. And the combination of his attitude and her tiredness pissed her off just enough to make her a little more adamant.

"OK, fine. I fucked up coming here tonight. But this is my job. I'm sorry I pissed you off, but could I talk to you again? Tomorrow maybe?"

Luke finished his glass of wine, "I'll be in the garden bar. It's where I am every afternoon as long as the sun is shining. You're welcome to come along if you want. And I'll chat if I feel like it. OK?" Saz didn't have much choice, his grudging offer was better than nothing. She got up to leave and Luke took her hand as she passed him, "Oh, and come to think of it, I don't actually think you ought to call my father, adoptive father. He's slightly less fond than I am of complete strangers poking around in his private life. Particularly where it touches on the sorry story of how his barren first love led to the adoption of the prodigal poof."

"But he's your business partner, isn't he? I thought from what Marc said, that the two of you had a good relationship now?"

Luke poured himself another glass, "We do. And I don't

want your nosiness fucking it up. Now off you go, I'll see you tomorrow. If I'm really lucky. Maybe I'll be in a better mood then, happier to part with my darkest treasures."

Luke waved her away and Saz walked from the room feeling uncertain and not a little uncomfortable. Clearly he'd used up all his pleasantries on Carrie and she'd been left with the nasty side that Marc had spoken of.

Downstairs in the main bar the music was still throbbing through the assembled bodies and it took Saz quite a while to prise Carrie and the brunette apart, but she managed to get Carrie's keys eventually. And to throw a compassionate smile towards the tall blonde sitting alone at the end of the table, mournfully watching Carrie monopolize her friend. Saz left the building, glad to be in the quiet of a bird-call street, trying to work out what she'd just experienced.

When she rolled back to Carrie's place at four-thirty in the already warm morning, soft light was prettifying Camberwell Green into something slightly closer to Camberwick Green, Windy Miller passed out beneath a blanket of *Evening Standards*. Saz collapsed with extreme gratitude onto the sofa. Sleep came easy and smiling. Until Carrie stumbled home an hour later, finger on the doorbell three minutes longer than was necessary and little brunette in doe-eyed tow.

TWENTY

Eventually Saz gave up trying to ignore Carrie and her new friend and slipped out the front door of the flat. Two hours later she was in her own kitchen, freshly showered and ready to go to work. Or as ready as her scratchy-eyed, no-sleep body could be.

It was fairly easy to get the full name of Gerald Freeman's unofficial companion in the early years of the '70s. The narcissistic nature of the print media meant those who ought to have been carefully guarding their precious archives easily swallowed the idea of a PhD thesis on the evolution of the gossip column and welcomed her into their offices. Saz sifted through about eighty old magazines and a similar collection of newspapers, the smug coyness of the *Jennifer's Diary* entries matching euphemism for euphemism with the more tight-lipped broadsheet references. What all the "close friend", "charming assistant" and "delightful companion" references boiled down to was the rather more basic *Private Eye* observation that it was clear the esteemed Gerald Freeman – businessman, entrepreneur, industrialist, good party man – was getting his end away with Sukie Planchet, a little bit of a girl from somewhere north of Sunderland, residing at the time in the wilds of Notting Hill, long before the area attained its faux-trash ambience so popular with the trust-fund babies.

With a few photos and the full name it was an easy step along the electoral register for Saz to locate the one Sukie

Planchet resident in London. She had assumed there couldn't be more than two or three in the whole country, if that, but it was always better to start in London. The chances were that anyone who'd experienced an enjoyable few years in the big city wasn't likely to return to the North East the minute the '70s globally cooled from summer of love into winter of discontent. Saz figured if she drew a blank in London then her next step would logically be the Home Counties, that nursing home for all former party goers, where reformed groovers slip quietly into a dark night of their own gin-and-tonic devising. Fortunately Saz's tube pass mentality wasn't stretched beyond breaking point: Sukie Planchet had taken the opportunity of growing up to relocate across London, Central Line direct. Ladbroke Grove to Bethnal Green in twelve easy stops.

Saz chose a direct doorstepping approach this time. Partly because she just couldn't be bothered lying for a second time that day, but also because the electoral roll information had thrown her a little. From what she'd read both of the "companion" in the old newspapers and from Sukie's own love letters to Sir Gerald she had expected the young raver to grow into a happy little middle-class housewife with a couple of perfect children at private schools and a nice cottage in Norfolk for sunny weekends, maybe a place in France if the husband was doing really well. In the few thoughts she gave to the possibilities, the most she had imagined was that Sukie might have used the novel clothing style she'd exhibited in the old photos to become an artist or designer of some sort. Or, if she really had enjoyed the mistress life, Saz thought she might even be interviewing a copycat Cynthia Payne in furthest Norwood. She hadn't expected to be making a visit to a Peabody Housing Trust estate, to see a single woman, no children named on the council tax roll, who listed her occupation as "Religious Educator – Unemployed". Saz figured if the worst came to the worst she could always claim the Lord had sent her.

She didn't need to bother. In a reverse Jehovah's Witness action, Saz knocked on the door and Sukie answered it almost immediately, heavy gilt-embossed bible open in one thin hand and Jesus holding tight to the other. "I don't know who you are, I don't know why you're here, I have no money to buy what you're selling, but what I have to offer you is prized above rubies. Please, come in."

Saz suppressed an involuntary shudder, a combination of an innate fear of evangelism and her even greater concern that if this was the way Sukie always answered her door, she was damn lucky she was still around to open it. Then she followed Sukie inside.

Prototype wildchild, social climbing blasphemer, drunken adulterer – and now clean living, headscarfed ambassador for Christ in one easy water-walking jump. Sukie had thought she was happy, persuaded herself the free love years of easy living were worthwhile, and then one morning she'd woken up and seen the error of her ways. It was that simple. The good Lord picked her up, dusted her down and sent her on His way with a gentle "Go and sin no more". The basic whore-to-nun conversion which Sukie was delighted to tell Saz all about. At length. With liberal biblical quotations thrown in for backup, though rather more of the raining-down brimstone and fire on Sodom and Gomorrah kind, than the wishy-washy liberalism of loving your brother as yourself. Sukie obviously found the pre-Jesus testament a little more appropriate to her message.

After the third parable designed to press home exactly the same point, Saz was almost prepared to give the Jesus thing a go if it would only shut Sukie up long enough to allow her to get a question out. Only so many ways to say the same thing and Jesus's buddies appeared to have come up with all of them. Basically be good, be very, very good, do not pass temptation, get out of limbo free, go directly to heaven. The camel's hump/needle's eye concept was not exactly new to Saz, her big sister having passed through a thankfully brief born-again phase when they were in their teens, just around the time Saz could really have done with an understanding sibling to discuss her own rebirth as might-be dyke. Cassie's redemption lasted as long as her virginity. Then she left home, engaged in an intense battle with the Prince of Darkness, discovered the joys of lust – it took Gary about two hours and cost him four pints of snakebite – and Cassie's shining faith was put away with the rest of her childish things.

Saz took less than five minutes to realize that while Sukie was one of God's very own children and therefore quite capable of conducting a three way conversation – Saz, Sukie and Jesus – she wasn't, unfortunately, totally nuts. If she was going to get any information at all out of the tiny but very forceful woman in front of her, it either had to be via terribly clever subterfuge and brilliant questioning, thereby uncovering the past in tiny glimmering increments of truth, or she would need to opt for blatant honesty and hope for the best. Saz was exhausted, hanging out for a proper night's sleep, and not feeling especially clever.

She opted for brevity and truth. "I've come to talk about Sir Gerald Freeman."

Used to deceit as by far the best way to coax unwilling candour, Saz was more than a little taken aback when Sukie sat right down beside her on the sofa, her tiny frame barely registering on the uneven old cushions, grabbed Saz's hand and hissed into her face, spitting just a little as she did so, "Bad man. Very bad man. Let's just pray for him, shall we?"

And the torrent began again. Sukie held both of Saz's

hands so tight in her own that Saz wondered her rings weren't fused together with the force. The older woman closed her red-rimmed eyes and began the litany of Sir Gerald's evils. "For the fornication and filth he forced upon me and so many others, dear Jesus, we ask your forgiveness—"

There was a pause, growing into an uncomfortable silence until Sukie squeezed Saz's hands even tighter and Saz realized she was supposed to offer a response. She dredged up long forgotten years of tedious R.E. classes and muttered an embarrassed, "Forgive us, oh Lord." Then stuttered out an "Amen" just in case that was necessary too.

Sukie turned her fierce gaze on Saz, nodded and continued. Saz was relieved when Sukie shut her disconcertingly pale blue eyes, the better to commune with her Lord.

The list of Sir Gerald's transgressions was seemingly endless, if a little tamer than Saz had been hoping for. There was sex, of course, more sex than she would have thought Sukie would be willing to admit to, but it seemed there was nothing the reformed zealot wouldn't share with her Lord, not even the night she crept from the sleeping Sir Gerald's bed directly to his best friend's bunk while on holiday with the two of them in Ibiza. Quite how Sukie blamed this particular piece of devilment on Sir Gerald, out for the count on his daily diet of gin, whisky and a whole lot more gin, Saz wasn't quite sure. Nor did she want to stop Sukie mid-flow and question her, thereby risking the chance of losing another important tale of the old man's wickedness. Or even just the juicy gossip. If Saz was going to have her fingers crushed by a woman wearing a "Thank God for Jesus" T-shirt – revealed when the threadbare pale pink cardie was ripped off for the prayer session – then she

might as well treat the experience like an aural tabloid. All
the juice and none of the air brushing.

TWENTY-ONE

Half an hour later Sukie seemed to be winding up her prayer-fest. Saz had been treated to a litany of rage directed against Sir Gerald, his friends and pretty much anyone who'd come into contact with Sukie in her time as his mistress. Saz had taken most of it in, occasionally attempting an interruption that might draw Sukie round to the purpose of her visit, but inevitably being bludgeoned into submission by the vehemence of Sukie's outpourings. The woman was small but frighteningly strong – vocally as well as physically. The period of the rant did at least give Saz an opportunity to examine the room: floor-to-ceiling postcards of every famous artwork ever to depict Christ or any number of pious martyrs, tripping cheerily off to their gruesome deaths. Clearly her hostess wasn't taking a fundamentalist line as far as graven images were concerned.

Sukie quite obviously wanted to force Sir Gerald back into purgatory for a good few years yet, but after thirty-five minutes she seemed to have run out of steam. Even she couldn't really have thought that being related by marriage to a former Chancellor of the Exchequer was that awful. She did, after all, have an extra large card of Saint Paul sitting in the arms of a plaster angel on the mantelpiece. While Sukie had dwelt largely on Sir Gerald's own failings, she'd only touched on a couple of her own. She made a passing reference to "claiming that which was not strictly mine" and another to "the youthful abandonment of adult responsibilities", though her own faults were only admitted where they were prompted by what she called Freeman's "disgusting appetites". She didn't, however, mention his wife and son.

So before it was too late and the attempted conversion began in earnest, Saz whispered, "And what about the family, Sukie? What about Sir Gerald's son. Did you know Patrick?"

The reaction was immediate. Sukie dropped her hands, grabbed her bible from the stool beside them and shoved a page under Saz's nose. *And when Rachel saw that she bare Jacob no children, Rachel envied her sister, and said unto Jacob, Give me children, or else I die.*

Saz looked at the page, looked back at Sukie, "Um . . .I don't actually think Sir Gerald's wife had a sister."

Sukie sat down, exasperated, "No, you silly girl. It's not meant to be taken literally." Which was rich coming from the mouth of a woman who not half an hour before had been raining down excessively real eternal damnation on her ex-lover's degenerate head. "Sir Gerald took the baby for himself, his wife wanted a child, he wanted a child, it didn't happen. Not for the two of them. They were not blessed with progeny."

"So he adopted a baby and brought it up as his own?"

"Like the foundling Moses."

Saz was rapidly running out of biblical knowledge, but even she knew that Patrick hadn't been simply found in a reed basket. And as a Peggy Lee fan she had her doubts about Moses too.

"Do you know any more about where the baby came from?"

"There was an arrangement."

"Who with? Did he know the mother?"

Sukie was staring off into space, evidently lost somewhere in the late '60s.

"Sukie?"

She shook herself and looked back to Saz, "I do apologize. I don't – I mean I try not to remember... these things. Sometimes it's better to leave them in the past."

Saz hardly knew what to say given how much of Gerald Freeman's past Sukie had just happily given away, "Yeah, but... with what you've already told me about Freeman... well..."

Sukie's pale blue eyes suddenly seemed incredibly clear, "Why do you want to know about the child?"

"Ah – I'm a friend of Patrick's."

"Girlfriend?"

"No. He's married."

"Like father like son," Sukie intoned fatalistically.

"Not in this case. We're just good friends." Saz didn't see this as an ideal moment to come out and continued with the purpose of her visit. "When Sir Gerald died—"

"It was all over the papers."

"Yes, well, Patrick went through his father's things and found out some stuff about his adoption. Things he hadn't known before."

Sukie shook her head, "The sins of the fathers..."

Saz was rapidly losing patience. "Exactly. And so now he wants to know who that father is, who his birth parents are."

"I'm not sure what this has got to do with me."

"You knew Sir Gerald."

"But he's dead now. Raking through the past? I don't know. Gerald will have to deal with his own misdeeds. It's not up to us. I have sins of my own to bear with. Vengeance is mine..."

"Saith the Lord. I know. But surely you can understand, Patrick wants to know about his father."

Saz realized what she'd said and scratched the old burn scars on her half-numb fingers in irritation. She could see the way Sukie's mind worked, and cut her off before she could start again. "Obviously I mean his temporal father. Here. In body. He just wants to know the truth. You can understand that, can't you?"

Sukie suddenly looked very tired, her afternoon's rant had obviously taken it out of her, "Yes, dear, of course. The truth. It's something your generation seems to be very interested in, isn't it? Digging up all the long-forgotten secrets. I'm sorry to have to tell you there's very little I know. While I was Gerald Freeman's harlot I was kept well away from the family, from the good ones."

"But you must have talked to him about them sometimes?"

"Occasionally, yes. And not with a great deal of charity, to my shame. I did know about the boy, I knew he wasn't Gerald's, as you said – the boy was adopted. It was a big secret, of course. Gerald didn't want anyone to know."

"Did you ever meet him, Patrick? As a child?"

"Just the once, when he was in town for the day with his father. Pleasant enough little boy."

"And why did Sir Gerald tell you about him? Can you remember?"

Sukie smiled and Saz suddenly saw a flash of the young woman she had been before time washed her out.

"We used to call it pillow talk. He could be quite lovely sometimes, you know. Very open and loving. Not that it ever lasted for long. Gerald told me they'd adopted Patrick early, when he was a very tiny baby, I think. Richard Leyton had a hand in it."

"The solicitor?"

"Yes. Never very fond of me, that one. Always on at Gerald to get rid of me. Spoilt his image." She clutched her bible closer to her, a hot water bottle against the cold memories, all hint of her fleeting smile gone. "I wasn't exactly top drawer stuff. Richard Leyton thought Gerald could do better – even in a mistress."

The venom in Sukie's voice seemed a little more than was merited merely by an acquaintance who had disapproved of her thirty years ago. Saz wondered if perhaps Sukie had known Leyton better than she was letting on. But Sukie would not be drawn on further questions. "I hardly ever saw the man, dear. All I can tell you is that whenever I did, he made me feel very uncomfortable indeed."

Sukie didn't have much more to tell. The adopted baby, the solicitor, the wife's complicit silence, all these Saz had guessed at, though it was useful to have them confirmed. Particularly Richard Leyton's involvement. "Gerald did love the boy, I'm sure of that. But he wanted the child to be his own. Really his own. I expect that's why they wanted it to stay such a secret, that if they didn't talk about the adoption openly, it might become the truth, he'd be theirs. But these things aren't always as easy as we might hope. Gerald minded, I think. Much as he loved Patrick, he minded the child wasn't really his. Couldn't ever seem to forget. People can be funny like that, you know."

At the door Saz leant back from the noise and heat of the busy road, gave Sukie her card and asked her to call if anything else occurred to her.

"I do hope not, dear. I don't like to think too much about my dark days."

"Just in case." Sukie shook her head and Saz figured it was unlikely she'd hear from her again. "Well, thanks anyway. I appreciate your help."

"You're very welcome. God bless you."

Saz turned to smile at the tired woman still clutching her bible to her chest. Sukie was looking out at the street, watching a fraught mother dodging buses and taxis as she tried to cross the noisy road with a couple of children, one in a pushchair and the other pulling against her tight grip, screaming for sweets or an ice cream, screaming for attention.

Sukie frowned as she closed the door, speaking to herself as much as to Saz, "I would have done it, you know. Given him a baby, made a family for him. If he'd ever asked."

TWENTY-TWO

Sara left the hospital by the side door. This was not the way she came in. Sara was brought up the main front steps, she was brought in kicking and screaming. Because she was mad and so they had to bring her through the main door. Sara was a bad girl. She knew this from what she had been told, not from what she remembered. They have helped her inside. Made her better here. Sara is quiet now, and good. Sara does not make a fuss, has learnt how to behave. It wasn't so hard, not really. She just had to adjust. And here they have helped her to adjust. There have been people here who would talk to her. Once she learnt what to say, how to speak nicely. Once she learnt how to be a good girl and do what was expected of her, then there were plenty of people to talk to.

Sara was well enough to leave by the side door, the quiet door, the east exit. She could be trusted not to make a scene, trusted to be by herself. Sara was no longer a danger – not to others and, most important of all, not to herself. She would live quietly now. Sara would forget those darker days. She was easy now. It was a relief to everyone. They had done a good job. Sara had done a good job. It was well worth it.

She walked by the sea, and the walk back home was slow. But then Sara was much slower too. They had slowed down the world that used to rush by so quickly. Sara was always running to catch up in her other life, speeding to make it, to get there, and not sure where it was she was heading for, but rushing headlong anyway, rushing before it was too late. She did not need to run any more. She walked slowly and simply, one foot after the other, with concentration, one step following another. Don't let the mind wander away, wandering is dangerous, just keep the thoughts on the steps. And so she did. Sara was successful. She could walk all the way to her home. Her bag was not heavy, she didn't own much. And even though she walked along the sea front, the waves were no longer rough. They were not taunting her. They simply went in and out, like breathing. That was all they did. They were just waves and Sara now knew that they were not powerful. Sara understood the nature of power better than most.

TWENTY-THREE

Saz went directly from Sukie's flat to Brixton for her meeting with Luke. The bar wasn't quite so salubrious in daylight. The silver and purple combination was too well lit in the afternoon sunshine and even the heavy cleaning job that went on every morning couldn't quite disguise an underlay of inevitably sticky floors and a back-of-the-throat hit from the acid leftover scent of alcohol, poppers and grass. But the garden out the back, where a surprisingly genial host offered her a bowl of thick chips and a cold beer, was warm and shaded by juicy grape vines and a fig tree.

"A fig tree? Fantastic."

"Fruit's all right too. Not brilliantly succulent or anything but it's bloody well sheltered out here and fairly sunny, so there is fruit, looks and tastes like figs."

"It's gorgeous."

"Yeah. The old lady who ran the pub before we took it over spent all her time out here. The pub itself was shite, but this garden – well, let's just say she wasn't stupid enough to let her punters get anywhere near it."

Saz looked round at the paved courtyard, stuffed full with pretty young things, eating and drinking and laughing far too loud.

"You're doing well out of it."

"My customers aren't old blokes smoking roll-ups and making a single pint last half the afternoon. This lot think they're incredibly fucking amazing because they even recognize a bloody fig."

A burst of raucous laughter from three barely-dressed babes in the corner underlined his sentiments and Saz diverted the conversation to Luke's parentage before his irritation with his clientele slipped into bad mood.

Basically their conversation simply confirmed what she remembered of the night before. Luke was willing to acknowledge that what he'd told Carrie was true, but he wasn't especially interested in re-hashing it all for Saz's benefit.

Pleasant host turned to bored and indifferent when Saz tried to get more from him. "And you didn't want to follow this up yourself? Find out more about your birth parents?"

"No."

"You don't have any curiosity at all?"

Luke shook his head, finished his beer and nodded to the glass collector to bring him another one. He didn't offer to get another for Saz, "Look. I only said I'd talk to you to set the record straight. If you want to poke around looking for stuff about your friend's birth parents, go ahead. I've made my peace with my past. I'm honestly not interested."

"But the woman I saw today seems to think Richard Leyton was really quite dodgy and—"

Luke interrupted her, "Who did you see?"

"My client's father's old mistress. I just went to see if she knew anything about him being adopted."

"And did she?"

"Not much. But she didn't have many good things to say for either my client's father or Richard Leyton."

"She actually made accusations against him?"

"No, not at all, nothing like that. She just didn't like him."

Saz wondered for a moment whether she ought to

mention the concept of buying babies, but decided she didn't want to risk alienating Luke further. Maybe his reconciliation with his adoptive father really had been so positive that he didn't want to jeopardize their relationship by delving into the truth of his own past. And then again, there was something about the way he jumped on her story about Sukie that made Saz question just how much she wanted to tell him anyway.

Luke grabbed the new beer brought out for him, polite thank yous obviously weren't his strong point, "Well, I know my father never had any problem with Leyton. And some people would say helping others to adopt was a gift."

"Well, yes, of course. But when people do that these days, it's all so open, acknowledged. No one's lying about it."

"And so that's OK?"

"I'm not concerned about the morals of adoption, Luke, I'm concerned that people haven't been told the truth."

"Well, not people, your client. I already know the truth about my family."

"OK, my client. But it looks like Leyton had a hand in his adoption, and in that of my other friend."

"So why doesn't he or she ask their adoptive parents what happened?"

"My friend doesn't want to hurt his mother. His adoptive mother. He doesn't want her to think he's looking for more than her. He's never been interested before."

"What's changed his mind?"

"He's going to be a father himself."

Luke laughed, "Ah, the sadly predictable workings of the traditional mind."

Saz decided not to expound on the very untraditional circumstances that had prompted Chris's new interest, "So you're not willing to help me at all on this?"

"I really don't see that it's any of my business. Or that I

can help you anyway. I don't know that much myself, I have
a good working relationship with my father and I don't want
to fuck that up by asking him to tell me things he'd rather
not divulge. And I'd prefer you didn't either. You're going to
have to find some other avenue of information for your
clients. There are some adopted people who aren't com-
pelled to search the ends of the earth for their blood
relatives. I simply don't have that desire. Anyway, look, I've
had enough of this shit, it's a gorgeous day, let's not waste
it talking about all this. I think a change of subject's in
order, don't you?"

Saz didn't agree with him, but didn't see how she could
protest.

Luke pointed to a new development on the other side of
the back wall, "See those flats over there?"

"Yes."

"The estate agent is a mate of mine, I've got a key. The
show place is amazing – do you want to have a look?"

"Why?"

"No reason – well, I have invested a bit in the renovations.
Wouldn't mind if you liked the look of what you saw and
mentioned it to a few friends?"

"Ah – no. Thanks anyway. I'm not sure that any of my
friends could afford designer places."

"Or that they'd want to?"

Saz smiled, "No, I know one or two whose leanings tend
that way. None with an awful lot of spare cash though.
Sorry."

Saz finished her beer and left Luke. Though their conversation had ended pleasantly enough – albeit on his terms
and not hers – she felt bad about the difficult patch in the
middle. She was aware she hadn't really thought through
the question of how adopted children might feel, that
perhaps she had been insensitive to expect him to want to

know as much about his birth parents as Patrick and Chris did. In fact, she was troubled to realize that as Luke had proved himself completely uninterested in helping her, it seemed much more likely that he had only agreed to meet her today to find out how much she knew. And, if that was the case, she'd better tell Carrie to keep her mouth shut in future. Just after she'd told herself. She decided to hold back on discussing the babies-for-money question with Chris until she knew a bit more. And until she knew something more about Richard Leyton's involvement. A return trip to Georgina Leyton's offices was looking more and more necessary. Unfortunately.

Then it was home, dinner, ordinary conversations about Molly's day at work, how Luke had tried to interest her in a new flat, thoughts about the baby, medical matters, arranging dates to dine with friends and family. All perfectly normal with just a hint of panic beneath the surface. Saz was beginning to find the pressing urgency, the five and a half months' distance from parenthood a terrifying prospect. After all the time of talking about the possibility and then planning for it to happen, the actual reality was much more terrifying than she could ever have expected. She hid her fears from her girlfriend though. Saz didn't think Molly really needed to hear her worries about what was now their inevitable future. Instead she drank her way through most of a bottle of wine, chatted about everything and nothing, steered clear of the confusing adoption talk and shrugged off her future fears in the warmth of their mutual ease. Molly managed almost half a glass herself before she gave in to media-hype terrors and settled for foetus-friendly mineral water.

They sat together while night settled across the Heath

outside. The balcony doors were open and even so, the room was still warm with the day's lingering heat.

Molly pulled at Saz's hair, "Take your clothes off."

"Why?"

"Aren't you hot?"

"Yeah."

"So take your clothes off. It'll be cooler. And I can stroke your body. I want to see you naked."

Saz complied with her lover's request. But she did so uncertainly. After the miscarriage and then the first three months of this pregnancy, feeling obliged to tread so carefully around Molly while they waited to know if the foetus would make it, she was still learning how to be with Molly's body again, how to be just flesh and no thought. But it wasn't a concept Molly had forgotten.

"Saz, honestly, you don't have to touch me as if I might break any minute. I am pretty strong, you know. I'm only pregnant. It is perfectly normal. The world is full of pregnant women shagging like rabbits."

"I know that." Saz frowned, stretched herself full length along her lover, her weight evenly distributed across Molly's much taller body, "I mean my head knows it, I know how fit you are, know you're taking care of yourself. But I can't help it, I try to just look at you as only Molly and I can't seem to. I look at you and I see that you're pregnant."

"Are you having a go about my tummy?"

Saz burst out laughing, "What tummy? God, Moll, most of the women we know would kill to have a body like yours."

"That's all right then."

"You know I think you're gorgeous."

"So you haven't gone off me?"

"Of course not, I'm just scared I might hurt you. Hurt the baby."

"Saz, you won't. Why should I be any different to every other woman in the world?"

"Because you're mine."

Molly nodded and then added uncertainly, "And because this baby's yours?"

"Ours."

Molly shrugged, adjusted herself beneath Saz, "Yeah, but yours really. Technically. Genetically."

"Well, that's debatable, but if so, then yeah, it is even more scary. I feel extra protective of both of you. I look at you and think how much I want to look after you."

Molly smiled. "So look after me. I know what my body can take, and it can take a hell of a lot more than just this soft kissing and cuddling shit. I'm sure it's not good for me to be so frustrated."

"No, I don't suppose unrequited wanting is terribly good for your blood pressure."

Molly bent her knees up, tightened them around Saz's waist, "No good at all. Trust me, Saz, I'm a doctor."

Saz trusted Molly. In the move from talk to skin they ignored the insistent ringing of the telephone. Twice. The first time Saz simply waited for the answerphone to pick up, the second she left Molly's skin long enough to turn off the ringer on both phones. Saz was believing in the doctor, not the messages piling up on her machine. Trusted Molly enough to leave her back aching from the hard floor, her calf muscles taut with slow-released tension. An hour or so later Saz had proved her trust enough to really upset their upstairs neighbour. For the past couple of months he'd been more than a little relieved that the "noisy shaggers downstairs" had finally decided to shut up and fuck quietly like normal people. The poor guy had been single for the past year. Fourteen months too long.

Once Saz had put Molly to sleep in their bed, rubbing her

back until she heard the familiar sound of her sleeping breath, slow and regular, she went to listen to the messages.

The first was from Sukie, a small voice, slightly concerned, "Miss Martin, I'm just a little worried ... maybe I shouldn't have said so much about Gerald. Or Richard Leyton. Perhaps he's made his peace now anyway, Gerald. Well, both of them, maybe. I think ... I'd rather you didn't ... I don't really want to be involved ... perhaps you'll call me back?"

The second call was also from Sukie, a hang-up this time. It was now well after one in the morning: according to the well-spoken BT lady, Sukie's second call had been at 22:15 hours. Saz decided to ring her in the morning. While the night might belong to the devil, she was fairly certain Sukie would rise early in the fresh-broken morning to get on with another full day of praise.

She went back to bed and lay against Molly's warm body, wondering for awhile about Sukie. What could have happened to turn such a groovy chick so far from her original course? Saz wasn't completely sure she believed the idea that Jesus had simply found her, all the people she'd ever known who had taken up any extremity of faith – from born-again Christianity to born-again lesbian separatism – had done so after a life crisis of some sort. Sometimes a wonderful crisis like falling in love, but a major turning point all the same. She was still wondering what had prompted Sukie's conversion when the past two nights' lack of sleep and the energetic return to fucking form finally caught up with her.

TWENTY-FOUR

By a quarter to ten the next morning Saz had been for her run, showered, dressed, washed and put away their dinner dishes from the night before, made Molly's breakfast, joined her in the shower to demonstrate yet again her trust of Molly's medical knowledge, walked with her to the tube and was impatiently waiting for ten, by which time Gary would be at work and she could ask him what he'd found out.

Pre-pregnancy, Saz had been used to extremely early rising to run, followed by a morning asleep and then working all afternoon and most of the evening. Now, though, she was trying to adjust her patterns to a more usual time-table – initially to suit Molly and get her through the worrying first months – and now because the growing baby reality meant that she was really pushing to get on with Chris's truth as soon as she could. And Patrick's. And Luke's for that matter. The fact that she looked longingly at their bed any time between nine a.m. and midday didn't stop her using the time as profitably as possible. It just made her bloody irritable when others appeared a little less urgent than she would have hoped. She tried calling Sukie a couple of times but there was no reply, nor an answer machine. Obviously steering clear of all the technological works of the devil.

Gary may have kept lax office hours, but he didn't disap-point. "Now promise me you're going to be careful with this?"

"You've found her? The mother?"

"I've found a Lillian Hope. In Cornwall, near St Ives – which is where your doctor was writing from, yes? She's probably the right age, possibly the woman you're after. Then again, your Lillian Hope may have left Cornwall the minute she gave up her baby and this might just be one who happened to be there at the same time."

Saz was excited, "Yeah, sure, all possible, just give me the story, Gary."

"Well, I can't find any record that this woman registered a baby around the time of Patrick Freeman's birth."

"Maybe she didn't. Maybe his adoptive parents did."

"Yeah, maybe. Anyway, assuming it's the same Lillian Hope – and as this one has only moved house twice since 1963, I'd say it was close to likely – I think I might have found your lady. There are only four other Lillian Hopes registered in Cornwall at the moment. Two got the name by marriage anyway, one died last year at the age of ninety-seven – so I don't imagine she's Patrick Freeman's mother – and the other one is a transsexual who changed her name ten years ago. She too seems something of an unlikely bet."

"And you've got her phone number and address?"

"Oh yes, I'm such a star at totally illegal data retrieval. I'll fax this lot over to you, shall I?"

"Please. Thank you. Gary, you're brilliant."

"Mmm – and Saz?"

"Yeah?"

"You will be careful with this, won't you? I understand this is a big deal for your client, but it's going to be a pretty big deal for this Lillian too. Go gently. It's not as if you're contacting her through one of those adoption agencies. You did say he'd heard nothing through them yet, right?"

"Yeah."

"Well, those people are trained to do this kind of thing.

Maybe this woman doesn't want any contact. She hasn't exactly made much of an effort to find him, has she? You have thought about that?"

"Gary, I can't imagine that either Patrick or Chris have thought about anything else since they first decided to start looking. I will be careful. Promise."

"Good. I'll leave it with you then. Now if you need anything else, you'd better get on to me in the next fortnight."

"You're going on holiday?"

"Finally and permanently. I've got a telly job."

"No!"

"Oh yes. Romantic lead, six-part series. Every chance it'll go to a second. I'm playing the 1970s' lover – excessively sexy, gorgeous, shag-fodder."

"Bloody hell, that's brilliant. But . . . Gary?"

"What?"

Saz heard the wariness in his voice. Gary had spent so long slagging off mainstream television she couldn't believe he wasn't getting quite a bit of flak for this decision. "Whatever happened to 'fuck-the-system-I-believe-in-theatre-for-the-people'?"

"Yeah, well, call me a turncoat, pragmatic, Clause-4-discarding middle way Labourite . . . but I've quite got my heart set on being able to pay my mortgage right now. It's called growing up, Saz."

"Tell me about it."

"But hey, I am playing a poof."

"Oh well, that's all right then."

"And I'm still undermining the system by passing on illegally collected information."

"That too."

"And that's enough?"

"Could be."

"OK. And I'm playing Alan Davies' love interest."

"Enough said. Good work."

Saz hung up laughing at the thought of the man who tempted her sister's body and spirit away from Jesus to the sins of the flesh attempting to do the screen version. With a man. Two straight men. That ought to cheer up the girlie viewers across the land. It certainly counted as innovative casting.

She thought for just a moment about what to do next and then she picked up the phone to call Patrick. She reasoned that while he might well have preferred the news to be gently broken in person, he would rather know sooner than later that there was a possibility of finding his mother. She didn't even get as far as dialling the whole number when she was interrupted by a ring on her doorbell and the appearance of two police officers who very carefully told her that Sukie Planchet had been found severely beaten in her flat. And would she mind just answering a few questions?

Sukie had been so badly injured that she was now unconscious in intensive care. And Saz was not only assumed to be the last person who had visited her – "She had your card on her, Ms Martin" – they also knew that Sukie had called her late last night. Apparently the young policewoman thought ten-thirty at night was late. Saz didn't hold out much hope that she had a raging social life when her official duties were done. It took Saz a few minutes to work out exactly why they were asking her how she knew Sukie. But when she did, she wasn't very impressed. "Fuck! You think I hurt her?"

The policewoman started to stutter an apology but the older policeman with her was all calm professionalism, "Not at all, Ms Martin. We're just interested in your reasons for going to visit her. You did say she wasn't a close friend?"

"She wasn't a friend at all. I'd never met her before yesterday."

"So why were you there?"

Saz gave her reasons as sparingly as possible, the briefest of resumés of Patrick's situation and nothing at all about either Luke or the Leyton law firm. On the other hand, she gave Molly as her alibi with copious details.

The policewoman took Molly's work number and did her best to reassure Saz, "I don't imagine anyone thinks for a minute you had anything to do with it, Ms Martin. I can't imagine a girl would hurt anyone like that." Saz wondered how recently the policewoman had graduated to be quite so naive, but she smiled gratefully anyway.

Her less trusting colleague continued with the story, "The main problem at the moment, Ms Martin, is that we couldn't find any next of kin."

"No one?"

"No. We tried the churches – she's clearly very religious."

The younger woman interrupted, "You know, the flat, all those cards? But we went to the four local congregations and none of the churches knew anything about her."

Saz concentrated her attention on the policeman, hoping that by doing so she would get them out of her place as soon as possible. "From what she told me, I didn't get the impression that she had much faith in organized religion. I think that's why she was so happy to have a chance to pray with me."

Completely oblivious to the mounting irritation of her partner, the young policewoman went on, "And Miss Planchet hasn't got a job either. Then, when we asked around, her neighbours also said they didn't know her. Not well, anyway. And you know, all her things were in such a mess, the whole flat was totally turned upside down. I've never seen anything like it."

It was only after the policewoman had started on her graphic description of Sukie's injuries, quite possibly inflicted with the plaster angel Saz had noticed the day before, that the older policeman finally managed to shut her up and get to the actual point of their visit. "So we were hoping you might come to the hospital to identify Miss Planchet for us."

"But you know who she is, you just said."

"We know she was found in that flat. We can only assume she is Miss Planchet. But it's not definite."

"I really don't know the woman."

"But you've spoken to her. She let you into her house quite happily."

"So this way you can kill two birds with one stone?" The minute the words were out of her mouth, Saz regretted them, "Sorry, I mean, you need me to identify her and this gives you a chance to check up on me too?"

The policeman simply smiled and offered her a lift to the hospital.

Saz sat in the back of the police car, unable to clear her mind of the picture of a pale, thin woman in a faded, pink cardigan, offering both her Bible and an outstretched hand, welcoming her in. Welcoming in whoever beat her up. The policewoman chattered throughout the journey and, while Saz was happy to pick up what information she could, she wouldn't have wanted to be in the young woman's shoes later, dealing with a disapproving old-school colleague.

Evidently an old man who lived in Sukie's block had called them out at five in the morning when he took his dog for a walk and noticed her door was unlocked. The policewoman thought Sukie was lucky to have been found so soon. Saz thought the policewoman had an odd concept of what constituted good fortune. They'd checked through Sukie's records, gone through the mess of papers scattered over her floor. Unfortunately almost all of them were God-relevant and none offered any clues as to family or friends. When they found Saz's card in Sukie's Bible, they decided to contact her. It had taken all of four hours to eliminate the possibility that Sukie might be identified by anyone else. Saz hardly felt that half an hour of prayer and another hour of discussion made her the ideal witness to Sukie's life.

Saz stood beside Sukie's bed. The policewoman wasn't exaggerating. Sukie had been comprehensively beaten up. In the brief two minutes she was allowed at the bedside, Saz's stomach churned at the thought of the extreme violence that resulted in the bruised and battered body laid out before her. And she was well aware that her reaction was only to what was obvious, to the dark-mottled and broken skin. According to the variety of drips and monitors Sukie was hooked up to, a great deal of damage had also been inflicted under the surface. As she turned away she comforted herself with the thought that the small, wiry woman had at least fought back as well as she could – the broken and bloody fingernails were a sad testament to that.

After a brief detour to the ladies' loo to throw up – shock and a sick sense of guilt uniting against her body – she confirmed that the woman in the bed was indeed the Sukie Planchet she had met the day before. She gave the police her mobile number and, refusing their offer of a ride home, made straight for Patrick Freeman's restaurant. Saz had no idea of what was the right order to take the new developments. She would tell Patrick about Lillian Hope, definitely sometime in the next few hours, but not until she was capable of talking rationally. Too many things were happening far too fast all of a sudden and Saz knew she wouldn't be able to deal with the potentially good news until she'd at least attempted to make some headway with the really bad news. She also knew Sukie had been beaten up after she'd mentioned to Luke that Gerald Freeman's ex-mistress had talked to her. While it sickened Saz to think this could have had something to do with Luke, it also seemed a little too immediate to be mere coincidence. She wasn't ready to speak to him again yet – not until she was more certain of her suspicions anyway – but she did think it was maybe time to have another go at Georgina Leyton. This time with Patrick by her side.

TWENTY-FIVE

Saz sat hunched on the tube oblivious to the tourists and Oxford Street shoppers looking forward to another hot afternoon in the sticky capital, and then pushed her way through an irritating swathe of slow strolling lunch-timers to Patrick's Soho workplace. Ignoring the outraged *maitre de*, she walked directly through the muted crowd of elegant diners into the kitchen, grabbed Patrick away from the stove, in the process ruining a perfectly good venison steak that required split-second timing. She was well aware that this intrusion risked his famed wrath but, exhibiting the potential of a much greater anger herself, she demanded he leave the twenty covers still to be dealt with, take the rest of the day off and go with her to Georgina Leyton's office. She took a brief moment to explain who Sukie was, well aware that Patrick had specifically asked not to be told about his father's mistress, but certain that this was one lack of delicacy he was going to have to deal with. Faced with Saz's combination of intense fury at the ghastliness of the attack on Sukie and agreeing with her awful sense that this didn't just seem like a random act, Patrick agreed to leave the restaurant. They would, however, have to exit by the back door; there was no way he was going to walk through his own dining room and depart in the middle of lunch when half a dozen people were waiting for the delectable scallop dish that had been excessively praised in three different reviews only the weekend before. Not while they were paying thirty quid a head for the privilege anyway.

Sukie had confirmed Patrick's assertion that the solicitor had been a constant figure in Sir Gerald's private and public life. She'd also implied he'd not been the nicest of people. Patrick had discovered the adoption letter from Leyton to his father, and now they'd found the other letter about Jonathan Godwin. If they'd been able to find information in the mess Patrick had made of his father's study, then Saz simply didn't believe that Georgina Leyton hadn't come across anything among her own father's things. She hoped that with Patrick Freeman beside her, she'd be able to prompt a little more co-operation from the solicitor.

Saz and Patrick made it to the Leyton offices in a record six minutes and near silence. After a whispered telephone conversation, the receptionist told them they were welcome to go through to Ms Leyton's office. She hadn't been expecting them, of course, and therefore they were extremely lucky to get a window in her very tight schedule, but she would naturally be delighted to see Patrick and his friend. The beautiful boy receptionist used the word friend like a weapon. This time Georgina Leyton was wearing a pale pink suit, something business-like and yet also very sheer at the same time.

She looked at them both with a small smile, "Nice to see you again, Ms Martin. I didn't realize you knew Patrick?"

Patrick answered her, "She's doing some work for me."

She welcomed Patrick with a warm and effusive hug, then offered Saz an exceedingly weak handshake. She showed them to separate seats; they went exactly where they were told with no demur. Georgina was obviously very good at directing people. She pulled Patrick over to herself, settling him into her own ergonomically perfect chair and lifted herself onto the desk in front of him. Patrick was therefore offered a gloriously clear view of Georgina's perfect, smooth, summer-bare thighs. Saz was directed to a half-size sofa, placed in front of the desk where a client's chair would normally have been. Even if Georgina hadn't had her back to her, Saz would have been at a disadvantage. As it was, perched uncomfortably on what felt like a bench for penance-hungry religious ascetics, Saz was suddenly the ungainly little sister intruding on her big brother and the very experienced babysitter.

Ignoring Saz completely, Georgina then embarked on a five minute catch-up period with Patrick – introduced with a brief note to Saz that they'd known each other for years, had often met through their fathers. The conversation involved a wealth of information about how well Georgina was doing, how high she was flying and, naturally, how fantastically energetic her sex life was. Eventually she returned her ice-blue gaze to Saz who felt even more uncomfortable than she had the first time she'd tried to make headway in that office. Obviously Georgina Leyton found ill-at-ease clients a boon. "Saz, isn't it? Unusual name. Now, what can we do for you? Of course, anything to help Patrick . . ." She left the sentence hanging in the air while she held his hand in hers and then kissed it, and Saz wished Patrick had been sitting beside her so he also could see Georgina's smirk.

Saz explained that now Patrick's father had died, he wanted to find out what he could about his birth parents. And that she also had another client in a similar situation – and the link between both her clients was Richard Leyton. Then she watched in amazement while Georgina started to cry, big fat tears rolling down her perfect cheeks. Shaking her head she took Patrick's hand, "It's so awful, isn't it, darling? To lose one's father. Of course you must be so upset. I do feel for you – and to have to add in this search as well. How can you possibly cope?"

Patrick mumbled something about getting on with it because he had to, and Saz re-routed the conversation back to the search for relevant information. But Georgina was having none of it. She shook her head and expressed the depth of her eloquent sympathies. Patrick was grateful; Saz tried to ask her about Richard Leyton's involvement in the adoption; Georgina said how awful it must be. Every time Saz tried to ask a direct question about her father's role in any of the adoptions, Georgina came over all moved and distressed. And for some reason Patrick said practically nothing at all, just took Georgina's manicured hand and excessive sympathy as if her attention were the sum total of his needs and the only reason he'd popped in.

When Saz, irritated beyond belief by Georgina and infuriated by Patrick's lack of assistance, finally asked outright if they could possibly have access to Richard Leyton's papers, she was met with absolute incredulity that she could be so gauche as to ask Georgina to break every oath in the solicitor's rule book. She refused to contemplate anything so far from common practice. No, she would make it her business to go through all the papers herself and pass on anything that would possibly be useful. It was the very least she could do for her old friend. Though, of course – she added, looking directly at Saz – it was unlikely there would be anything much as her father had been most particular about security.

It took a good fifteen minutes more for Georgina to adequately convey the vast depth of her enormous sympathy, using each new bout of compassion to evade another question from Saz, by which time the receptionist was standing at the door, practically dragging Georgina from the room. A cab was waiting to take her to City Airport, Geneva wouldn't wait. But it seemed Chris and Patrick would have to. Georgina hugged Patrick again, commiserated some more and would have been out the door without a further word if Saz hadn't physically stood in her way.

"Look, Georgina, I'm sorry, but you can't just run off like this."

The small woman stood her ground, looked calmly at Saz with perfectly shaped pursed lips, her sympathy-eyes quite dry, "Of course not, Ms Martin." She turned and smiled at Patrick, rubbed his shoulder with an over-fond hand that ended up on his cheek. "Of course I don't want to just leave like this. But I do have a meeting to get to and you did arrive unannounced. Still, as I've already said, I promise you both, the minute I get back from Geneva I'll make it my absolute priority to go through everything my father left behind." She held Patrick's hand again, "You have my utmost assurance. If, even by the slightest chance, the files I have contain anything at all about this matter, I'll pass on the teeniest scrap of information to you." Her cool fingers wandered back to his cheek again, "Now, I'll be back on Monday and believe me, I'll make it my only mission the minute I'm free."

They followed her out to the lift. Saz got in with mounting fury that this woman, whom she assumed knew so much more than she was letting on, was able to walk away, having given them nothing at all. They both watched in silence as she climbed into her taxi, Patrick waving pleasantly as it joined the throng of traffic heading east. They turned down the street and into Regent's Park, Saz silent as she tried to contain her day's worth of built-up anger, Patrick walking alongside her, not quite certain what he'd just experienced, even less sure of how to talk to Saz about it. They headed for the nearest shaded bench and sat down.

Saz, looking straight ahead at the gathering ducks and

pigeons, waited a beat until Patrick seemed almost comfortable beside her and simply asked, "And you fucked her for how long?"

Patrick exhaled an exhausted groan, "About six months. Five and a half months too long."

"Christ."

"I was young."

"And stupid."

"That too."

"She's horrible."

"No. Not really. Just a bit . . ."

"Cold? Calculating? Manipulative?"

"She's bit fucked up actually, Saz."

"Yeah, right. I just love it when men excuse women for being bitches by saying they're crazy."

"It works for her."

"I don't doubt it does. And why didn't you bother telling me about the two of you?"

"It didn't seem appropriate."

"Bollocks."

"I didn't think it would matter."

"You didn't think it would matter that we needed to get her at a disadvantage, we needed to get information from her, and it wasn't until we got there that you realized she knew you so bloody well she could wrap you round her little finger?"

"You didn't exactly get the better of her yourself."

"Thanks a lot, but at least I fucking well tried. I don't get it, Patrick, she's hardly your type."

"She's not."

"But she's got a great body?"

"Great mind too."

"Obviously."

There was silence again for another minute, then Saz added, "She's fucking scary."

"Because she's posh, or because she's too good looking?"

"Because she's lying."

Patrick nodded his vehement agreement, "Oh yeah. She's certainly doing that."

They sat in the warmth of the late afternoon for another ten minutes until, her fury subsided, Saz realized she could no longer put off the next bombshell. While four big Canada geese beat the ducks to the Japanese tourists' chunks of broken bread, Saz quietly told Patrick that Lillian Hope, the woman listed on his birth certificate as being his mother was, very likely, alive and well and living in St Ives.

TWENTY-SIX

When Saz first told Patrick the news about Lillian Hope he
had wanted to get on to the M4 immediately. His initial
shock and eagerness gave way to anger that Saz had chosen
not to tell him sooner, though his fury faded when she
reiterated her very good reasons. After all, Georgina was
now winging her first-class way to Geneva and wouldn't be
back until late on Monday. Obviously Saz hadn't known that
earlier, but Patrick eventually agreed it was useful they'd
encountered Georgina's duplicity sooner rather than later.
She had a harder time persuading him that this precise
moment wasn't ideal to make an impetuous break for the
west. It was five o'clock on the Thursday evening before a
summer bank holiday weekend. While the guaranteed ten
hours stuck in rapidly overheating traffic would at least
have given them plenty of time to work out the best way to
approach Lillian Hope, Saz reasoned with Patrick that it
might be a little more sensible for them to spend an evening
with their respective spouses, rid themselves of some of the
day's frustrations and get in a good night's sleep so they
were ready for the physical and emotional demands of travelling all the way to Cornwall to meet Patrick's possible
mother. She suggested they attack the new dilemma with
clearer heads the following morning. Patrick finally
accepted it as the great plan that it was. A great plan and
therefore doomed to failure from the beginning.

For a start, Saz had to deal with Chris who was feeling

left out and more than a little pissed off that she seemed to have found Patrick's mother but not his own. He was aware his reaction wasn't rational, that Saz was having a harder time getting information about him than she was about Patrick – not least because now his mother had returned home he couldn't offer Saz complete access to the family archives.

"Chris, you have to understand, this is a lead for you, of sorts."

"How?"

"Well, this woman was actually cared for by Lees. She may even have met Leyton. It might be that she knew other women who gave their babies to them." Saz didn't think now was the right time to mention the baby-buying. "There's a good chance she'll be able to give us something about your mother too."

"I think you'll find that's a very slim chance actually, Saz. I asked my mother if she'd ever seen a specialist before they adopted me – you know, like Patrick Freeman's mother saw Lees?"

"And?"

"Yes, she did. But the doctor was called Keane. Not Lees, not even in Cornwall."

"Oh, shit."

"Yeah, right. Look, I'm sorry. I'm just feeling a bit bloody jealous actually, I wish it was you and me driving down to Cornwall to meet my mother."

Saz looked at Molly sat across the room from her, small baby bump barely discernable beneath her T-shirt, "I know you do Chris, I do too. I'm disappointed they didn't have the same doctor, but we still know they had the same solicitor. Maybe this woman in Cornwall knows something about Leyton. It's better than nothing, isn't it?"

"Only just."

Molly wasn't able to offer much consolation, but she did add Keane to her medics research list and then cooked Saz and Chris an exceptionally sticky mushroom risotto. Small consolation, but not entirely negligible.

Patrick's evening was considerably more fraught. His eldest stepdaughter, Martha, was a fourteen-year-old schoolgirl trying desperately to pass herself off as anything but fourteen. Twenty-one sounded good. And like her mother had been, she was also worryingly successful at it. Which meant they became immediately worried when she didn't come home. Not at nine when she was expected. Not at ten when her best friend arrived home to the fury of her own parents. Not at eleven when the police were called and expressed their distinct lack of concern; the duty officer had teenage daughters of his own and was surprisingly sanguine about the whole matter. And she was still not home at midnight when Katy called back to tell the same duty officer exactly what a load of pointless tax-payers'-money-wasting cunts the lazy fucking lot of the bloody police force were. Luckily he was equally sanguine about her bad temper.

By the time Martha did stumble home at two in the morning – distinctly worse for the gin, whisky and cheap lager combinations she'd spent the evening trying out at an undisclosed friend's house – Katy took a good four hours to blame Patrick for most of her ills. She'd complained about his workaholic nature, berated the weeks he'd given over to sorting out his father's estate, poured scorn on the concept of yet another television series in the autumn – something else to take him still further away from his family – and finally reserved her strongest vitriol for this ludicrous parent hunt.

"For fuck's sake, Patrick, don't you think that if she is

your mother she'd have tried to find you by now? If she'd ever wanted to? What makes you think she's going to welcome you with open arms? Why the fuck can't you just leave the poor bitch alone?"

It wasn't very fair and it probably wasn't true and Katy didn't even mean it in the moment she said it, but once she was in a rage, there was little that could be done to halt the flow of furious bile. Martha had been packed off to bed after her third vomit and so Patrick received the full brunt of Katy's vented fury. And because Patrick had no reason to feel as guilty as Saz did, and because Katy had spent her evening in a state of heightened anxiety quietly turning into nastiness, and because their relationship had always based itself as much on their excessive passions – both pleasurable and viciously cruel – as on the joys of family life, their fight did not simply end with a slammed bedroom door and sleepy dawn apologies.

When Patrick picked up Saz at eight the next morning he had not even had the two hours of semi-peaceful sleep she'd managed to fall into just after dawn. Katy woke with an evil hangover and a grumpy, uncomprehending daughter to deal with, and the bitter awareness she'd let her mouth run away with her. Not for the first time – which she covered with a face of continued bitchiness because Patrick was leaving the house before they'd had a chance to deal with Martha together. Molly woke ill again and pissed off that Saz was going away, leaving her to her lonely nausea. Breakfasts were skimpy and caffeine-fuelled, goodbye kisses were rushed and perfunctory.

Fortunately neither of the women left at home knew their partners were on the sunny motorway heading into a blue sky west, roof down, music far too loud, and an unspoken bond of quietly wicked delight at being able to run away. The traffic queuing to join the M4 had never looked so good.

TWENTY-SEVEN

For most of the past twenty-five years Lillian Hope had lived alone. She did not enjoy the closeness of other people, physical or otherwise. She attempted relationships but they'd never made her happy. Other people had not made her happy. She had tried intimacy – in her experience it was not worth the pain. Lillian was big and constant and good. But she did not enjoy the closeness of other people.

She was known to be reliable and trustworthy, but she was not known well. She ran a Bed and Breakfast, clean and comfortable, no frills. Her B&B was not in any of the major guides, it would not rate four stars. Or even three. It was candlewick bedspreads and blankets, not duvets, thin cotton sheets. The sheets were expressly not nylon. Lillian's place may not have been terribly modern, but neither was it a tacky cliché. She enjoyed caring for her guests. Liked to be busy. Lillian fed extra special breakfasts to the nice guests. Fed good breakfasts even to the not-so-nice ones. It was rare that Lillian dealt with not-nice guests. They were not welcomed back the following summer.

Many things might rank a guest in the unwritten list of not-nice. Prime among these was asking about family. Lillian would happily talk about their families until they'd run out of relatives; she did not want to discuss her own. Lillian was her own family. For very many years she had been both mother and child to herself.

At first, after almost four years of the redbrick, Lillian

lived in a house with seven others. Equally broken, bent
people, battered people. It was a halfway house to
nowhere; people did not leave to move on, they left only
to return to the redbrick institutions from whence they
came. Theirs was a house that would be home that was
halfway into society – though no one ever quite made it all
the way back. They would yo-yo from halfway to redbrick
to scared foray into all the way. And then come running
back. There were no success stories. Until Lillian. For ten
years Lillian was beneath the state, not of it. Three years in
the place of redbrick, and many years more semi-comatose
in the halfway house. And then one day it was time for her
to be out of there. Freedom or rejection, she could not work
out which, it came to her as a surprise, a shock. They were
not able to keep her in the halfway house any longer, the
halfway house was closing, the community would care for
her. It didn't, there were no resources, and people who had
spent years protected from the hopscotch monsters slipped
through yawning cracks in pavements and fell into dark
night streets in London and Glasgow and Manchester. But
Lillian was saved.

Lillian's guardian angel was an old lady who couldn't
walk up four flights of stairs any more. A yellowing card in
a newsagent's window and Janet took the place of the
mythical care in the community. Lillian moved into Janet's
Bed and Breakfast, odd-job girl too old for the title, but still
not grown enough in life to be a woman. Janet didn't bother
with women or girls, instead she taught Lillian to be a
landlady. Janet did not ask questions, was quite honestly
not interested. Janet had enough unanswered questions of
her own, she did not need to add to the list. What Janet did
do was teach Lillian to cook full English for sixteen in half
an hour, scrambling four eggs for ten people, using stale

crusts to soak up the bacon fat and buttering the fresh loaf before slicing it.

Lillian learnt all her sadly lacking life skills from Janet. Lillian learnt getting by and making do and reserve. Lillian had never had enough reserve and even her three years in the redbrick was not long enough to teach her the value of keeping her mouth shut. Seven years of halfway house taught her only form-filling and DHSS ruses and carefully locking your door at night. But Janet taught Lillian how to look after her own heart. It was a lesson she could have done with ten years earlier, but still not too late to learn.

After four years Janet died and left the house to her protégée. There was a court case and Janet's flesh daughter – the one who hadn't laid eyes on her mother for six years – tried to reclaim Lillian's home. She was unsuccessful. Like Lillian, Janet understood the system too. She had kept back so much that Lillian never knew. There was more told in that court case than Lillian had ever heard from the old woman's mouth herself. More than she needed to know. In the end, though, the legalities were in order and the house was hers. The daughter took half the furniture and all the old pictures, but Lillian didn't mind. There was some refurbishment to do anyway. A spring clean was well overdue.

The following winter Lillian redecorated in time for the early season and welcomed her first guests on Maundy Thursday just as Janet had always done, plenty of hot water to wash their tired feet, weary from the long walk uphill from the bus station, and then a cold supper waiting for them on the dining table. Scotch eggs and corned beef sandwiches, ready-buttered cheese scones, bulk-bought Arctic rolls individually foil-wrapped. She knew how to please her guests.

Lillian took in the same families year in, year out. She remembered their foibles, likes and dislikes. Lillian valued the regularity, the safety of welcoming the same people to her door year after year. Knew who would put up with the late summer rain, knew the would-be painters and their desire for that perfect stroke of light. Lillian watched their children grow. She was happy to share an afternoon cup of tea with the mothers and grandmothers, back from the front for a rich tea and a little gossip about the new daughter-in-law, the old second cousin. The holiday-makers were free with their news and freer with their mouths, and their joy in the unburdening meant they rarely noticed that Lillian did not gossip, Lillian did not give her stories in return. And even those who did notice were used to it. They imagined that perhaps Lillian had no news. Pictured themselves as her news. They comforted themselves with the thought of their own largesse and were easy in the expansive wealth of her wide comfort. It seemed to be a fair transaction. They would not disrupt Lillian, they were happy with the status quo. So was Lillian. Or, if not happy, then happy enough. It would do. All you need is all you need.

And there were casual guests too. Even in the height of the season Lillian had always tried to keep one room back. Not a very good room, but twin beds and clean sheets and a basin with running water. Just in case someone came begging. A tired couple all the way from London, an Asian family perhaps, obviously turned away at three or four other places, still quite a rare sight down here, slowly dawning on them why they'd been told Cornwall was like England in the '50s. Not just the safe and clean beaches then. Someone who would only want the room for a night, who would eat a fast breakfast and be gone by nine. Lillian was always glad to help out, to provide unexpected succour. She knew what it felt like to need a room and have nowhere to go.

She was glad she could do something for Saz and Patrick when they stood on her doorstep. They could obviously do with a break. The girl looked like she hadn't slept in a week; his shoulders were tense, his face drawn. Of course they could have the room. It wasn't anything special, but it was probably the best they were going to get, this time of year. And by the way, didn't she recognize him? From the telly?

TWENTY-EIGHT

On the journey down to Carbis Bay, Patrick had decided he
was going to have to stay in Lillian's B&B if at all humanly
possible. Saz thought this was a very dodgy idea to say the
least, but Patrick had no intention of allowing her to dis-
suade him. They negotiated their way around the plethora
of roundabouts and past the families spilling from the pavements into the road, all trooping home from the beach for
a fish and chip tea, small children weighed down with sandy
buckets and spades and salty water wings, exhausted
parents weighed down with salty, sandy, sun-burned
children.

Saz tried one last time. "Patrick, the woman who runs this
place might not be your mother. We don't know anything for
definite. And even if Lillian Hope is your mother, there's no
guarantee she's here right now. She might have gone away
for summer herself."

"It's the height of the fucking season, Saz. If she's not
here right now then she's a worse fucking landlady than she
is a mother."

"Yeah, OK, maybe – but I still don't think we should just
barge in there and confront her, for all you know, she might
not want ..."

Saz broke off abruptly as Patrick swerved dangerously
close to the oncoming traffic in an attempt to avoid
knocking down a little girl on a half-size bike, trailing behind
her parents who each held a tiny baby in their arms.

"For fuck's sake! What the hell do they think they're doing? They bloody well shouldn't be allowed to breed. Fucking morons! Christ, if they can't keep their attention on one bloody kid, what the fuck are they doing having another two? Jesus fucking Christ!"

As Patrick honked the horn ferociously and screamed abuse at the startled parents, Saz decided she'd be better off keeping quiet herself. There was nothing she could do to calm Patrick's seething nerves, and clearly any more discussion would only rile him further. She sat beside him, eyes glued to the map in front of her, quietly indicating left and right turnings, and hoping that the calm she was trying her best to pretend and to communicate to the man beside her would somehow get past his frazzled aura and help them both through the next hour or so.

Half an hour later they pulled up outside Lillian Hope's B&B, and Saz sighed with relief at the "No Vacancy" sign in the front window. But Patrick made her go and ask anyway. At the very least, he reasoned, Lillian might open the door and he'd get a chance to look at her. Against her better judgement, Saz walked across the small lawn, bordered with a flourishing jungle of huge geraniums and lush begonias and, breathing hard herself, lifted a nervous hand to ring the doorbell. Moments later her heart plummeted at the sound of shuffling footsteps coming down the stairs and the door was opened. Of course, the woman answering the door might have been the cleaner, a housekeeper, Lillian's assistant, Lillian's best friend or even, appearances to the contrary, Lillian's own mother. But if the tall, rounded, greying woman who stood in front of Saz wasn't Patrick's mother, then she looked out of Patrick's eyes by pure chance, and Saz had already used up her week's quota of lucky coincidences.

"Oh, hi. I know your sign says 'No Vacancy', but we are desperate, and I just wondered . . . well, maybe . . ."

Saz didn't know what she wondered. Patrick had insisted she go to the door but he hadn't come up with a clever reason for asking for a room at a B&B that clearly indicated it had none. An interminable ten seconds later Saz's basic lying skills returned, and with them her manipulative ability. Baby. Mother. Adopted babies. Young mothers. Saz put the lot together in a heart-string tugging story. They'd come this far, found Lillian only through deceit and subterfuge. Patrick was right, it was a bit late for her to start going all social-worker-conscience on him now.

"Yeah, and um . . . I'm having a baby." Not a huge lie.

"Just over three months."

Saz rubbed her too-fit tummy and hoped the woman in front of her hadn't been one of those women who looked five months pregnant from two months onwards.

"And I haven't been well, so we thought . . . well, actually," Saz shrugged her head back towards the car where Patrick was sitting staring at the woman. "He thought, we should go away for the weekend. Only there's nowhere to stay. I mean nowhere. And I'm shattered." Also true.

"So . . . do you have anywhere at all? Even a single room? Or know of somewhere else we can try? Please?"

The older woman assured Saz of their great good fortune, "As it happens, love, I do keep a room back. You and your chap look like you could both do with a bit of a rest. It's nothing special, but it is a room, and that's more than you're likely to get anywhere else. Now you park the car round the back and come on in."

Mary, Joseph and not-Jesus were in luck.

Saz saw a dangerous silence fall on Patrick when they left the car on the gravelled courtyard at the back of the house. She had initially been concerned that he might blurt out what they believed to be the truth the minute he set eyes on Lillian. Worryingly, his reaction was just the opposite. Patrick's mouth was tightly closed around grim, thin lips, his clenched teeth delineating an even stronger jawline than usual. After his voluble rantings all the way down the A30, this hushed calm was disconcerting to say the least. Patrick retrieved their bags from the boot and started to walk round to the front of the house.

"Patrick, I can take my own bag, it's not heavy."

"Hell no. You're three months' pregnant. What would she think of me?"

"She'll think I'm three months' pregnant like I told her, not a bloody invalid. Give it here."

Patrick shook his head, "I'll take them."

Saz didn't understand the sudden development of a sense of chivalry. Not until they stood in the hallway of the house and she felt him flinch as the woman came towards them, her hand held out to shake his. He nodded his head at the tall woman, shrugged his shoulders and indicated the bags. As if they were glued to his hands. The woman was evidently used to taciturn husbands, because she winked at Saz with a conspiratorial half-smile and led the two of them up the stairs – which Saz was delighted to see were carpeted in a dark blue runner. In fact, as far as she could tell, the decor of the whole house seemed quite distant from the usual garish pinks and oranges so favoured by most British land-ladies. Perhaps Patrick's mother had his good taste as well as his eyes.

They were shown into a tiny twin room in the attic of the house, painted an easy cool blue, just enough space for two narrow beds, a half-sized sink and a waist-high ward-robe with a tea tray perched precariously on top of it. The woman indicated which of the beds had a firmer mattress for Saz and then told them to take a look out of the little window. "Best view in the house, that is."

The window looked out past the tiled roofs of Carbis Bay down to the coast, a wide stretch of golden sand. The rolling waves and green shoreline to her right reminded Saz of the beaches she'd seen a couple of years ago in New Zealand. She shuddered at the thought and turned away. The view was wonderful, the memory was not. The woman went on to tell them about breakfast, the bathrooms downstairs, the closest shops, the nearest restaurants. Saz could feel Patrick's hackles rise beside her and knew it was time to get this woman away from him if he wasn't to explode. Ferment was probably inevitable, but she'd rather it was in a time and place she had a little more control over, if at all possible. Feeling frightened and exhausted herself, she knew she wasn't up to handling a full scale investigative row just yet.

"OK. Brilliant. Thanks. Look, I might just have a lie down first. Before we go out for dinner. If that's OK with you, love?"

She placed a cool hand on Patrick's arm. Cool and very firm.

"Yeah. Sure. Whatever."

The woman spotted her cue to leave. She could see this warring couple needed a little time to themselves. "Well then, you've got your keys. As I said, the front door is locked at eleven; if you're in after then, make sure to double lock it behind you. Anything else, just give me a yell. If you shout loud enough, I'm bound to hear you. There's not any other Lillians stopping with me."

Saz had to ask, "So you are Lillian?"

"Lillian Hope. Definitely not Lily. So don't go shouting that or you'll get no answer. Good. I'll leave you to it then."

She held out her hand to Patrick who stared at her a half second too long, then took her hand in his.

"Yeah. Great. Thanks Lillian."

Saz wondered if Lillian could feel his shaking hand.

TWENTY-NINE

Saz and Patrick decided to take their landlady's advice and drive into St Ives to find somewhere for dinner. Except that wasn't quite how it worked out. Instead they found themselves driving round and round a one-way system looking for an elusive parking place. With Patrick getting nastier by the minute. The one-way system was obviously designed to be impenetrable to foreigners and clogged still further by hoards of barely-dressed teenagers lining the pavements and spilling out into the narrow cobbled roads. Saz had hoped that getting Patrick out of the tiny attic room, dinner perhaps on the shorefront, with a shared bottle of wine over which they could plan their next move, might calm his mounting agitation. She hadn't counted on the pretty seaside town she'd happily holidayed in with her parents taking the intervening twenty years to turn itself into a cross between Alton Towers and the Ministry of Sound. Saz felt old just looking at the thronging youth and Patrick wanted to mow the lot down. Except he kept following arrows that directed them into steep winding lanes too narrow for the wide new car and he had to reverse and try again. Patrick was far from happy. Saz was nervous. And bloody hungry. The shortbread biscuits in the room had done little to soothe her grumbling stomach, even though she'd eaten both packets the minute Lillian had closed their door.

An hour later they finally parked the car, found a

restaurant with a stunning moonlit view of Porthmeor
Beach and the night-lit Tate. Two hours after that they'd
eaten a meal that even Patrick admitted was well above
passable. Saz thought it was bloody fantastic. Patrick may
have sneered at her ordering sausages and mash when they
were within spitting distance of the sea, but he happily
forked a good half of her mashed potato down his face. All
in the name of research, of course. It was good mash. He
wanted to know what potatoes they'd used. Saz said he
should leave her bloody dinner alone and ask in the kitchen.
Patrick told her to shut the fuck up, he was paying. He may
not have been in a great mood, but at least he was using
his mouth to eat and speak, not to grind his teeth to a
jawline of powdered enamel.

They also shared a bottle of champagne.

As Patrick said, "It's not every day you shake hands with
your mother for the first time. Hell, let's really push the boat
out." Celebratory words, voice fat with bitter irony. Patrick
would be driving them back to the B&B later and Saz knew
things were going to get a hell of a lot messier before he
was calm again so, much as she would have loved to get
completely slaughtered and use the pale straw bubbles to
forget the whole reason for them being there, she insisted
on a half bottle. It didn't help her client's mood any, but it
did save him from shooting his mouth off too unpleasantly
when the chef came out from the kitchen and asked for his
autograph. On his apron. And the napkin. And the tablecloth. Saz thought he might be getting Patrick's handprint
on his face if he pushed it any further, so she explained as
politely as possible that they had an early start in the
morning and hurried Patrick out to the car. It took them
only four wrong turnings in dark country lanes to get back
to Carbis Bay and on the way Patrick gave Saz her first
compliment.

"You're brilliant, you know that?"

Expecting sarcasm, Saz asked a wary, "Why?"

"The way you got me out of that restaurant."

"What about it?"

"Well, Katy would have kept me there until that syco-phantic wanker really fucked me off. She actively pushes me into the punch-ups, she doesn't try to save me from them."

"Patrick, I wasn't trying to save you from a beating, I was trying to save him from one."

"That bloke was an arsehole."

"Good mash though."

"Yeah. Bastard. But anyway, good work."

"Thanks. It's always been my aim to be someone's minder."

They sat in the little upstairs room for half an hour trying to decide on their next move. It was no clearer than it had been over dinner. If anything, the proximity to Lillian made Patrick's pressing need to confront her even more urgent. Finally Saz knew she could put it off no longer. There was no way Patrick would allow either of them to sleep if they didn't deal with it that night. She did at least manage to persuade him to allow her to go downstairs alone.

"Patrick, you're so bloody hyped up I just don't trust you. Either you let me do this my way, or we don't fucking do any of it. I'll walk out and leave you here by yourself. Then you can shout at her as much as you want, only you won't have me beside you making it OK. I mean it. My way, or not at all."

It was midnight, Saz was tired, the line between per-suasion and threat was even more blurred than usual. They sounded remarkably similar. The main problem being that Saz's "my way" didn't exist. She had no idea what she was going to say to Lillian. The walk down four flights of dark stairs didn't provide her with any astonishing insights and Saz knocked on Lillian's door half hoping that her hostess had scuttled off for a rampant night out with the youth of St Ives.

It was quarter past twelve when Lillian opened the door to her private part of the house. She looked smaller and softer in the pale blue dressing gown she'd hurriedly pulled around her. Saz felt sick. Tense nerves and exhaustion and irritation at Patrick and concern for this woman. Concern for them both.

"Um, Lillian, I know it's late and I'm really sorry to bother you . . ."

"Is something wrong with your room?"

"No. Nothing like that."

Lillian frowned, "I can't do midnight snacks, you know."

"No. Look, I really need to talk to you. Do you think I could come in?"

In answer Lillian pushed the door further open, turned and walked ahead of Saz down a short passage into a sitting room. These rooms had evidently not been redecorated when Lillian had done up the rest of the house. Her own domain was landlady-traditional. Yellow-flowered wallpaper, red-flowered carpet, a heady selection of well dusted china ornaments and a blazing coal-effect electric heater, coals glowing merrily though the heating itself was turned off.

By way of explanation Lillian waved her arm around the room, "I inherited this house, from the original landlady. I did the rest of it up as best I could, but I didn't have the heart to change her part of the house. And I'm pretty much used to it now."

Saz sat on the gold velour armchair and as she did so the one absence in the cluttered room came into clear focus.

There were delicate ornaments and dried flowers and lace doilies crammed onto every surface. But the family photos were glaringly absent. There were no posed portraits, hair-combed perfect from the '60s, no sweet children grown into unruly teenagers in the '70s, no proud mother at the firstborn's nuptials, latest grandchild, happy couple on their silver wedding anniversary. Nothing at all on yellowing photographic paper in a gilt-edged frame. It might just have been that Lillian didn't care for family photos. Or that she had none. Saz felt the knowledge she held in her clamped-shut mouth was choking her. She was going to have to spit it out before the intestinal knots looping themselves in her stomach ended her dining-out days forever. Lillian was sitting, calmly waiting for her to speak. Almost too calmly. Even in her state of heightened tension, Saz found herself thinking that Lillian's detachment was a little weird. She couldn't imagine herself waiting this patiently as a stranger forced her way into her sitting room and demanded to have a talk in the middle of the night. Then again, she couldn't imagine what it might be like to open your home to complete strangers for nine months of every year. Perhaps Lillian's guests often insisted on midnight conversations. Perhaps Lillian knew what she'd come about. Maybe she'd been waiting for this moment for nearly forty years herself. Maybe it would all be OK after all. Saz's mouth opened and, as so often before, she heard herself speaking before she'd even decided what she was going to say.

"It's about your son."

"I'm sorry?"

Saz opened her mouth again and the words fell out, "I need to talk to you about your son."

"What son?"

"Patrick Freeman. Sweeney. The guy from the telly."

Lillian continued to look at her as if she were speaking a very foreign language.

"The man I'm here with. Patrick. He's your son."

Lillian shook her head, "I think you must have me mistaken for someone else."

"But you're the only Lillian Hope."

"Other than my great-aunt Lily who's been dead for twenty-five years."

"Well, then Patrick is your child. I mean, he's your adopted son. Your birth son, who was adopted."

This time Lillian spoke very slowly, as if Saz were particularly stupid, "But I don't have any children."

Saz didn't know what to say. Maybe Gary was right and all the things that seemed to prove she was the right woman were just coincidences. Or maybe she was the right woman but Lillian had blanked her son from her memory, had spent so long convincing herself that she didn't have a child that now she actually believed she'd never even given birth. Then Saz had a very worrying thought, what if Lillian really hadn't wanted the baby? What if Patrick was waiting upstairs for a made-for-TV reunion, soft focus tears and welcoming hugs, but the reality was the exact opposite? She didn't think she could bear to deal with Patrick's reaction if that really was the case. Except that Lillian didn't look like someone who'd just had her deepest secret revealed. She looked like someone who honestly wanted to help. And didn't know what the fuck was going on.

"I'm very sorry if this upsets your husband, love . . ."

"He's not. He's my friend."

"Well, whatever. But the two of you must have made a mistake somewhere along the line. Your friend can't be my child. It's not possible. I don't have any children. I did have a baby. Years ago. Or at least, I gave birth to a baby." Lillian's speech wound down to a slow staccato. She spoke quietly into the middle distance. "But I didn't have the baby adopted. I couldn't have. I mean, there was that option, to adopt, before I gave birth, but I didn't want to have it adopted anyway. I was going to keep it. I wanted to keep the baby. Only that's not what happened. My baby was stillborn. I don't have a son."

THIRTY

The birth was to have been Lillian's beginning, a hand-made genesis, and she had decided for herself that it was possible. She would show them her cool sanity and perfect demeanour. Lillian had planned to be a model of exceptional behaviour, the paragon of dark corridors and bright, white rooms. The child would go, after the first couple of days with her as quiet mother, to her aunt in Falmouth. Lillian would allow the child to be taken with no fuss and no tears. It was right. This transfer would be carried out just as she had agreed with Doctor Lees. He would be amazed at her surrendering calm. Days and weeks would follow and through all of them Lillian would be the good girl, so that at her December review the board would have no choice but to agree to her sanity. Quiet perfection flowing from herself to all the others and then she would be free and healthy and welcome to return to the world. It would be nearly Christmas by then and the baby would still be small enough to forget the time of separation. Lillian was to be the good girl and all would be right with the world. It was her birth plan.

But then the pains came and it was so much more than she could ever have expected. But not simply the hurt as the child began the first separation from the mother. Lillian knew something was not right. Felt that they were not talking to her as they should. Where were the reassurances that it would all be fine in the end, the cajoling coercion that this was a pain worth breaking through, breathing through? And from inside the circle of her terror she realized they did not mean to let her keep this baby. Her aunt might take the child, but Lillian would not get away in time for this Christmas or the next, they would never believe her to be neither mad nor bad, there would be no re-birth. They would not be convinced of her reason, because it did not suit them to change their minds. The changing of her mind did not suit them. All this she knew from their whispered words and stilted walk, the uneasy gait of the silent nurses, the mother nurses most of all, those who had children of their own at home looking at her in pity and timing her contractions unwillingly, each new pain stretching their baby-bond sympathy.

And so the timed torment carried with it not merely the physical wrench, but also an emotional rip and tear. Lillian would not let the child out, she would not go the long way into labour, they would have to cut her apart to set this child free. She would keep it safe within her own flesh. If it was the only way she could keep her baby, then that is what she would do. But of course she couldn't. Her body betrayed her to the enforced will of institutionalized desire. Lillian eked out each contraction, numbing herself with the intensity of her desire to hold on, hold in, did not want this ripping away to be painless. Did not want this ripping away to be.

Finally she could hold the birth back no longer and the baby was born in wailing blood. There were only Doctor Lees and one nurse in the room; it was the middle of the night, the others had long ago been sent home. The child did not cry. Lillian cried. Lillian did not know the nurse, a young woman new to the building, drafted in for the late-night shift. Lillian had thought she knew Doctor Lees, but this white coat was a cold version of the gentle man who had held her hand through the last five months and discussed the possibilities. The baby was born and they did not show the child to her, did not slap the slippery infant to make it scream, healthy lungs attesting its presence to the world. There was silence in the white room and a heavy gas mask over Lillian's mouth.

When she woke in the middle of the night she was sick and bleeding. And no longer pregnant. Her breasts ached with the rest of her flesh. But for no reason. There would not be a reason. At first Lillian thought her recollection must be wrong. Doctor Lees' words running through her mind must be lies created from her own suffering. But as the early sun pierced the morning rain, Lillian knew his words clear in her head: "Your baby is dead, Lillian. Your baby was born dead. I'm really very sorry. There is no baby. You should sleep now. Go to sleep. Rest." And as she breathed, gasping full through the ether, she also heard his quiet mumble to the nurse, "It's probably for the best, in the end."

When Lillian awoke the next morning she did not at first believe the dream her body told her. This could not have happened. The long waiting, the final thirty-six hours of heavy labour, and all of it for nothing. Pain and waiting with no result. Simply to be given another end, return to dark.

Lillian never saw the dead baby, did not hold her child. They had not offered to let her. She was drugged and beyond understanding anyway. The corpse foetus was taken away and dealt with and kept far out of sight, incinerated along with all the other waste matter from a day's work in blood and guts. There was no funeral, there was no goodbye, no need for a tiny white coffin. There was nothing. It was not a real child, so why should Lillian grieve at all? Time and silence would heal the loss. Lillian would get over it. No one need ever know. It had not been a wanted child in the first place. That was the reason she'd come here, after all. God moved in the most mysterious of ways and who knew when Lillian would be ready to care for a baby? If ever. It wouldn't be fair on the poor little mite. Now she had to concentrate on forgetting all about it and try to get herself well again. That was a far better aim. She should trust them, they knew about this, Doctor Lees understood. Lillian was not a bad girl and, if she tried hard, she could be a good girl. Then Lillian could be in the world again and this nastiness would be over. All the pain would be far away in the past. She really should let it go.

Except Lillian couldn't let it go. Because she knew it was her fault. She had killed the baby with her own wanting to keep it. Strangled the child with her desire to hold it in. Rather than let them take the baby away, Lillian had made the child die. Only yesterday it had been turning and kicking, she'd felt it vibrant and ready inside. And Lillian had ruined everything. They were wrong. She was a very bad girl indeed.

It was another two years before Lillian climbed out of the darkness of her imagined wickedness and was ready to leave the place of crying. Though she never left the place of guilt.

THIRTY-ONE

They could have just looked at each other's eyes. Same pale green, same rounded shape, same face of dark-ringed tiredness. They could have just gone with gut feeling and blood certainty and the complete fucking weirdness of the whole thing. They could have relied on the fact that as well as feeling drawn to each other, there was also a terrifying distance, almost revulsion. An uncertainty which was clearly not the circumspect dance of polite strangers.

They could have agreed this looked more than likely, though the old story told otherwise, though a residual hope of trust in the system told otherwise. And then they might have taken things very slowly, eased themselves into the possible, gently found a way to be that was interim and waiting and careful. But Patrick wanted to run out into the street slaughtering officialdom. Conduct his own personal massacre of the white coats and the social workers who made decisions on behalf of the irredeemably decision-free. They could have believed what they both seemed to just know anyway. But that simple assumption wasn't enough for Patrick. He wanted proof too.

It was fortunate, therefore, that he also had money. The pause until morning was too long, but it was waited out all the same. Coffee and no-sleep and grated cheese melted onto thick white bread, which only Saz could eat, and then half-started conversations that were left hanging in the air because until they knew the truth there was no point in answering questions properly, giving whole details. Why would Lillian want to know about a fourteen-year-old boy's school year? What need did Patrick have to learn that her father had been a tobacconist who'd died when she was twelve? Who cared when Lillian's birthday fell? She already knew Patrick's birth date. The conversations were waiting until daylight and the analysis, not of past experience, but of present actuality. Of flesh and blood.

Saz, though, had plenty of questions she was dying to ask. About Lees, about Richard Leyton. She wanted to know about the institution Lillian had been in, to ask about the other women there. To enquire if there might possibly have been a woman expecting a mixed-race baby, back then when the child would have been half-caste, delivered with even less welcome than the other babies. But it was too soon and Lillian was too shell-shocked and Patrick too angry. Furthering Chris's search would have to wait until the midnight revelation began to feel a little closer to normal.

The search for a private clinic willing to do the blood and DNA tests at such short notice had them jamming the phone lines of the whole far west. It was Saturday morning. Most private clinics were open for privileged patients only. Or urgent ingrown toenails – a snip at three hundred pounds a time. Patrick made several calls to friends in London, then still more to friends of friends all over the country. Saz asked Molly to speak to a couple of trustworthy doctor friends. And when that proved useless, she demanded her girlfriend contact a couple of other less trustworthy ones who might be of more use. Molly thought it wasn't wise. Counselled more speed, less haste. And then less speed and more care. Explained the impossibility, the lunacy of demanding such important proof at short notice. Molly told

Saz she was asking the impossible. Saz handed the telephone to Patrick who pointed out that Molly's impossible
and his own were quite different – his had cash to throw at
it. Anything could be bought for the right amount of money.
Babies could be bought for the right amount of money. He
got no further argument. Lillian made twelve full English
breakfasts and eventually remembered to drink a cup of tea
herself. She added three sugars. And threw it out after the
first mouthful.

At eleven-thirty, after maybe twenty phone calls, Patrick's
rising disgust with the corrupt health system was finally
confirmed. They were to drive to Plymouth. Hair, saliva and
blood samples would be taken. They could, of course, go
to further extremes later if these did not prove conclusive.
But it was unlikely that would be the case as blood and
saliva were most authorities' ready reckoners of reliable
parentage. A technician would take the samples to have
them immediately analysed by her friend who worked in
police forensics. It was by far the fastest way they could
hope to get an answer. It would involve a bit of subterfuge,
some lying and possibly even minor theft – and the whole
thing would cost just two hundred pounds less than Molly's
first IVF treatment. Patrick and Lillian would have their
answer by the end of the day. Or tomorrow morning at the
very latest. Definite. Promised.

Lillian left each of her guests a hand-written message in
their rooms and Saz reluctantly agreed to stay in the B&B
just in case Mrs Dawkins came back from the beach with a
migraine and needed someone to keep the others quiet. She
waved goodbye from the front door, one hand waving, the
other with fingers crossed for good luck. Lillian's wide frame
uncomfortable in the new car, even with its easy seats and
soft welcome – perhaps because of it. Patrick kept his eyes
glued forward and his hands white-knuckled to the wheel,

not sure whether to hope this was reality or a mistake. Not sure it was possible all this could have happened in such a short time.

Saz closed the door after them and surprised herself with a release of tensed, held breath. Tight shoulders fell to almost ear level and she sank to the hall floor. Though she had initially wanted to go with them to help dilute their tension in some way, another body-buffer hoping somehow to make it easier, part of her was also relieved to be forced to wait. Their journey wasn't likely to be your average Saturday afternoon picnic in the teashop of English tourism. She hoped Lillian was used to speeding drivers – silent and furious.

Five minutes later Saz shook herself from a sleepy stupor and went into the kitchen. Twelve full English breakfasts left a hell of a lot of dishes behind them. And even a cold bacon and sausage sandwich, liberally spread with mustard and brown sauce, did nothing to raise her flagging energy levels. But the thick slicing of the crumbling fresh white bread and the art of getting a wide bite into her mouth without spilling grease all down her clothes did take her mind off Lillian and Patrick for a whole three minutes.

Saz sat by the phone for most of the evening. Molly called twice to see if there was any news. Saz called the hospital to check on Sukie and was told there was no change, she was still very ill. Neither Patrick nor Lillian called. Saz waited by the phone anyway, the thin diet of summer Saturday evening television for company – though even a fourth screening of a youthful Schwarzenegger in *Terminator* was preferable to the fretful complaints of Mrs Dawkins. Linda Hamilton was a damn sight better looking for a start. Saz greeted the migraine-free moaner when she knocked at Lillian's door in search of clarification. Yes, Lillian would be back by the morning. No, there was nothing to worry about, just a minor family matter. Yes, of course Lillian would be able to prepare breakfast for the Dawkins family. And naturally, though Mrs Dawkins understood Lillian had endured a personal crisis of her own – no, Saz was sure she couldn't go into details – Lillian would, of course, put the needs of her guests first. They were paying after all. Saz ushered Mrs Dawkins from Lillian's part of the house, shutting her up and sending her off to her room as quickly as possible. One more irritable complaint veiled in mock-concern and Saz would have felt obliged to take Mrs Dawkins' migraine-prone, penny-pinching face and slap it. Really fucking hard, in a manner she was sure Lillian didn't usually use, even on her more irritating guests.

At midnight Saz finally gave up waiting and decided she might as well try to sleep. Certainly her body's need for rest looked set to overcome her racing brain's interest in answers – her usually racing brain which had slowed now to a stumbling jog as the past week's combination of tension and lack of sleep dumped themselves on her in a red and yellow room at the bottom of a house of sleeping tenants. She laid herself out on Lillian's couch, the alarm set beside her for six-thirty. Even if Patrick and Lillian made it back in the middle of the night, whatever the result Lillian might not be in a fit state to play the perfect seaside landlady. It was more than likely that eight in the morning would see Saz as the provider of twelve full English breakfasts, five of which were for the Dawkins family. She really needed the rest.

THIRTY-TWO

Lillian had planned the funeral so many times. The funeral she had not even thought to ask for. Not even the good girls had funerals for stillborns; they were foetuses whisked away before you'd even noticed. For your own good. Un-mothers, helped back to bed for a few days' rest and then bundled into a warm coat and sent home to get on with it. Get on with life. And hopefully a kind neighbour would have moved the pretty little baby clothes lovingly collected over the last nine months, closed the door on the pastel-painted room, tidied the cold flat. And in the tidying left it colder still. Not that Lillian had anything like that kind of attention.

She did not think she was unusual. She waited in the hospital, floating on waves of medication and neglect, well beyond the reach of talking or analysis. Getting by on largactyl and ECT and time. It was a very long time before Lillian knew, from the TV documentaries and the newspaper supplements and the radio programmes, that she had been neither bad nor mad. Just one of those girls. Lillian had gone into care when she was twelve, mother unable to cope after her father had died. Taken first to a brief run of foster homes and then, as her demands became greater in wanting a real family, there had to be a new plan for Lillian. As she grew older and began to ask for what she wanted, started to demand what she perceived to be her rights, they had no alternative but to place her in the first of many institutions.

They could not give her what she wanted, so they would give her what they wanted instead.

Lillian then understood that quiet and good weren't getting her anywhere, so she might as well go for loud and bad. Finally a small affection was eventually shown by a visiting teacher, one she found she could talk to. Small affection returned by the easy gift of her body. At least he talked to her as if she was intelligent enough to converse, listened when she talked back, actually appeared interested – maybe he even was interested. But then his interest was noticed and he was moved on and Lillian stayed silent to protect him from the growing child. They did not like Lillian's silence. If she wouldn't tell them who had done this to her, how could they help her? From Lillian's point of view, nothing had been done to her. For the first time in a long while she didn't feel like a victim, she felt like he'd helped, been her friend. So she kept her silence and her refusal to speak was deemed yet another demonstration of her wickedness. From wickedness, and in silence, it was an easy metamorphosis from bad to mad.

Another institution, another language to learn. But first there was the baby to be born. Plans to be made, her aunt to care for the child. Lillian's heartbreak was mad, her pregnancy was bad and there was a free bed in the dark hospital and Doctor Lees was ever so understanding. Lillian didn't know why they thought she was unwell – it was simply words she wouldn't use – but she understood they must know better, they had mapped the labyrinthine corridors, they wore the white coats, they knew how to walk outside. Lillian was no longer interested in going outside, the heat was building up out there, she stayed in the cool of the high walls, signed the papers they offered her and waited. Growing quiet, quiet growing.

Lillian was not the kind to cry loudly – she remembered

what crying loudly had done to her. She did not talk it over
with friends or family because by the time she was ready
to leave there were none. But for years Lillian had imagined
the lilies and the incense and the tiny white coffin. Planned
out each little detail. Made the ending real until eventual
acceptance came with exposition and Lillian began to put
the baby away. To clear the memory of the nothing, the no-
memory she had been left with.

And now it was nearly forty years later and Lillian did not
need to plan the funeral any more. The dream had come
true and it looked nothing like she had hoped. There was
no funeral. It was far from making sense and yet it was also
perfectly understandable. Far more understandable than
when they had tried to get the loss of the baby into her cold
and closed mind. The grown child sat beside her, talking
twenty to the dozen, spewing out a torrent of abuse against
the people who had allowed this to happen to both of them,
interrupting himself to ask another question about Lillian,
about her family, about how she had even found herself in
that cold building in the first place and then on again,
another furious rage against the iniquity, the wickedness
that had allowed this to occur. She sat beside Patrick
growing quieter. Growing more Lillian. Part of her had
always held onto the myth of reunion. The possibility of
this might-be baby, come back to hold her and love her and
to be mothered. And now here he was. Both ludicrous
and perfectly normal. Lillian wasn't crazy. Her sense that
the child couldn't be gone, her never-spoken conviction
that they must have made a mistake, was confirmed. The
baby didn't die. Lillian wasn't mad.

And it wasn't that all the pain didn't matter, and it wasn't
that their lying hadn't been corrupt and wicked. But Lillian

had been right. She sat listening to Patrick's fury and even while acknowledging the bitterness, the soft warmth of relief blanketed out much of the pain. Perhaps it would come later, when there had been time to adjust. But for now, she had her child and her sanity. Which was rather more than she'd ever expected.

Lillian sat silently shaking beside her son who drove slowly and carefully through the night, Patrick glad of the new car with its comfortable seat for his crying mother, very glad of the new car with its automatic gears that left him one hand free to hold hers as he drove. And really fucking angry.

THIRTY-THREE

Lillian and Patrick arrived back a little after three in the morning. Saz, part sleeping, mostly listening for the slam of car doors, was in the hallway by the time Lillian put her key in the lock. Matching pairs of tired eyes confirmed her unspoken question. Saz made tea and reassured Lillian about the comfort of her guests – including Mrs Dawkins and family – and then heard their story. Summer traffic had taken the first two hours and then they'd met with the technician who was to help them. The bottle-red matron who greeted them wasn't quite the girlie lab rat Patrick had been expecting. Nor was her manner. She took blood and hair and a £500 cash sample of Patrick's money: "I mean, I'm OK to wait for the rest of the money until later in the day. You can go out and get the remainder while we're waiting for the results from the police lab, but there's no way I'm even going to start without some of the cash upfront. All right?"

Patrick handed over £500 and Shirley laughed out loud at his offer of a cheque for the balance. She gave him directions to the nearest cash machine instead. Satisfied that she'd have her money as soon as possible, Shirley slapped on a pair of latex gloves and got on with the job. She took their hair, blood and saliva samples and then told them they could bugger off for the rest of the day.

"Audrey's got a rush job on just now. I called her half an hour ago to check her schedule. She reckons she'll probably be able to get on to this lot in her tea break and then slip it in with a bunch of other stuff that's going on in her lab. But they've got heaps to do, some murder or rape or something like that. I don't know, Audrey's job's a damn sight more bloody exciting than mine, all I ever get is . . ."

Patrick felt Lillian tense beside him and realized he needed to shut Shirley up before she gave out any more gruesome details. And he had no doubt she would if they gave her half a chance, "Right. So you'll get our stuff to her and we'll wait to hear from you, is that it?"

"That's it, love. There's a couple of nice little restaurants I can point out. I mean, it might be quite awhile. I hope you two have got something to talk about?"

Patrick looked at the short, fat woman addressing him. Hair that Lillian was later to describe as "harlot-red" floated in a bouncy top-knot above an apparently innocent face: smiling mouth, dimpled cheeks, eyes cold as fuck. It was impossible she hadn't guessed why they were there. She simply couldn't be that stupid – which left only one reason for her question. She was actually enjoying their discomfort. His anger rising, Patrick clenched his fists tight, digging short strong nails into his palms. They needed this. He gave Shirley his mobile number, took Audrey's number in case Shirley couldn't get through to him for any reason, and wrote down the names of the three restaurants "a man of your tastes might find almost passable".

As they left the lab Shirley shouted after them, "You won't forget my money, will you?"

Patrick smiled and nodded back at Shirley and then turned to look at Lillian. Her face was screwed up and her arms folded tight across her chest. "Are you OK?"

Lillian nodded. "Just get me out of here."

Only once they were safely in the car did she relax a little. "I'm sorry, I just knew I was going to have to slap her if she didn't stop soon. Nasty piece of work, not enough to get all that money out of you, but she has to humiliate us both as well."

Patrick burst out laughing and opened his hands to show Lillian the stigmata of his own fury. He put his arm around her as she crumpled into tears and he wondered how it was he'd become such a twentieth-century boy that he needed to waste so much money proving an already clear truth. Though even in the comfort of that moment, he realized that proof was a vital component of vengeance. And somebody was definitely going to have to pay for this.

This Patrick explained in great detail to Saz back at the B&B, while Lillian slept off the strain of the past day. "I'll kill the bastard. You just find out where he lives and I promise you, I will kill him."

"Patrick . . ."

"No. I mean it. This Lees bloke – really, I want to slaughter the bastard."

"I know you do, but . . ."

"Then you find out where the fuck he is, so I bloody well can."

"I'd rather we contact him and get more information. There are others in your position, you know. Chris hasn't even made it this far yet."

"I don't give a flying fuck, I just want to meet the bastard."

"Oh for God's sake, Patrick, shut up. Of course I know how to get hold of this doctor. If he's still alive."

"Yeah, well if he is, he's not fucking alive for long."

Saz sighed and ignored his ranting, "Yeah, right. That'll help no end. If by some stroke of luck and astonishing bad management this bloke hasn't been struck off yet, he's easily found through a medical register. Even if he's retired. That's not the problem."

"Well then, what is the problem?"

"For Christ's sake, will you calm down?"

Patrick shook his head, "Fuck no. This is forty years' worth of pissed off. I'm hanging on to this one."

"Listen, Patrick. There's no way I'm going to let you have anything to do with this. Not now. Not as long as you're thinking like this."

"And you'd rather I behaved like what?"

"Nothing. Just be exactly as you are. I don't expect anything else. You have every right to feel the way you do."

"I'm glad you think so."

"But it doesn't actually help anyone, you know. It's too nasty and it's too bloody close and, for fuck's sake, this is clearly not something we should be dealing with ourselves. We should take you and Lillian straight down to the police first thing in the morning and hand the whole lot over to them. Including that poncey bloody Georgina's role in it, because believe me, she knows something about all this."

"We can't."

Saz spoke through teeth clenched in irritation and exhaustion, "Patrick, this isn't a vigilante outfit. This is only you and me. And Chris. Maybe Luke too. And for all we know it's not just you lot. There might be other women, other children involved."

"There's bound to be."

"We can't just race round the country reuniting mothers with babies they thought died years ago, it's fucking insane. There's got to be a more ordered way to take care of this. The man's committed a crime, for fuck's sake. I've done my part of the job, we've found your mother. Now I'll clear it with Chris; he's going to have to tell his adoptive mother about this some time anyway, then we call the police and leave the rest of it to them."

"I promised Lillian."

"Promised her what?"

"She wouldn't have to talk to the police."

"Why the fuck not?"

"You've seen the woman, Saz. She's clearly not the most balanced of people at the moment—"

Saz forbore to mention it was now abundantly clear where he got his own great reserves of sanity from.

"She's got a pretty damn tenuous grip on her life as it is. And she's terrified of the system. She spent nearly four fucking years of her life in that loony bin. Not a nutter, but persuaded that she was. She won't talk to the police about it. We spent fourteen hours together, just her and me, all that time driving and waiting, and nothing to do but talk about what might be coming, and I guarantee you, there's a fuck of a lot more she's still not said."

"Patrick, that would be true of anybody, for God's sake. You've just been re-united with your mother, and in hardly the most ideal of circumstances. Even if the rest of Lillian's life had been a fairy tale, this would still be really shocking."

"So we should do what she asks."

"We should do the right thing."

"What? And turn all this over to the likes of my little social worker?"

"You make her sound like my little pony."

"She is. She's practically a child herself, for God's sake. She doesn't know anything about all this."

"Neither do you."

Patrick stood up, squared his shoulders to Saz, his hand on the door, "All I know is that I promised my mother she wouldn't have to deal with any police or any social workers. I promised her I'd take care of this. You and I would take care of this. Now, if you find other mothers, your friend Chris's mother perhaps, or that Luke, and they're willing to talk to the police or social workers or whoever, then fine. But if Lillian can't do it, then she doesn't have to, and I'm not going to make her. And neither are you, got it?"

Patrick slammed the door before she was able to argue any more and Saz stood up, stretched, walked around the little room, scratched irritably at the scars on her hands and then sat down again, completely frustrated. She understood Patrick's position, had guessed at the extent of Lillian's fear, but this was ludicrous. It was also dangerous. She knew Patrick's fury was no empty threat. If he did get hold of Lees, there was no knowing what he'd do. And she didn't think a minimum of grievous bodily harm was readily excusable in court, not even with the sound reasoning Patrick had to offer.

THIRTY-FOUR

Molly was waiting with information for Saz, information she clearly felt very uncomfortable about passing on. She knew about Doctor Lees, not because Saz asked her to check on his present status as a medic – though that had been Saz's first request when she called to say she was on her way home – but because she'd spent most of Saturday afternoon going through Eva Freeman's medical records. And then gone into quite a lot of further research.

"It made fantastic reading. It's amazing how much we've learnt about fertility in the past forty years. The incredible amount that's changed in so short a time. I mean, I'm a walking advertisement of that, right?"

"Yeah, Moll, you are, but these records . . .?"

Unfortunately for Saz's sense of urgency, Molly really was interested in the subject. Saz, who'd been interested in reproductive sciences only as far as it pertained to her own procreative desires, wasn't especially enthused about any of it right now. Molly had made it to pregnancy, Chris and Patrick's adoptive mothers hadn't. That was the extent of her involvement in the subject. She was far more interested in the fact that Eva Freeman had been in contact with Doctor Lees.

"Lees wasn't her own doctor though, was he?"

"No. She was referred to him much later." Molly shuffled through the case notes in front of her, "According to this lot, Gerald and Eva tried to get pregnant straight after the marriage. Your bog standard, perfectly happy, straight couple. Not a question in their minds that it might involve anything more than just a matter of ordinary old sex."

"But it was no good?"

"Sadly for your disgustingly prurient nature, Saz, their sex life doesn't come into these strictly medical notes."

"I meant the attempts to make babies."

Molly glared at her girlfriend, "I know that. I thought bringing a little levity to the discussion might remind you that I'm your partner, not merely your research assistant."

Saz had wondered when this might be coming, though she'd hoped to forestall the time-not-spent-on-relationship discussion until after she'd got the information she wanted from Molly. She tried to head her off with straightforward contrition.

"Sorry."

No good. Far too late and certainly not big enough. Whatever was going on, Molly wasn't likely to be appeased that easily.

"I mean, I barely got a kiss when you walked in the door; you didn't even ask how I was feeling."

Saz tried again. Few words. Heartfelt. "I am sorry, Moll." Still no go.

"And the first thing you said was how exhausted you are, and then you just asked me to tell you all about Lees."

Saz bit her lip, clenched her teeth, scratched at her left hand scars, sighed, felt guilty, sighed again, felt more guilty and therefore, guilt breeding its own bad temper, still more agitated.

"Molly, I'm sorry. I am really fucking sorry. I know I'm being a crap girlfriend."

"Crap mother-to-be as well."

Saz ignored that. The potential parent was a whole other

argument and even in her stressed state, Saz knew better than to go anywhere near that one.

"But I do need to get onto this. Patrick is being very scary. Really. The whole journey back he was ranting and screaming about doing this bloke in. I don't know how serious he is, but I also don't think he's joking a whole fuck of a lot."

"So you said."

"And I did ask how you are."

"You asked how well I am. That's asking about the baby, that's not asking about me."

Saz groaned inside and reminded herself to speak to some fathers, quick. She obviously had a lot to learn about being the non-pregnant partner. And she still went with apology. It was right. But it was also faster than argument.

"OK. I'm sorry I didn't ask about you. I'm learning how to do the pregnant thing at the same time as you are. I know I'm being obsessive about this, but I do really feel that time is of the essence here. And though I am worried about Patrick's excesses, it's not just about that. I'm very aware that I've made hardly any headway with Chris, nor do I have any idea how I'm going to, since we now know his adoptive mother wasn't connected to Lees."

"She was."

"What?"

"That's one of the things I found out. Keane was Lees's partner. They fell out in the late '60s, but worked together for years before that."

"Fantastic! Can we get hold of him?"

Molly shook her head, "Sorry, babe, he died in '78."

"Shit."

"Look, Saz, this is getting all a bit out of hand. Are you're sure you can't take this to the police?"

"I've had this argument with Patrick already. It was my first suggestion."

Molly dropped her pissed-off frown long enough to raise her eyebrows. "That's not like you."

"Yeah, well, even I learn eventually. Only Patrick won't let me. And I called Chris just in case he wanted me to, but he refused as well. Doesn't want to have to tell his adoptive mother, not yet anyway."

"And people saying no has stopped you before, has it?"

"Well, what can I do? They're both adamant I can't go to the cops; Patrick won't even let me tell Helen or Judith. I explained they're mates and so they don't really count, but he's having none of it. My hands are tied. It's their story, not mine. I need to find another of these women, maybe Luke's mother was one of them. If Leyton was involved with his adoption, there's a good chance she's been done over by them too. I just need to find one other, someone who's prepared to go to the authorities on this. Or, better still of course, I could get actual proof that Lees and Leyton were selling these babies."

"But you need to know how to get to the woman first."

"Yeah, I do. And I am sorry that means I'm treating you like an unpaid researcher, but you do see that the sooner I get this sorted the sooner I can get back to being normal with you? And the sooner I can stop Patrick becoming a homicidal maniac?"

Molly grinned, "Hell, yeah. Wouldn't want that."

Saz took Molly's hand from the case notes, "And I do want to know how you are and how the baby is and I don't want to keep going away and I am really sorry ..."

Molly pulled her hand back, obviously not wanting to be placated that easily. "I know. We can do sorry later, all right?"

Saz hastily agreed, inwardly weighing up which

expression of remorse was likely to be demanded this time, time or money. Or both. Even while she knew it made her very selfish indeed, Saz hoped it would be money. She had a whole lot more of that than time at the moment. Then she fixed her eyes on Molly's and gave her her undivided attention. The least she could do was to look like she was concentrating. Concentrating hard and feeling like a bitch at the same time. And exhausted. And frustrated. Sounded like good practice for motherhood.

Saz drew her thoughts back to Molly's words. She was talking very slowly, as if telling a story she didn't really want to tell. Saz started to feel uncomfortable. Something was clearly not OK. Something more than she'd been expecting.

"Anyway, after a couple of years the Freemans realized nothing was happening. She went to her doctor – private, of course – who referred her to one specialist, and then another, and then another. She seems to have tried everything."

"And all of them no good?"

"Nothing. Three years, no baby, no sign of a baby, not even a miscarriage to show that perhaps it could be possible."

Saz was surprised by Molly's cool description, by her attitude in general. "God, Moll. That's all a miscarriage is? Just a sign you might be able to have a baby?"

"To a medic? Yes. You're asking me to be a doctor here. Not to talk for myself. I'm not telling you how she felt. Or how I feel for that matter. You've asked for the information. I'm giving it to you. This is really difficult and I'm trying to do it as best I can, all right?"

Saz sorried for the hundredth time that day and Molly went on. "In the end they went to Lees. I don't know how they got referred to him, the notes don't say. In fact, they jump from one specialist straight to Lees with no indication of a referral at all."

"Yes, but according to Lillian, he was resident at that institution. He was in charge."

"Doesn't mean he couldn't have also had a private practice in London, babe. How do you think this lot make all their money? They don't just stick to the one job like me."

"How do I get hold of him then? Do we know?"

Molly looked away, sighed far too heavily for Saz's comfort, "Sadly, babe, we know all too well."

"Why sadly?"

Molly half smiled, then turned the smile into a groan, shook her head, moved her mouth as if to speak, and closed it again. Then, with great effort, she started. "There's no easy way to explain this. Your Doctor Lees, the one you think sold Patrick to the Freemans, well, seems he likes to have a partner to work with, someone else to help develop his ideas. When he and Keane stopped working together he became Barbara Richard's partner."

Saz blinked, as if clearing her eyes might make comprehension easier. It didn't. She felt sick. Shocked and very sick. "What?"

"Sleeping partner. Silent partner. He started the practice twenty years ago, though he retired from any actual involvement after the first couple of years. But he's still named as one of the directors of the practice."

Saz finally managed to stutter out, "Our Barbara?"

"You really thought I was in a shit mood just because you hadn't been around? Fuck, Saz, you're never around. That's hardly news. I've been trying to think how I could tell you this for half a day now. I had to sit here with this by myself for the past twelve hours."

"No, look, it can't be, Moll. This is ludicrous. That sort of coincidence is just too freaky. It's too bloody unlikely."

Molly shook her head, "Not really. You know there aren't actually that many places to go to for fertility treatment. Sure, there's plenty of clinics setting up; it's a great money maker, especially with the failure rate. And all that hormonal desire. But there simply aren't that many places with a really good reputation, not many recommended by other medics. Yes, it's a coincidence that we ended up going to a clinic that he's been involved in, but it's not a huge one. It's really not that unlikely. His clinics are known for being positively undiscriminating in who they help to procreate. Lees has helped set up four other clinics in London and a couple in other parts of the country. Chances are, with so many refusing to help 'non-traditional' couples, we would have wound up at one of them. It's what he does."

"What he does?"

"He cares about people having babies."

"Cares about?"

"Saz, please, you're just repeating me. It doesn't help."

Saz raised her head from her hands, "Yeah, well, funnily enough, Moll, I didn't exactly have him down as a good guy."

"No, I know." Molly shrugged, "Maybe he was selling babies forty years ago, perhaps it was the closest he could get at the time, but the man's always been interested in fertility issues. Even when he was at college, he turned out some specialist thesis on it: 'Procreation for the Traditionally Infertile'. It's his baby, so to speak."

Saz still didn't get it. Didn't want to get it. "How the hell do you know so much about him?"

"Once I'd realized who he was, I stayed up half the night on it. Luckily his website doesn't keep normal office hours."

"I feel sick."

"I don't feel too hot about it myself. I wanted to tell you face to face. I wanted to have you here when I told you, so you could make me feel less awful about it."

Saz knew that was exactly what she would have to do. Molly was the pregnant one after all, but she had no idea how she could make either of them feel less shocked, less disturbed.

Molly handed Saz a printed sheet of paper, "Here's your man, babe. Samuel Lees is seventy-four. He lives in Maida Vale and has a country house in Dorset. He's been officially retired for the past nine years, though he's often called on to speak at embryology and fertility conferences. Even though loads of people think of him as a maverick, he's still highly respected in the profession. He's been married twice, single since the mid '70s. He's got three grown-up children of his own, all created in the traditional method and, most importantly, he's a fierce proponent of the fertility-on-demand school. All of which means, well . . ."

Molly faltered and Saz finished her sentence, "It means Samuel Lees is why you're able to have our baby."

"Yeah, indirectly. He is."

THIRTY-FIVE

As they lay in bed together, Saz and Molly talked briefly about Chris and decided it would probably be best not to share the disquieting news with him. Not yet. There was an unspoken awareness that they did not really want to discuss Lees's influence, that perhaps by acknowledging his involvement in their pregnancy, the unpleasant sense of his presence would become more tangible. They did, though, need to decide what to say to Patrick. Saz had told Molly of his furious rant about Lees and they both agreed the last thing Saz wanted now was Patrick charging over and confronting him directly.

"Moll, he wants to kill him and maybe it wouldn't be such a bad thing."

"You can't mean that?"

"Of course not. But I hate this, hate how it taints our baby."

"No, it doesn't, Saz. Nothing's touching the baby. What we need to do is protect Chris from this for now and protect Patrick from himself as far as your Doctor Lees is concerned."

"He's not mine, thanks. But you're right. We can't let Patrick go crazy on this one. I mean, it'd be shit to have to take Lillian over to Wandsworth every Saturday."

"Traffic's terrible over that way."

"Terrible."

"You'd better not tell him then, babe."

"No. Best not."

For most of the past week Saz had been craving time with her partner. In her state of permanent tiredness, it was all she wanted. Easy hours, a meaningless evening together, time that looked like nothing at all – dinner and a bottle of wine, an evening out, even a night in, just watching TV or a video. Being at home together, just the two of them and the bump. Hours available to simply hand-hold, to be the kind of easy physically close that might then lead on to still further physical closeness. But Molly's revelation allowed none of that. An image of Lees sat between them on the squashy sofa, pushing apart their warmth-inclined shoulders. The thought of Lees as their true progenitor kept their usually-entwined legs from each other as Molly slept fitfully on her edge of the bed and Saz lay wide awake, uncomfortable and agitated.

Six-thirty on Monday morning and she was exhausted. Already. Again. Exhausted when she'd lain down and tried to sleep and exhausted when she'd dragged herself from bed an hour ago. The first night for the past six days that she'd been able to just be at home and there was no rest to be had. The worry genie had been released when Molly coupled their baby with Lees's name and now Saz couldn't forget about him until she could investigate further. Though Molly made dinner and they did share a bottle of wine – Molly had one glass, Saz the other four – she wasn't able to relax at all. Working on a case about someone else, no matter how deeply she became personally involved – and Saz usually got in too far – there had always been home to hide away in, Molly to run to for succour and relief. Home was security. Not now. Without the clinic Samuel Lees had founded fifteen years ago, Molly and Saz would not be having their baby. They had undertaken a serious search to find somewhere that would help them achieve their goal. Not merely for Chris to be a donor for Molly's baby – that would have been easy, they could probably have done it themselves, at home – but to actively make it possible for Molly to carry Saz's and Chris's baby to term. To do something they knew the traditionalists would find horrendous, to do something they themselves had only imagined and talked about, hoped for. It was all too close.

And the running didn't help. It often did make a difference, giving emotional as well as the expected physical benefits. At the least, the morning three miles usually cleared her head of the fear-detritus, of the unfounded imaginings, but not today. The running didn't help and Saz couldn't stop anyway. She'd started with her usual route and had then counted down another circuit and now found herself hitting yet another round. Slower now, of course, but still moving on, she'd looked at the track that wound through the trees to the path that led back to their road and, before she'd had time to clearly acknowledge what she was doing, had thrown herself on again, back to the main track of the open ground.

Breath coming in sharp bursts, warm early morning air stabbing sharp at the back of her throat, raw now with the exertion of forced breath for too long. Oxygen dragged into her lungs by a hungry diaphragm, snapping back with each breath determined this should be the last it strained so hard for, disappointed each time as Saz ran on. Ran on anyway. Despite the scream of her pounding heart, forced to beat at far more than the healthy target rate, the seventy per cent of maximum Saz could usually hear within herself without bothering to count beats. It felt like she was now far closer to eighty-five or ninety this morning. She ran on. Disregarding the cramp in her left calf, acknowledging the pain and then running right through the stitch in her right side, beating her body into a submission she could never wholly claim from her mind. Not a happy Saz.

She knew she'd have to get on with this by herself. Not that she could have relied on Patrick for much more anyway. They now had all the information that could usefully be expected to come from his parents' files. In fact, she'd actually completed the job she'd set out to do for Patrick. And as Lillian refused to go to the authorities with their DNA information, it no longer needed to concern either mother or son directly. Not for the moment anyway. Saz would have to pay a visit to Georgina Leyton by herself and see if she couldn't get something closer to the truth. Another chance to visit the lair of the designer-clad harpy didn't exactly thrill her to the core. She might just have to take Carrie with her as a distraction against the sleek wealth, if nothing else.

Saz was having to acknowledge that the one she'd assumed was the bad guy was not solely bad. It wasn't easy. Lees had also, albeit indirectly, made it possible for her and Molly to have the family they craved. Saz could just have chosen to accept that she'd found Patrick's mother for him and therefore she was quite at liberty to now leave the matter. Tell Chris she didn't know where else to go, that he was going to have to talk to his adoptive mother about it. But it wasn't that simple. The dividing line between right and wrong was even less clear than she usually found it. Much as part of her wanted to run away, to just play happy families and refuse to look at any of this, Saz had no choice. China shops and blind bulls came to mind. But so did another image. The unstoppable process of birth. There was nowhere to go but on.

And home. For a long shower and a brief opportunity to rest her overworked body. Her hamstrings would be hell by the afternoon and she didn't want to be tripping over her high heels when she took Carrie to visit Georgina. At least one of them needed to be presentable, and Saz feared that if Carrie had spent the past week in bed with the new brunette, it was more than likely going to have to be her.

THIRTY-SIX

Walking into Georgina Leyton's offices with Carrie beside her gave Saz a strange sense of power. If she herself wasn't quite able to break through the well-built defences, she was sure that the added weapon of Carrie's highly sensitive bullshit detector would be a valuable adjunct to her plan of attack. Except that she didn't yet have anything quite so comprehensive as a plan. But there was the disquieting sense that she couldn't simply wait for matters to run their course now. She was going to have to be proactive, if only because it might give her some small measure of peace of mind to feel as if she had a little influence over what was happening to her family. She was aware that a semblance of control wasn't anything like the actual thing, but it was going to have to do. She couldn't go on with no sleep for another week.

Saz intended to introduce Carrie to Georgina as another person Richard Leyton had arranged to be adopted. She hoped that Georgina would know enough about her father's involvement with Lees to be confused by Carrie's story. Either she would know Carrie couldn't possibly be one of Lees's sold babies, or she would be surprised to be confronted by a child she didn't yet know about. Either way, they were hoping that in her confusion she might give something away. Saz planned to then demand that Georgina tell them anything she'd found out about Lees and her father's involvement with him. From their meeting the week before,

she had convinced herself that Georgina actually knew
much more about her father's affairs than she'd been prepared to reveal. Saz hoped she might manage to shock
Georgina – maybe even prompting the odd revelation or
two. But she was also fairly certain that all those years of
good breeding and training in cold confidence would come
into play pretty quickly and Georgina's perfectly shaped
mouth would close on any further revelations – which was
when Carrie's other uses came into play. With her finely-
honed wheedling skills, Saz figured that if anyone could get
around the officious receptionist, it would be Carrie. The
plan was to leave the younger woman alone with him for
as long as possible – Saz expected Georgina would want to
talk to her by herself anyway – and any information Carrie
could get from him was bound to be useful when they came
to analyse what they'd learnt and work out the next step.
Carrie, with no real concept of a career having made it into
her adult life, had become the temping queen in the past
couple of years. Whenever she could be bothered to work;
on the occasions Saz's demands for rent became too pressing; or she couldn't get a chunk more cash from her
childhood-absent-therefore-guilty-as-hell-daddy.

People loved Carrie in their offices – all they ever wanted
from a temp was someone willing to get on with the job
and, if she didn't really know what she was doing, to at
least pretend that she did. Pretence of competence kept the
office managers happy and the bosses soothed. And pretence of competence was Carrie's forte. Her vast experience
in a wide variety of offices meant she could assure Saz that
a quick once-over of the reception area would furnish them
with all she needed to know about whatever computing
system the firm was using. It might also, if they were really
lucky, even provide them with information on the alarm
system. Carrie could never be held back for long from a

good cops and robbers fantasy and Saz's story of Georgina's behaviour had Carrie fuming long before she met the woman, which is what Saz had hoped would happen. While she didn't intend their day's work to go as far as actual breaking and entering, Saz had known there was no way Carrie would refuse to help once she'd heard the description of Georgina, let alone what else Saz suspected Georgina knew. There was little Carrie hated more than a posh girl in designer clothes, primarily because she knew she would always look better in whatever they were wearing than they could manage themselves, genetic predisposition to Knightsbridge shopping or not. Carrie, then, had already determined she would use her time at the offices as efficiently as possible. To her, this meant getting the alarm combination out of the pompous receptionist at the least. Saz wasn't sure that even Carrie could achieve quite such a feat of deceit, but then again, she wasn't going to discount anything that might help in the end.

When Saz called Georgina's office to make an appointment to see her, she was surprised to be put through without demur. She had expected a polite brush-off at the very least. Georgina told Saz that she had been through some of her father's things and, while she'd found nothing that pertained directly to Patrick's adoption, she did think that perhaps they should have a clear talk about the matter. The threat in Georgina's voice was so thinly veiled as to be practically naked, but Saz ignored the tone, took several deep breaths, clenched her fists and then awarded herself a row of shiny medals for not taking the bait. She accepted the offer of a meeting as graciously as possible. Not an easy acceptance, forced out between gritted teeth, but at least her words managed to stay perfectly polite.

Saz had arranged to meet Carrie outside the office building at two-thirty. Two twenty-five came and she had to

look twice at the woman crossing the road towards her
before she knew for definite that it was Carrie. The woman
was Carrie, but it wasn't a version she'd seen before. Saz
had made an effort to dress up a little herself as she had
no intention of repeating the last two disastrous meetings
when Georgina had easily claimed the high ground in cool
ice-maiden pose. But while Saz was now wearing a perfectly
respectable summer linen suit, Carrie had outdone herself.
The woman crossing the road towards Saz was dressed in
white – all white, all silk. Long flowing trousers, a shirt so
fine it was almost transparent and a soft white jacket that
did up with a single button to cover both Carrie's modesty
and the three tattoos on her left arm. Her hair was scraped
back into a smooth chignon, she wore only one earring in
each ear, her nose and eyebrow rings were gone, her
makeup was understated and pretty pink soft, and even
her trademark purple diamanté sunglasses were missing.
On her head was perched a traditional pair of Ray-Bans.

"Bloody hell, what the fuck happened to you?"

"Thank you, Saz, you look lovely too."

"But . . . Christ . . . I told you to dress up, not look like
you'd just stepped off a yacht in Monaco."

"Posh people always wear white, don't they? Just to show
they don't care about having to wash everything after
wearing it for half an hour. Or getting someone else to wash
it for them. You think this is too much?"

"Fuck no, you look fantastic. It's just . . . well, where on
earth did you get this lot? I wouldn't have thought you'd
have the money."

Carrie laughed, "Saz, you're such an innocent sometimes.
That's the whole point of M&S."

"This lot is from Marks?"

"They're almost interesting these days, darling."

"Yeah, but it still must have cost a hell of a lot."

"Saz, you're not listening. I got this all from Marks. So, assuming your bastard receptionist doesn't tip a pot of coffee all over me this afternoon, it'll all be back on the returned racks at Marble Arch by six o'clock this evening. Sort of costume hire, really."

"Only without the money bit?"

"That's right."

THIRTY-SEVEN

While Saz had expected stonewalling from Georgina, she hadn't known anyone could be so good at it. And still smile. Offer coffee. And cake from Fortnum's. Compliment Saz on her suit, her healthy tan, her lovely new shoes. Be really bloody nice, beautiful, charming, and far too damn clever. Saz said again that she believed Richard Leyton had been involved in Patrick's adoption by the Freemans. Georgina insisted that she had been through all her father's papers and found nothing. Saz showed her a copy of Leyton's letter confirming the adoption. Georgina acknowledged it was definitely her father's letterhead and even more definitely her father's signature – "That little loop on the R, that's Daddy, certainly." But no, of course she hadn't found the original of the letter herself, in fact nothing else about the matter at all. "Obviously my father and Gerald Freeman wanted to keep this business about Patrick a secret. I suppose, Ms Martin, my father must have had a few things he wanted kept secret. Even from me. It's been quite a disappointment, I can tell you. I was so certain I was Daddy's little girl. But I guess we all get it wrong sometimes, don't we?"

The disingenuous smile was startlingly obvious. Saz discarded the thought of bringing Lillian's revelations into their conversation because she felt that letting Georgina understand how much she did know, even if it managed to startle her out of some of her complacency, would mean giving away too much too early. From her position of semi-ignorance, Saz needed all the leverage she could get. That Lillian and Patrick had demanded she keep their secret was also part of her reasoning – though by no means the most important. If she'd thought it might help, she would have been willing to break their trust, especially now that she felt this was as much her own case as Patrick's. Means to a still more meaningful end.

Confronted with the dead-end honesty offered her, Saz tried the second branch of her attack. She told Georgina that she'd brought Carrie with her because she believed her to be one of Leyton's adoptees. The suggestion was greeted with complete disbelief. Georgina had glanced only briefly at the well-dressed young woman Saz had brought into the building with her. Glanced at, and then dismissed her as irrelevant when she asked Saz, and only Saz, to follow her into the office – for reasons of confidentiality, of course. Why Georgina thought Saz had brought anyone with her wasn't clear, though she did refer to Carrie several times as Saz's "friend". Friend with an emphasis. Friend that suggested she'd done a little checking of her own into Saz's life. Saz found it disquieting, but thought it best not to disabuse Georgina of her mistaken view. The longer she left Carrie alone in reception, the more likely Carrie was to make good progress. Besides that, she wanted to talk to Georgina about Carrie, not with her.

Saz knew from Molly's information that Lees had left the institution where Patrick was born in the late '60s when his interest in embryology and fertility issues was becoming more acceptable in mainstream medicine. She therefore assumed that his baby-selling activities had been curbed while he put his energy into the new field of research; at least he could follow this one openly and with society's approval. If Georgina knew anything at all about her father's involvement with Lees, she must have known that Lees's tenure in Cornwall ended in 1968 and that his other work took up all his time from then on. Carrie was in her late twenties, though she looked a good three or four years younger. But any face-value judgement would place her as a baby of the '70s, so much so that when Saz said they believed Carrie's adoption had also been arranged by Leyton, Georgina expressed what Saz thought to be her first honest emotion of the afternoon. She looked – and sounded – relieved. Her shoulders, which had been tensely, if beautifully held, relaxed from the loose collar at her pretty neck, the slight frown in her otherwise clear forehead disappeared, and she blurted out what sounded almost like a real laugh. "Don't be ridiculous, she's far too young! My father couldn't possibly have had anything to do with her."

She then caught herself, though just a little too late, and quickly backtracked to explain how all her father's clients were so old, how Daddy never dealt with younger people, the few adoptions she knew he had been involved in – which she hastened to add had all taken place with the complete knowledge and compliance of all the appropriate authorities, and not with this Doctor Lees that Saz seemed so keen to discuss – were in the '50s and one or two in the '60s. Way back when there were so many more babies available for adoption. Naturally, that all changed in the '70s with widely available contraception and abortion. Saz didn't really need the thesis-full of information about the changing face of modern society's procreation methods, but she did enjoy watching Georgina give herself away. If Georgina's initial statement didn't quite rate as empirical data, Saz was happy to store it in her really-bloody-likely file. At the very least, Georgina's revealing expression of relief confirmed Saz's suspicions, placed her firmly in the camp of knowing a damn sight more than she admitted to. And it made Saz feel fantastic. Getting a little closer to the truth was, of course, her stated aim for being in the building. And it certainly seemed as if she was achieving that. Managing to make Georgina sweat was merely a delicious by-product. It was Saz's turn to sweat when Georgina asked if maybe she, Georgina, shouldn't speak to the young woman herself. While Saz knew Carrie's ample lying skills were more than up to the task, she didn't really want to expose her to too much of Georgina's scrutiny. Not least because she didn't trust Carrie to keep her temper if Georgina pushed too far. She fobbed the solicitor off with a brief explanation of what she knew would be Carrie's terrible disappointment to hear that Leyton had not arranged her adoption, and how she thought that information would best come from her, not in the less comfortable surroundings of a strange office. If it wasn't the ideal answer, it was at least the one Georgina accepted, no doubt she was just as eager as Saz to part company.

Saz exited the office still more certain that the woman knew about Lees' and Leyton's involvement – quite possibly because Saz's first visit had prompted her to go through her father's files. She was a little concerned that Georgina seemed to know a bit more about Saz than was ideal, though it also pleased her that she seemed to have riled Georgina enough to prompt her to make any enquiries at all. And she left the building with Carrie. Carrie left the building feeling – and looking – very smug indeed. Saz didn't yet know what they had, but she knew from the smirk on her ex-girlfriend's gorgeous face that whatever Carrie now knew, it had been worth going in for.

They walked into Regent's Park, semi-naked bodies lying all around, exposing their deathly white Londoners' skin to massive doses of welcome radiation, and Carrie explained. "I just chatted to him for a bit at first."

"What about?"

"Switchboards."

"What?"

"Theirs is Swedish, it's bloody tricky. One of the most complicated actually. And they only had it installed a month ago. I've worked with a couple though, gave him a few tips."

"And had him eating out of your hand? I wouldn't have thought he was that easily pleased."

"He's not. The Wimbledon tickets are what really got him going."

"What Wimbledon tickets?"

"Good question. I told him your girlfriend works for the LTA. Said we get free tickets every year."

"And he believed you?"

"Why shouldn't he? He works in a world where people fly off on Concorde to shop for the weekend – or that Georgina does anyway – I don't imagine he found it too hard to believe you'd get him tickets."

"For next week?"

"Details Saz, details."

"Details count."

"I told him I'd send a bike in the morning. Detailed enough for you?"

"Not bad. So what else did you get out of him other than his unfeasibly excessive love of tennis?"

"Saz, it's not only dykes who like tennis, you know."

"I don't like tennis. And neither do you. And neither does Molly come to that."

"Yeah, but I wasn't going to contradict his view of the stereotype bollocks. Not when we were getting on so well, anyway."

"You got all this in half an hour?"

"You were gone almost forty-five minutes and I got all

that in ten of them. And it gets better. Didn't you notice how much nicer he was when we left?"

"All I noticed was that he looked like death warmed up."

"Yes, well, that's because he took a little poorly while I was there. Went off to the bathroom to throw up, in fact. He must have been gone – well, all of about fifteen, twenty minutes, I reckon."

Carrie opened her bag and, ignoring the supine sun-bathers around them, started to pull things from it as Saz looked on in amazement.

"I have here the three alarm combinations necessary to get in and out of the building safely, Adam's password into the company's filing system, and" – Carrie flourished a healthy handful of jangling keys – "both the spare set of building keys and the spare pass key that opens all the offices on Leyton's floor. Georgina's office chief among them. Impressive or what?"

Saz grabbed Carrie's arm, looked for a bench to sit on and marched her over to it. She checked briefly to make sure it was more or less clean so she didn't ruin their good clothes and then sat down, pulling Carrie down beside her.

"Careful, this has to go back by six, don't forget!"

"Carrie, the suit does not matter."

"I beg to differ . . ."

"Shut it! OK. It's impressive. It's all very impressive. The suit, the hair and most of all, your incredible feat of thievery. I'm impressed. I'm stunned. I'm fucking amazed. Now keep your bloody voice down and explain just how it is you managed to pull off such an act of astonishing wickedness."

Carrie started to speak and Saz interrupted her, "And please, tell it so I don't have to call Claire from a police station and get her to bail us both out before she goes to bed tonight."

Carrie grinned and leant in towards Saz, "You remember the brunette?"

"Is this relevant?"

"Very. She's a naturopath."

"And?"

"Well, you know how you thought Adam looked like death warmed up?"

Saz uttered a cautious, "Yes."

"I made him sick."

"Carrie, you make me sick half the time. What's that got to do with the brunette?"

"In addition to being a great shag, she also knows loads about herbs. All sorts. Which ones to use for . . ."

"Headaches, period pains and menopause. Of course she does, you can get that from any health shop. Give me traditional drugs any day. Damn sight faster for a start."

"Well, actually, I was thinking more of the herbs you can take for increased sexual desire."

"I would have thought you'd be the last person who'd need help there."

"Nah. Always ready to give anything new a try. Anyway, she also knows about emetic herbs."

"What's an emetic herb?"

"Makes you throw up."

"You gave him something to make him throw up?"

"Yeah, it's bloody lucky he's not as dismissive of herbal stuff as you are – I offered him a nice refreshing cup of tea. He drank it down, pronounced it deeply enjoyable and ten minutes later went off to the bathroom to commune with the porcelain."

"Carrie, that's awful."

"Worked though."

"Yes, but . . . will he be all right?"

"He'll be fine. If he was at a Roman orgy it would be

perfectly acceptable. Eat, vomit, shag, eat, vomit, shag someone else."

"OK. Enough. Sounds a bit bloody dodgy to me."

"Ah yes, Saz, but hey," Carrie tossed the keys on to Saz's lap, "think of how much thinner and more attractive he'll be to the other lads when he goes out tonight."

"So he's gay?"

"Saz, how many straight boys do you know that go clubbing on a weekday night?"

THIRTY-EIGHT

As Carrie said when they let themselves into the office, it wasn't as if they were actually breaking and entering. They weren't breaking anything. So it was really only half a crime. Carrie's nonchalance hadn't rubbed off on Saz. In fact, it was her very ease with the whole concept that unnerved Saz so much. On their way back to Georgina's building, she made several attempts to instil some sense of danger into Carrie's plans for the evening. To little avail.

"But there must be security cameras?"

"No video. Too expensive. Half the buildings in London just have them for show."

"You wouldn't think they'd scrimp on something like security when they've spent so much on the building itself."

"Nah, they've put a lot of faith in the alarm system. It's very flash, Adam said."

"He was particularly free with his information."

"I asked nicely. Like I was interested. Didn't treat him like a bimbo receptionist – unlike some people I could mention."

"I wasn't rude to him!"

Carrie smiled, "No, but you probably didn't make much of an effort. I know you when you've got a bee in your bonnet about something."

"I had other things on my mind the first time I met him. And even more the second time. That bee you so glibly refer to happened to be the fact that a woman I'd spent the afternoon with had just been beaten senseless by some still-to-be-found tosser. No doubt someone intimately connected with Georgina Leyton herself."

"You don't know that."

"No. But I know Georgina's involved somehow and therefore I hardly have time to waste exchanging pleasantries with the staff."

"Naturally. But the poor boy's bored senseless. I think he just liked having someone to talk to."

"You certainly found his good side."

Carrie winked, her face a somewhat scary leer in the half light, "Trust me Saz, everyone's got a good side – you might just have to turn them over a couple of times to find it."

Carrie let them into the building and Saz tried very hard to persuade herself that Carrie was right about the video camera which automatically followed them as they hurried across the foyer. Once Carrie had turned off the main building alarm, they then took the stairs up to the Leyton offices as Saz had no intention of finding herself stuck in a lift should anyone suddenly decide to pop into the office at three in the morning. At least they could always run down the stairs. Again Carrie used two different keys and a password to disable the alarm and get them into the reception area; it really was a very complex system, practically failsafe – though not once she'd established it was also a system she'd worked with several times before – and stolen the keys and password. They made straight for Georgina's office where Saz opened the filing cabinets in a far more traditional way – with an old-fashioned skeleton key. She then spent the next twenty minutes going through Georgina's files, which was not quite as easy as she might have expected. For a woman who appeared so impeccably groomed, Georgina Leyton's filing cabinets were in a hell of a mess. Then again, Saz's recent presence in her life might have had something to do with the chaos – Georgina may well have been prompted to riffle through anything she had on Patrick just to make sure she knew as much as she should. As much as she needed to know to stay ahead of Saz. Carrie meanwhile attached herself to Georgina's computer. Saz was going nowhere near it. Not while Carrie was trying several different passwords to get in. And another three. And another. Each time hoping she wasn't about to be ejected from the system completely. She found it on the tenth try. And kicked herself for not thinking of it sooner.

"Bloody hell, Saz, you've really got this girl worried."

"Why?"

"Her password is Lees."

"Brilliant. Let's hope she stays worried."

"OK. Here goes."

The two women worked on in concentrated silence and as much darkness as they could manage. The huge glass windows had no curtains or blinds and London's lack of real night gave them a glow of dull orange to work by. Saz supplemented the street illuminations with a tiny torch and Carrie did her best to turn the monitor as far as possible from the window, shielding any extra light spill by sitting right up against the screen, eyes glued to the coloured dots as she quickly scanned through Georgina's correspondence for the last week.

"Nothing here, if she's been writing to anybody about your enquiries she's been doing it by hand."

Saz didn't look up from the file she was going through, "Or e-mail."

Carrie smiled, "For a girl who hates these things, you do think awfully logically sometimes. We'll make a technophile of you yet."

"I don't hate them. I just don't understand them. Doesn't

mean I don't know they exist. I do live in the real world you know. Molly has e-mail at work."

"Hampstead's not the real world."

"Carrie, shut the fuck up and get on with it. I don't want to be still sitting here when the cleaners come in."

Carrie did as she was told: she followed a labyrinthine path through a technophobe's nightmare and, barely containing her gloating pride at her own prowess, recalled all Georgina's e-mails from the past fortnight. Messages both received and sent that Georgina believed she had safely deleted. Carrie scrolled through them, the various letters about wills and inheritance, memos regarding divorce settlements and alimony payments. A couple of personal notes to what had to be Georgina's boyfriend – or if he wasn't her lover, then she was talking very dirty to a complete stranger.

"God, I love the Internet, all that stuff out there and you think you've got rid of it, deleted, wastebasketed, whatever. But it's really just hiding in the ether, waiting for someone to call it back into being."

"You make it sound like magic."

"It is. If you know how to use it. And – fuck me, but baby I do!" Carrie jumped back from the screen, light spilling into the room, "Saz! Get over here and look at this."

"This" was a tersely worded series of e-mails between Georgina and Lees, Georgina more and more concerned, his replies calming her, insisting nothing was on record, nothing could be proved and that Georgina was over-reacting. Carrie's initial enthusiasm was dampened a little when she realized there was nothing solidly incriminating. "Sorry, I thought I'd found something more exciting than this."

"This is exciting."

"It doesn't tell us anything for definite."

"It tells us she's bloody worried. It confirms the address

Molly had for him. Best of all, it tells us he doesn't take Georgina seriously."

"And how is that good?"

"Means he's not worried. She is, so she knows she needs to be careful. He doesn't know that yet. Which in turn means he's much more likely to make a mistake. I reckon Lees is my next port of call."

Carrie went into the last e-mail, from Georgina to Lees.

"Fuck. Look. Sukie."

Saz looked and what she read made her feel sick.

"I can confirm that Ms Planchet is currently not in a position to disturb you."

Saz shook her head, said nothing.

"What's wrong, that's good isn't it? You did think she might have had something to do with Sukie getting beaten up?"

"Thought it, but really hoped not. And it's not like this proves anything for definite. It's legal-speak, it could mean anything."

"But it is what you suspected."

"Yeah. Bitch. Maybe that's what Sukie left me a message about. Wanted to tell me she'd been in touch with Lees." Saz sighed, ran her hands through her hair, "Keep going, girlie, it's good we've confirmed what I thought, but we need something bigger than this to get her."

Saz found the bigger thing twenty minutes later. Drawing a blank in the messy filing cabinets, she decided to try the cupboards. At the back of the second she found several dated cardboard boxes – Richard Leyton's notes. And struck gold with the first box she tried. Halfway down the pile there was a thin file. Inside were just six sheets of paper. The top one was a copy of some form of adoption certificate.

For Patrick Freeman. It stated that he was in perfect health, gave the time and date of his birth – 30th August, the date he'd always been told by his adoptive parents – Lillian's name, and finally a brief outline of the emotional difficulties his mother was currently facing, and her delight that her child would be going to a good home. Saz read the last statement with huge relief. Until then she hadn't really acknowledged how concerned she'd been that the Freemans might have known the extent of Lees' duplicity. While actually buying the baby in the first place was bad enough, what really disturbed her was the possibility that his parents might also have known that Lees had told Lillian her baby was dead. That they might have been party to the entirety of the lie. At least it was not quite as bad as both she and Patrick had silently feared. At the bottom of the page was a reminder that the "demand for the adoption arrangement fee" would follow with a separate invoice – at a suitable interval.

The following pages were of other babies, in chronological order. Some with full birth certificate and details, others with the thinnest of resumés. Saz wasn't surprised to see that one of the babies was Luke. His mother's name was listed but not the father's. A pencilled amendment stated the mother had refused to give out this information – Saz thought briefly of how hard it might have been for her to keep that to herself. Especially with both Lees and Leyton pressing her.

The fourth page listed the baby adopted by Margaret and Peter Marquand. Saz saw the surname and gasped audibly, "I've found him."

"Who?"

"Chris. These are adoption certificates. Sort of. From Leyton. There's a bunch of them. This one is Chris."

Saz held the page out to Carrie, her hand shaking.

Carrie frowned. "Well, come on. Tell me what it says."

Saz looked down, terrified of what she was about to read. Hoping she could now name her baby's grandmother. Grandparents. Praying they hadn't known about the baby sale either. So scared of what she might have to tell Chris. The father wasn't listed. The mother was named as Sara Fisher. The baby had been born healthy. The mother was physically well. Only on this certificate there was no mention of an adoption fee. She read through the page three times and then gave it to Carrie who was equally perplexed, "I don't get it, Saz, if Lees and Leyton were making money every time they gave away a baby, what's so special about Chris? Why not him? Were they doing the Marquands a favour, or what?"

Saz shrugged and then, comprehension sickening her, let out a half laugh which turned into a groan as she covered her mouth. "Oh shit."

"What?"

"I think I might know."

"What?"

Saz sighed and held out her hand for the papers, "You just said it yourself. What's so special about Chris? Out of the four children we know about? He's the only black one. Mixed race. 'Half-caste' to them."

"Really?"

"Well, what do you think? Nearly forty years ago? Knowing what we do about these people, how they treated Lillian? They wrote her off as a nutter for years. They're hardly the most enlightened of souls."

"Fuck."

"Yeah. Fuck. Lucky they didn't know he was going to grow up to be queer as well."

The two women were silent for a moment, Saz wondering if there wasn't an alternative explanation that wouldn't hurt

Chris still more. And when that didn't come, she decided to ignore the nastier assumptions for the moment and concentrate on the good news that at least they had found a name for his mother.

Saz made copies of the letters and then placed the boxes back in the cupboard. Carrie printed off a few of the e-mails – "a few of the begging notes to Lees and then just the sexier ones mostly, you never know when you're going to want to do a spot of blackmail – I bet this bloke she's writing to in Geneva is married, she only ever contacts him at his office."

They left the originals of the keys back in the reception desk from where Carrie had stolen them, locking themselves out again with a variety of passwords and the extra set of keys Carrie had had cut that afternoon. Just before she returned the nice suit to the nice lady at Marks & Spencers. They ran silently down the stairs and Carrie reset the alarm and locked the door behind her. Saz couldn't quite believe how smoothly it had all gone, couldn't believe they had just got away with it – especially not with Carrie by her side who, even if she was fantastically useful, was also prone to having at least one personal crisis an evening. But not this time. This time it was all fine. In a sick relief kind of way.

The two women ran straight down into Oxford Street and then grabbed a passing cab. As they finally relaxed into the back seat, Carrie cuddled into Saz, "We're such a good team, you and me. Why did we ever split up?"

Not yet ready to be interrupted from her reverie on the iniquities of inequality, Saz wasn't in any mood for game-playing with her ex, "Because you dumped me, trampled on my heart, ripped it into tiny pieces and then refused to speak to me for a year. You bitch."

"Oh yeah, sorry."

"Nah, it's OK. I think I got the better deal in the end."

The taxi pulled up outside Saz and Molly's flat just as first sun hit the windows at the front of the house. Saz paid the driver quickly and walked a half-sleeping Carrie inside. She settled her friend onto the sofa, covered her with a thin blanket and then went through to her own room to give Molly an early wake-up call for her early morning shift.

THIRTY-NINE

Molly wasn't impressed. Not by Saz's soft wake-up kiss to her upper lip, full kiss on fuller lips. Not impressed either by Saz's less soft wake-up stroke of her summer-bed naked body. It was morning, she'd slept badly and could well have done with the extra half-hour allowed her by the alarm clock. She was least impressed by Saz's story of her night's exploits. It wasn't that Molly was especially fussed about having slept another night on her own. Long years of shift work and only slightly fewer years of shift-sleeping with Saz meant that she was perfectly happy to go to bed with a duvet all her own. What really annoyed Molly though, what had her storming back from the shower to loom dripping over a semi-comatose Saz, was the stupidity of breaking into a highly secure building in the middle of the night.

"For fuck's sake, Saz, when are you going to get it into your head? This is our baby! Things have changed, we have a future to think about."

"There's always been our future to think about."

"There hasn't always been three of us. What if you'd been caught? I'm hardly going into this hoping to be a single parent."

"We weren't caught."

"Or worse, if this woman really is such a bitch, who knows what she might have done if you'd bumped into her?"

"Moll, I hardly think Georgina is a gun-toting crim."

"But you are assuming she had something to do with Sukie Planchet getting hurt."

"Yeah, I am. Not that there's any direct proof."

"But you don't trust her?"

"Not as far as I could throw her."

"Well, that's my point."

"Yeah, OK. I don't trust Georgina. But that's not quite the same as thinking she might have hurt Sukie herself. Georgina's far more subtle than that. And anyway, if anything had gone wrong I would have been done for breaking and entering. That's all."

"That's enough."

"Yes, of course, but at least if we had been caught, I would have had to explain why I was there. I could have told the cops about Lees and what I think about Georgina's involvement. It wouldn't have mattered that I was breaking my promise to Lillian and Patrick."

Molly shook out her long dark hair, furious water drops spraying Saz. "You make it sound like you wanted to get caught."

"Of course I didn't. But actually, I already knew it wouldn't be the worst-case scenario."

Molly turned from combing out her hair, "And that is?"

"That is that you are carrying our baby."

"Oh thanks, I thought you wanted this as much as I do."

"I do. Of course I do, Moll. I just didn't want to have to feel so weird about it. So compromised. We don't know anything about what Lees has been up to in the years since he was last selling babies to other people."

"Yes we do, Saz. He's been selling babies to people like us."

"That's what I mean. His career progression doesn't exactly fill me with confidence in the man."

Molly sat down on the end of the bed. "Me neither. I don't

feel any better about this than you do. I hate that we've
uncovered horrible things about the man. But that was a
long time ago. We checked out the clinic, we went into this
with our eyes wide open. Lees has never actually worked
there himself, he only set it up. He's too important to
work there, he's on the board but never seems to go to any
meetings—"

"How do you know?"

"You think I didn't look into him more myself? Of course
I care about it too, it's a very horrible, quite yucky coincidence. But that's all it is – a coincidence. The man who
started our clinic happens to have been a baddie at some
point in his life. Who hasn't?"

"Oh, come on, Moll . . ."

"No, listen to me. I'm not excusing him. Of course it's
awful – criminal, unforgivable – what he did to Lillian. To
Chris's mother. But you know, he also did what those adoptive parents wanted. He gave them their baby."

"The Freemans paid for theirs."

"So did we."

"We're different."

"We think we are, but you know as well as I do that there
are plenty of people who'd think what we're doing is wrong.
And irresponsible."

"We're not lying about it, it's not illegal. This is different."

"I don't know, babe. In the end, no matter how legal we
are, we're still doing it for exactly the same, selfish reason
that everyone does. We're having a baby because we want
to. Because we can. Just like the Freemans, only they didn't
have the same resources as we do now. I'm not excusing
them, I just don't think of the whole thing in quite the same
black and white terms that you do. What Lees did then was
bad, what he's created since then has helped us."

"That's my problem. What I know now just taints it all."

Molly climbed back into bed beside Saz, her long wet hair falling over her girlfriend. "No it doesn't, hon. This baby isn't touched by any of that shit. You are. You've really gone off on this one."

"I hate it. I hate that it affects us."

"I know you do, but it was always going to be complicated, we knew that. You've found Patrick's mum. You've got a name for Chris's. Find out about her and you've done the job. That's it. Let it go."

"I can't. I know too much of other people's stories. I've got Luke's mother's name now, how can I not tell him about her?"

Molly got up again, picking up her towels to take them to the bathroom. "I don't know babe, but I can't imagine why you'd ever want to go near him again, assuming what you do about Sukie. This isn't just someone else's life you're digging around in, it's ours. And it worries me. You don't have any perspective – or even less than usual. I'm just scared that you'll go too far."

Saz watched Molly leave the room, unable to reassure her. As she'd said herself, she now knew far too much. And too little.

When she woke four hours later it was to the rich smell of breakfast. She pulled on a T-shirt, stumbled blearily from bed and walked through to the kitchen where Carrie was beaming at her over fresh coffee, bacon and eggs, mushrooms and grilled tomatoes.

"Good morning, darling. My, you do look attractive. I'd forgotten how delicious you are first thing."

"I doubt you ever noticed. What is this?"

"Breakfast. What does it look like?"

"It looks," Saz said, reaching a shaking hand for the

coffee, "like you've invaded my house. Did you see Molly this morning?"

"Nope. But I did hear her. Just hormones or is she always that grumpy?"

"Neither. She's concerned for me."

"Sweet."

"Very. So shut it and pass me that breakfast thing."

For a few minutes Saz ate in silence, then on the second egg, fourth rasher of bacon, she looked up, "This is brilliant. When did you learn to cook?"

Carrie shook her head, "Saz, this is breakfast, it's not cooking. You don't need Delia to tell you how to fry an egg."

Saz shrugged, her mouth full, hand reaching for a slice of bread to mop up the plate, "Don't tell Delia."

Breakfast over, Saz had a very brief conversation with Gary, giving him Sara Fisher's name – and nothing else other than a quick pep talk about how much faith she had in his investigative powers. She put the phone down, well aware that she was asking an awful lot for such a little. But he'd found Lillian, maybe he'd score on this one too. Then she and Carrie went into the sitting room where they spread out the smuggled papers on the table. They decided that Saz would deal with Sukie. She'd also contact Chris once she'd heard back from Gary, and then they would both speak to Luke, though neither of them felt up to telling him about his parentage in the top room at Bar Rage. Saz thought it would be far better done at home or on neutral ground, ideally with Luke as sober and coke-free as possible. Carrie was more concerned that a negative reaction might spoil a potentially good night out. They decided to leave the other unknown adoptees until something more was found out about Lees. Neither woman fancied contacting strangers out of the blue and turning their lives upside down for them. That was far more the province of Patrick's little social worker. Saz did, however, mean to deal with Lees as soon as possible.

"I want to meet him. I really want to know who I'm dealing with."

"How are you going to do that?"

"Not sure. Molly says he works from home now, so I guess I could just go and see him. Turn up, tell him I'm researching the clinic's work, flatter him."

"He's probably a bit more careful than that, Saz."

"He's an old man, he'll be happy to talk about his lifetime's achievements. I doubt he gets that much publicity; for obvious reasons he's had to stay pretty much in the background. And yet, all this playing God with other people's lives, some part of him must want to brag about it. Anyway, I'm hardly going to ask him to tell me about all the babies that he's sold. I'll just start him on the clinic and see what follows from there."

Carrie shrugged, "OK, if you have to. You know, Saz, I don't want to sound like Molly, but I have to say this isn't really your job any more. I mean, you could just pass all this information on to the adoptees and let them make up their minds themselves . . ."

Saz glared at Carrie, "You're right. You don't want to sound like Molly. Now, anything else, or shall we get on?"

"Yeah, there is actually." Carrie looked at Saz and hesitated.

"Well, what?"

Carrie pulled out a couple of pieces of paper from her bag, "Ah – now, you're not going to like it when I tell you what I've done, but you are going to like what I'm giving you."

"Get on with it, Carrie."

"Right. OK. I found these when you went to photocopy the other stuff."

"Where?"

"One of the other boxes. The next one down from the one you were working on actually."

"Why didn't you tell me while we were there?"

"You were already pissed off about Chris and the money stuff, I didn't trust you to keep your temper."

"Brilliant."

"Yeah... and... well..." Carrie winced, anticipating Saz's reaction, "I knew you wouldn't want me taking away originals—"

"Oh, for fuck's sake!"

"See? But I just think these are far more valuable to us as originals than copies. I knew you wouldn't let me bring them with us."

"So you waited until we got back to tell me. God, Carrie, you're devious."

"Yeah, but I think you'll thank me."

"Well, what is it?"

Carrie handed the two sheets of paper to Saz. The top one was a form confirming an adoption, just like the other ones Saz had been so pleased to find the night before. The adopted baby was Georgina. Adopted by Leyton to bring up as his own. Neither of the birth parents was listed on her form so Saz assumed Leyton must have arranged for their names to be kept secret. For the first time she almost felt a tiny degree of sympathy for the woman. She really hoped Georgina had known her own circumstances before they'd brought all this up and forced Georgina to rummage through her father's papers. It wouldn't be a great way to remember darling Daddy otherwise.

The second piece of aged paper was Georgina's birth certificate. It certainly looked like an original. And this one had both mother's and father's names on it. Samuel Lees and Sukie Planchet.

FORTY

December 1967 was a cold month with winter snow early to London, surprising the girl who'd assumed the south was warm and easy. Sukie Planchet was only just three months arrived from the north. She had come to London to find the swinging city, late-night party land, Peyton Place equivalent. Instead she found a bedsit in Kilburn: one tiny room two floors above an off-licence in which to eat and sleep, meter-run bathroom and tiny kitchen shared between five other bedsits. Three of them were occupied by young couples, the other by an old man who took a three-hour bath once a week and ate a single chicken leg each night. All that and a fantastic view of Kilburn High Road for the princely sum of six pounds a week. On her second day in town she found a clerical job at St Mary's in Paddington, ten pounds a week to file the juicy details of other people's internal lives. And another week later she'd found what she thought was love with Samuel Lees.

Sukie was seventeen, supposedly too young for sex but wanting it anyway. Wanting to drink and party and play and fuck and willing to take whatever was offered. Sukie was in town simply for the experience of being. There was nothing for her at home, she'd left with a ten pound note and headed south because she imagined London was where the real blessings were to be found.

Samuel Lees was her first blessing. In his late forties, unhappily married for the second time, with a daughter just six years older than Sukie, Samuel was her first and her greatest love. Samuel was the proof that real love really existed. She'd listened to all the songs, read the books, watched Emergency Ward 10 so Sukie knew the point of love was unrequited wanting. Samuel gave it to her in triple doses.

She could not call him at home, nor could she could call him at work. He lived in Cornwall but came up to St Mary's two days a week, and was also working in his private practice with infertile couples. It was his ambition to one day allow everyone who wanted a child the possibility to conceive. He was inspired and passionate and cared about little other than his work. Sukie had never met anyone so certain of themselves; he was John Lennon and Bob Dylan rolled into one and, better still, he was an adult. Father figure and first fuck – a lethal combination. In March 1968 Sukie was two weeks' pregnant. She knew immediately, though her own doctor took another month to confirm it. Samuel's method of confirmation was equally clinical. As he put his hand inside her, he explained that he had no intention of being trapped by a lie – or by a liar – he would see for himself if she was really pregnant. She was. Sukie had expected anger, but she had also assumed that he would take care of things for her. Refer her to a safe abortionist, make it go away, make it better. Which would have been OK with her. Not great, but all right, bearable. Certainly more bearable than the single motherhood that would have her returned ignominiously to Sunderland, to embarrass her parents and shock the town. Without the pregnancy though, Sukie imagined they could go on as before. She'd just had her eighteenth birthday, this was an aberration, but it would pass.

Sukie was in love with Samuel Lees, but even in that blindness she knew he would not leave his wife for her.

She knew that they would probably continue to have a relationship as long as she did not demand too much – to know when he might call, to ask for commitment to any pre-arranged date, a wedding ring. Sukie may have been young but she was not completely naive; the nature of Samuel's passion extended as far as her body. She didn't expect him to be interested in her mind as well. Sukie was in London to develop her mind; Samuel was one of the ways she was doing so. He loved to talk to her and she loved to listen to him. Sukie thought he was the epitome of all things modern and progressive, which was why she was so shocked when he refused to even countenance the idea of her aborting the baby. More shocked still when he smacked her in the face for even suggesting it. Samuel Lees had never referred a woman to an abortionist before and he had no intention of starting now. What he had not done for a stranger, he would certainly not do for his own girl-friend. Did she understand nothing of his work at all? He dealt in the giving of life, not its taking. That was all he cared about, making new life possible, allowing other people's dreams of family to come true. What's more, this was his baby, how could she possibly have thought he would sanction her murder of the child?

Put that way, Sukie agreed. Agreed he was right. Agreed because she also knew that if she didn't go along with him, she would not only lose the new life she'd planned for herself, she would lose Samuel as well. And Sukie couldn't bear for that to happen. She carried the child to term, left work when she'd reached six months and the bigger and bigger dresses could no longer hide what was referred to behind her back – and once to her face – as her "shame". And then she sat out the last three months alone in the bedsit. It was autumn and then winter again. She saw Samuel once a week when he came to pay her rent and give her five pounds for herself and the bottles of milk and great bags of expensive green vegetables he insisted she eat. His baby would not be grown on a glass of stout a day. Samuel Lees was a man well ahead of his time.

When the baby was due Lees moved Sukie down to a cottage in Cornwall. It was the first time she'd ever stayed in a place that had a telephone in the bedroom. Or in the hall for that matter. She was to call Lees the minute contractions started. He would deliver the baby himself and then take it on to the couple who were going to adopt it. At three in the morning, on a freezing night, Sukie went into labour. Alone. The baby she had not intended to keep came quickly but not easily, and Lees was sweating and crying as much as she was by the end of the delivery. Against his better advice, Sukie did hold the baby, very briefly, kissed the little girl's dark head of hair and then watched as Lees took her from the room.

Two hours later he returned to Sukie. The baby had been safely delivered to its new parents, Sukie's life could go on as before. Except their relationship was finished. He would check her over physically in the next few days and then again in a month's time, he did not want her to go to a hospital or to her own doctor, he did not want anyone else to know she had even been pregnant. It was over now, the baby was with people who wanted her, and Sukie was not to mention the child to Lees ever again. He would leave her in the cottage, there was plenty of food, warm blankets, a radio. A taxi would come in two days' time to take her to the train station. He left her ticket and five hundred pounds on the dressing table. He didn't kiss her goodbye when he left the room. Sukie cried for two days.

Four months after that Sukie met Gerald Freeman at her

new job as a clerical assistant for his London office. Sukie had remade herself. The money had provided a great flat, good clothes and the entry to a much better job – where she might meet a better class of man who would appreciate all that Samuel Lees had taught her. Sukie had become a much wiser little girl. A wise little girl who knew that if there were any advantages to be taken, she intended to be the one taking them. Lees had educated her well.

Occasionally in her later travels with Gerald Freeman, Sukie met up with Samuel Lees, who was always impeccably polite to her, as she was to him. They behaved as well as any two strangers might when introduced at a party, and if Lees sometimes wished she'd taken his money and returned to Sunderland, he never even hinted as much. Gerald did note though that Richard Leyton's doctor friend Lees had been a damn sight friendlier before he started taking Sukie out with him. He assumed that while the man had no qualms about selling babies, he obviously didn't like the idea of extra-marital affairs. Which was odd, but not unusual: Richard himself didn't approve of Sukie either.

If Sukie had known where her daughter had been taken, she might have assumed that Richard Leyton despised her out of fear that his child's identity might be uncovered. But neither she nor Gerald Freeman ever found out the real reason behind the change in Leyton's behaviour. And Gerald thought it was a bloody shame that they couldn't keep their censorious noses out of other people's business – and ordered another bottle of wine for himself and the girl.

FORTY-ONE

The nurse who let her in was not doing so because she felt sorry for Saz. It was Sukie who had gained her pity. She'd had no visitors other than the young policewoman who'd been returning twice a day in the hope of getting some information, any information. But the tiny battered woman in the flat bed was not speaking. Rarely anyway. She drifted in and out of consciousness, waking briefly and disorientated, waking to pray and then slip back. They still had her on the danger list and Saz wasn't officially allowed into the room.

But as the nurse whispered, "It's a wonder she's managed to hang on this long actually, love. And I don't see why she shouldn't get a chance to see the one friend."

She walked off muttering "bloody bureaucracy" and Saz thought maybe the woman would fancy getting together with Molly for one of her regular "patients not papers" sessions.

And then she saw Sukie and forgot about Molly. She actually looked worse than the last time Saz had seen her. The bruises across her face, around the wired jaw, had come out in full and she was a mess of deep purple with pale yellow tinges. Iris skin. Saz felt her stomach lurch as she approached the bedside, hushed ICU unit, dimmed lights and quiet, but for the electrical tracking of monitors. She sat beside the bed and waited. Ten minutes, fifteen. The nurse didn't return and Saz spent the stolen time wondering which part of her investigation could have led to the beaten-up mess she now saw in front of her. There was no clear link, no definite reason for her to feel responsible, but Sukie's beating had followed far too closely on her visit – an unpleasant coincidence which meant Saz felt far too much potential guilt to have an easy time waiting.

Then Sukie opened her left eye, the right clearly too swollen to move. Saz waited a moment, unsure if Sukie was waking or merely shifting in her uncomfortable sleep.

A cracked whisper spilled from the swollen lips, "Miss Martin?"

Saz leant into the bed, "Yes, it's me. I wanted . . . I came to see how you are. I'm terribly sorry."

Saz wasn't quite sure what she was apologizing for, wondered if maybe Sukie knew more than she did. The older woman's eyelids fluttered and Saz thought she had fallen asleep again, but then Sukie rallied and, with evident pain, opened both ice-blue eyes this time. Saz wondered if Georgina knew how much she looked like her mother. And with the daughter's features in her mind, Saz decided to open her mouth. She'd been wondering if she should tell Sukie about Georgina or not. Finally veering slightly towards the nurse's point of view – if Sukie really was that ill, what else could hurt her? And it was the truth after all. Saz thought Sukie probably had a right to know who her daughter was. Saz thought probably, maybe, not definite – hoped she was doing the right thing – and then did it anyway.

"Sukie? I've met your daughter. The child you had with Samuel Lees."

Sukie breathed in with pain, spoke with even more, "Georgina?"

In all Saz's moral deliberations it hadn't occurred to her

Sukie might already know. "Oh, yes. Georgina. I didn't realize you knew her. I didn't think—"

"I don't know her," Sukie sighed, whether from physical or emotional pain, Saz couldn't be sure, "Richard told her about me when she was eighteen. She came to meet me, but there was nothing. I wasn't what she was looking for. I'd already found Jesus by then, I wanted to help her to the truth too. She didn't want to know."

Sukie stopped to catch her breath and Saz wondered how likely she would have been to accept a born-again mother at eighteen. It couldn't have been the easiest of reunions – for mother or daughter.

Sukie was speaking again, "Then she came to see me again, not long ago, when her father – when Richard – died. I thought she had come back to me." Saz waited, Sukie flinched, a barely perceptible shake of her head, "But Georgina just wanted . . . to see me. To see if I'd changed since the first time we met."

"And had you?"

"Not in the way she wanted, I don't think. It was too late anyway, she couldn't see me as her mother."

"But she knows Doctor Lees?"

"Samuel always was a very charming man. I loved him dearly, I can understand that she wanted to know him. I am less – less of a catch."

"But surely you both had her adopted? She can't just blame you."

Sukie frowned, breathed in a couple of shallow, rasping breaths and replied, "Girls always forgive their fathers long before they pardon their mothers, don't they? Anyway, it was my sin, and my suffering. Sins of the mothers, you could say."

Saz didn't want to. Particularly as she believed Georgina was in some way responsible for the pain of the woman in

front of her. And whoever else Georgina had enlisted to
help damage Sukie. Saz didn't want Sukie to blame herself
for the pain she was now in. She wanted to help find the
culprit.

"The police want to know, do you have any idea who did
this? They think you let someone into the flat. Do you
remember who it was? Who came in and hurt you?"

*"As thy sword hath made women childless, so shall thy
mother be childless among women. And Samuel hewed
Agag in pieces before the Lord in Gilgal."*

"Sukie, it wasn't Samuel, he's an old man. It can't have
been him who did this to you."

Sukie nodded with difficulty, "No. Of course. I opened
the door and it was a man. Not old, not an old man. We
talked, he told me about himself."

"What did he tell you?"

Sukie shook her head, "I don't know. You were asking
me about the babies and then – I thought perhaps he was
one of them. The children. But maybe I only thought so
because you reminded me about them. I don't know."

"What's his name, Sukie, can you remember the man's
name?"

But Sukie was rambling now, caught back in the space
between letting the stranger into her home and waking in
such pain in the hospital. "And then he followed me into
the house and there was shouting, and I didn't understand.
And he hit me. I tried, but I couldn't stop him, he was so
angry, shouting so much. And then I thought perhaps it was
right, paying my dues."

"What?"

*"How much she hath glorified herself and lived
deliciously, so much torment and sorrow give her. Therefore shall her plagues come in one day, death, and*

*mourning, and famine; and she shall be utterly burned
with fire: for strong is the Lord who judgeth her."*

"Sukie, nobody deserves to be hurt. You have to try and
remember who it was, what did he look like? He can't be
allowed to get away with this."

"But he won't get away with it. He'll be judged too. In
time," Sukie shuddered, "I'm sorry, I can't do this. Not now.
I'm tired. I'm sorry."

Saz stood up, "No. I'm sorry. I've pushed you too much.
I shouldn't have. I apologize. I should go."

Sukie tried to lift her hand to Saz, "Wait. There's still time
for you, you know. You can repent too."

"No, really, look I should just go. I should have let you
rest, I didn't mean to upset you."

"Listen – *Behold I stand at the door, and knock: if any
man hear my voice, and open the door, I will come in to
him, and will sup with him, and he with me."*

Saz nodded, "Yeah, look, it's OK, Sukie, I'm sorry I upset
you. I'll come in again, soon. And if you do remember –
anything at all – you will tell the policewoman, won't you?"

Sukie was asleep before Saz had crossed the room.

Saz left the hospital and headed for Patrick's home where
she was due to meet him and Lillian. She intended to explain
about the break-in, confirm what they now knew anyway.
She also hoped that Lillian might now be in a calmer state
and would perhaps be able to offer some information about
Chris. From what Patrick had told her, Lillian had some
ghastly stories about the time she'd spent in the institution
where she'd given birth, but it had been long enough for
her to possibly have come into contact with women who'd
had children after her. Chris was three years younger than
Patrick. Maybe Lillian would remember his mother.

She sat on the tube and tried to remember Sukie's biblical ramblings, wondered if there was any meaning to them. *I will come into him and will sup with him, and he with me.* If she hadn't known better, she might have thought it was a garbled reference to Patrick. But while she knew he had an appalling temper and was possibly capable of extreme anger, probably even more than she'd already experienced, Saz figured his violence leaned more towards the emotional and verbal than the physical that had resulted in Sukie's injuries. She was stuck on the memory of Sukie's whispered rant, disturbed by the preposterous suggestion that Patrick might have had something to do with it. But once she'd started to see meaning in the words, she was unable to dismiss the ludicrous thought from her mind. Until she remembered that Luke also owned an eating and drinking establishment. And then she felt worse than ever.

FORTY-TWO

Saz sat at a corner table with Lillian and they both picked at fresh olive bread. Neither of them had much of an appetite. Saz was sparing in the details she gave to Lillian. Patrick could hear the lot once he'd finished with lunch, but the tired woman in front of her was obviously barely coping with the massive changes of the past week or so. She didn't need to hear about Sukie's suffering as well. Saz explained a little about Chris and then asked Lillian if she thought she might ever have come across his mother.

Lillian frowned, "I've been talking to Patrick about my time in that place."

"I know, and I am sorry if this brings back awful memories for you; it's just that we really don't have much else to go on. We think she was called Sara Fisher, at least that's the name Leyton gave for her. And Chris is black, but not that dark-skinned, so all we can assume is that one of the parents, either Sara Fisher or the baby's father, was probably black. Chris doesn't want to ask his adoptive mother about it; he doesn't want her to think she wasn't enough for him."

"That's nice of him."

"Yeah, but difficult for me."

Lillian leant forward in her chair, toying with a piece of bread, dipped it into the plate of olive oil on the table. "I wonder if I should do this at home?" Then she smiled, "Not a lot of call for fancy bread in the B&B trade."

"No, but it's interesting that your son went into catering too, isn't it?"

"Yes, I suppose it is." Lillian sighed, brought a shaking hand to her mouth, "Look, there was a girl. A couple of years after Patrick ... was born." Lillian shook her head, tried again, "It's just that – you see, I did want this, want my child. To have him back. But for so long now, I'd thought he was gone. You understand? And I'm not unhappy, believe me, far from it, but I just ... I remember every minute of his birth. Every single minute. It's never left me. And neither has the pain of losing him. And it's very hard to adjust, even though this has always been what I thought I wanted. So I'm just not sure ..."

"You're doing the right thing telling me about her?"

Lillian held her shaking hands together and nodded.

"But Lillian, I already have this woman's name. I'm not asking you to tell anyone else's secrets. And, as you say, it may be hard, but at least you do have Patrick back. This could be her chance to know about Chris. And if she was lied to, like you were, then I do think she has the right to know the truth. Don't you?"

"Yes ... no. I'm not sure. The truth doesn't solve everything, you know."

"Maybe not, but I think she has the right to decide that for herself."

Lillian sat there for awhile, just staring at the linen tablecloth. When she started to speak she was so quiet that at first Saz wasn't sure if she was meant to listen. But she did.

"Sara was older than I was. She came to the place a couple of years after me. She was already very far gone when she came in, maybe eight months. She was in her twenties, I think, not a child like I'd been anyway. But she was so strong, knew what she wanted all right. Of course that didn't last long. See, she'd had an affair with this black chap, she wanted to have the baby, didn't mind what they were saying. I thought she was amazing, so brave. She wanted to keep it. Really wanted to. I know you think it's strange now, but it was very hard then, quite different, and we weren't living in London, you know. Her family wouldn't have it. Bad enough she wasn't married, they could just about bear that, let her move back home, stay with them. But then she thought she ought to tell them, prepare them for the baby. And that was it, the last straw. Her father brought her into the hospital the next day."

"He had her committed? Because she was carrying a black baby?"

"An illegitimate child, a black child, in 1962, and the baby's father not even in the country. Oh yes. It only took her father and two doctors to sign the forms."

"Lees and Keane?"

Lillian nodded assent, "Probably those two, I imagine so. You have to understand, it was very different then. Things have changed so fast – they were able to say I was crazy because I was young and I'd run away and I was pregnant. So, of course, it was even easier for them to say the same about her. But Sara wasn't like me, she fought them, screamed the place down." Lillian smiled at the memory, "She was magnificent. Threatened them with all sorts. I think she would have done it too, taken them to court, made a fuss, if she'd had the chance."

"What happened?"

Lillian shook her head, "Same as me, love. They told her she'd lost the baby. Told her it was her own fault for fighting so much. And then she didn't fight any more. She learned to stay quiet. Her parents took her home not long after it was all over. I'm sorry, I can't tell you what happened to her after that."

Saz left Lillian with her thoughts, aware that she'd been digging deep in someone else's pain, and yet certain she was doing the right thing. Almost certain. She went to the kitchen to talk to Patrick. He wouldn't be happy that she'd upset Lillian again and he'd be even less happy when he realized she was once more trying to get him to talk to the police. But, having seen Sukie that morning and after hearing Lillian's latest story, she was even more certain that Lees and Georgina and whoever else was involved should be brought to some sort of justice, and that it would take more than just her own word to do so.

Patrick did his best to get on with the last of the lunch covers, not especially interested in Saz, despite her new-found evidence against Lees.

"No, I don't care, you can take those other people's adoption certificates or whatever they are to the police, do what you want. But not mine. Lillian is more than disturbed enough. And you don't seem to have helped any today either."

He pushed her out of the way and screamed at a few of his staff to underline the strength of his fury, practically ignoring her until Saz reluctantly shouted over the whirr of beaters and chopping knives and clattering plates that she believed she had a name for Chris's mother – another woman Lees had cheated of a child, according to Lillian – and what's more she had proof Georgina Leyton was Lees' own child. From his affair with Sukie Planchet.

A cry of "He sold his own baby? Jesus fucking Christ!" rang singing from the hot mouth of the crowded kitchen into the subdued atmosphere of the dining room. Suddenly Patrick Sweeney's carefully reduced sauce was the last thing his late lunch customers were interested in.

Saz knew they had no way of telling if Lees had actually sold Georgina to the Leytons or merely handed her over –

as a gesture of goodwill, perhaps. She was, however, relieved that the extremely non-paternal nature of his act gave her a chance to wake Patrick from the trance of his culinary creativity. No sauce was competition for news of that ilk. Patrick handed over the precious substance to a terrified underling who looked as if he was about to wet himself with the weight of responsibility placed upon him. Then Patrick hurried Saz into the glass hole that was his tiny, messy office.

Almost an hour of argument followed. Saz wanted to go with Patrick to the police, take Lees' details, the stolen documents – she was willing to admit the breaking and entering even – just to get him there with her and hand it all over. Patrick refused point-blank to even think about something that might involve Lillian further. He'd spent every spare hour with his birth mother in the past few days. They talked on the phone when he couldn't be with her. She'd been spending time with Katy and the children. And, as Saz could see for herself, Lillian was still really very fragile. It was proving to be a huge adjustment, clearly much more difficult than either of them had imagined in the first day or so in Cornwall. It was all he'd been able to do to persuade her to get in a temporary housekeeper for the B&B and stay with them in London for a couple of weeks. Lillian did want to get to know Patrick and yet she was quite obviously terrified, guilt-ridden, heart-broken, and also delighted, all at once.

And Patrick was starting to discover that she could be as stubborn as he was, that underneath the carefully manu-factured ease and calm, there was someone just as forceful as himself. Saz tried to say that it was to get justice for Lillian that they needed to take this on. Patrick countered that Lillian didn't want justice, she wanted peace. A peace she hadn't been allowed since she first discovered she was pregnant. And that was all she wanted. After her latest conversation with Lillian, Saz could hardly disagree. Patrick went on to say that this was one relationship he intended to take care of for all he was worth. And no, not even her friends, the police-dykes, would do as an alternative. If Lillian wanted to keep this quiet, for the time being or for ever, that was what he was going to do.

"Saz, I'm as fucked off about all this as you are. But none of what happened was Lillian's fault, and there's no way I'm going to let you allow her to be hurt any further." He did though, volunteer that there was one thing he was more than prepared to do, "I'll come with you to see Lees."

"Why?"

"So I can beat shit out of him."

It wasn't quite the offer Saz was hoping for. "Look, Patrick, I understand you're furious with him."

"Furious is a very thin word for how I feel," Patrick's head whipped round to look out at the work in the kitchen. He wrenched the door open: "William!" The sous-chef spun round, terrified, "If that sauce doesn't get the constant attention of your tiny, fucked-up, dope-addled mind, you're out of here in two fucking minutes, got it?"

The young man nodded his head, long golden dreadlocks trembling in the harsh fluorescent light. Patrick slammed the door again.

Saz stretched her arms out behind her, trying to reach some life into her tired back and neck. The latest display of Patrick's temper had made her mind up for her, "No, Patrick, I don't want you to go to Lees. I want to do this properly. For once. Molly's right – I'm always bloody charging in without anything to back me up. This time's different. I don't need to risk anything, we've got all the proof we need. Or at least all the proof needed to start a proper investigation. It's just . . ."

"What?" Patrick's tone wasn't that of one about to be persuaded.

"I wish you would agree with me."

"Well, I'm not going to. I'm not going to put my mother's delicate grasp of sanity in any jeopardy at all. No fucking way."

"OK. Then I'm going to the cops myself. I'm not going any further with this alone."

"You don't have to. I told you. I'll kill the cunt myself."

"Don't be stupid. You've got every right to feel aggrieved and bitter and God knows what else. But it's pointless. Sure, you might hurt him, but what good would that do anyway?"

"It'd make me feel a fuck of a lot better."

"Right. And then what? He breaks your mother's heart—"

"Ruins her fucking life."

"Yeah, and you beat shit out of an old man. Brilliant. He's seventy-nine, for God's sake, wake up. Frankly, I think that confronted with him, even your bitterness wouldn't let you hurt a man old enough to be your father."

Patrick was silent for a moment, shook his head. When he looked up again, Saz was scared by what she saw. "You're wrong, Saz. And 'old enough to be my father' doesn't wash with me. Not any more. I didn't know it was possible to feel like this. Not again, not after Marina died." He dropped his arms by his sides, no words for the extremity of emotion, "Just to feel too fucking much. So yeah, go ahead. Run off and tell your girlfriends my story. Go tell the cops all about it. Do what you want. Because I've held Lillian sobbing in my arms the past two nights, held her from when she wakes after the recurring nightmare where she buries the baby that isn't dead, hears it screaming from inside the coffin that's buried too fucking deep for her to ever dig up. You go and sort everything out, Saz. Because believe me, if you don't, I will."

Patrick turned on his heel and walked back into the kitchen, shaking out his arms and shoulders as if shaking off the image of his mother's pain. Saz stood for a couple of minutes, watched him barking out furious orders, deftly slicing into a bloody lamb carcass, then she left. Through the back door. She didn't want to see Lillian crying either.

Saz got home to a message to call Gary. She was hoping for some good news about Chris' mother – anything to make her day seem slightly less wasted. She didn't get it. Gary had found a Sara Fisher. He'd also managed to dig up a reference to her having been in the same institution at the same time as Lillian, and she would have been the right age to be the woman Lillian said she remembered. Assuming the certificate Saz had found in Georgina's office was authentic – and there was no reason to assume otherwise – there was every likelihood that the Sara Fisher Gary had found details about was Chris's mother. The young woman had hanged herself a month after she returned to her parents' home.

FORTY-THREE

There had been a time when Sara was bright and exciting. When people had expected so much both for her and from her. The clever one, the forceful one, the ever-so-bright one. But, of course in the end, she had been too clever. In the first place they had tolerated her intensity, her excess of charm, believed it was part of the package. How could they have a daughter so admirable without just a few tiny flaws? And really, an excess of intelligent energy was hardly something to complain about – especially when others had so much more to deal with. And Sara was easy to tolerate; even when she went too far she was prettier and brighter and cleverer than the rest, could always charm her way back into their good books, knew exactly who to be in order to reclaim the place of perfect one.

She was the only child, finally born after years of disappointment to desperate parents. Later, the father would blame the mother for loving her too much. He said the long wait for a baby made her want the child beyond what was normal even for a mother, that she allowed the little girl to get away with so much more than was right. Later, the mother would blame the father, saying he'd always been too hard on Sara, expected far too much from the girl, demanding from her both the intelligent vigour of a boy-child and the sweet compliance of a girl. Demanding and receiving. They were both right. They were both wrong.

Sara was the much-wanted baby of eager parents, a prin-

cess daughter who could do no wrong. Her mother and
father were good, God-fearing people and she feared God
with them. They were honest and hard-working and,
because they expected no less from her, she worked harder
still. They were intelligent people who would have done so
much more with their lives if only they had had the chance.
They offered her their own missed opportunities and, as
expected, she did better with her life. Sara's parents'
relationship was strong and passionate, even late in life,
long after most couples settle to sweet affection and calm
pleasantries. And from them Sara learnt desire.

She worked hard, studied harder and played hardest of
all. When she left her parents' house to go to London, she
left with their blessing but none of their sensible fears. She
simply did not know how to be afraid; they had bred
strength and she believed absolutely in the path they had
mapped out for her. The obedience that rewarded affection.
The hard work that led to the successful career. The open
soul that understood desire to be part of love. Happy, too,
to accept the repercussions of desire. It did not occur to
her that the parents who had taught her to reach out to the
world, could ever disapprove of what the world then gave
her to bring home.

It had not been a conventional relationship. It was a fling,
a dalliance, a brief but extremely enjoyable time – on her
part as much as his. There was nothing she wanted nor
expected from him – neither marriage nor responsibility.
Her parents had made a wonderful daughter; they had not
made a conventional one. When, after a while, the passion
had burned away for both of them, she easily accepted his
decision to move on. A month later, she found she was
pregnant, and Sara realized that it was not, after all, the
man that she really wanted. She had been trained to be a
woman of the new world, but even more so she had been

bred to fulfil the destinies of the old. She was her parents' child. The years of their own disappointed yearning, all that time when the only focus of their desire had been the perfect baby, finally found its culmination in her. Though she had not understood it until the day she discovered she was pregnant, from that moment on, Sara realized it was the baby that she wanted. And all that she wanted.

Sara had not been abandoned or cheated or deceived. She had been loved – and then left – in complete mutual understanding and agreement. And, as it turned out, he had given her all she wanted anyway – without her even needing to ask for it. So she did not contact him about the child, she had no wish to trap the man, no need to lure him back. From her mother and father she had inherited the desire to parent, but not an attendant desire to couple. And, because she could not see beyond her own happiness, she quite naturally expected them to be happy for her – which they were at first. A little disappointed, but eventually accepting. And because they were so accepting she told them the second secret and again waited for their eventual support.

Sara told her story and waited for their reaction. She waited a long while. And when the answer finally came from a place of bitter silence, she did not know how to respond. She could not understand their fury. Would not understand that the people who had been her perfect progenitors could also be unloving, uncomprehending. They had never before wanted anything but the best for her and she knew that this child was only that. It was beyond her comprehension to believe that they would carry out their threat. And so she stayed with them a day too long and then it was too late.

After the baby was born, after she was told the baby had died, Sara finally appeared to give in. Became the good girl after the months of fighting and unpleasantness. Her parents were disappointed, but also relieved; if Sara was no longer the bright and exciting girl, the shining star they had loved so well, nor was she the rebellious changeling-daughter who would not listen to reason either. Sara was behaving herself. Sara was biding her time. And when they let her go she returned to the home of the loving parents, and spent a few quiet weeks.

On a dull Tuesday afternoon Sara wrote a letter to the dead baby's father. She sent it to Samuel Lees asking him to forward it to the man – after all, Lees was the only one who had ever listened to her through all that painful time, the only one who had allowed her licence to grieve for her lost child. She saw him as an ally in a small way, she trusted him. Sara placed the letter in the post-box at the end of her street and returned to her parents' empty house. They were out doing the weekly shopping, special purchase of tinned peaches with thick cream to cheer up the unhappy girl waiting at home. As her mother and father caught the return bus in the High Street, Sara hanged herself in the pretty pink bedroom in which she had so long, and so willingly, played out the role of dutiful daughter.

The parents buried their daughter and each mourned alone, blaming themselves, blaming the other. They did not find each other again in their grief.

Lees read the covering letter and felt himself vindicated in his decision to send the child to a better home – clearly Sara had been unstable after all – and then he took the letter meant for the father and filed it safely away. There was no need to send it on to the man, he had not known anything about the baby in the first place, it would only upset him. But, of course it should be kept, because Lees was a scientist; full and complete records were of the utmost necessity.

And Chris grew up to enjoy his family and never thought to question his beginnings. Until he was beginning a child of his own.

FORTY-FOUR

Chris was incredibly calm and Saz didn't know what else to say. They sat in silence in Chris and Marc's kitchen. She'd called before going over to their house and spoken to Marc. Chris would be home within the hour and Marc had offered to give the bad news himself. Saz wanted to jump at the chance, would have given anything not to have to tell Chris they'd found his mother but it was too late. Except that she knew it was her job and so Marc let her into the house and she waited for Chris. The minute he saw her there he knew something was wrong, thinking at first that perhaps it was the baby. Saz reassured him that both Molly and baby were OK, and then explained it was another mother and child coupling she'd come about.

Chris listened very carefully, then spoke incredibly quietly, "And you're sure she was my mother?"

"No, not absolutely sure, there may have been another Sara Fisher – though Gary couldn't find one, not around the same time and age. And this one was in the same hospital as Lillian – who did remember her, remembered a Sara."

"Who was having a black baby?"

"Her actual phrase was 'a poor wee coloured mite' – but yes. And Sara Fisher's name is also on the adoption certificate I found in Georgina's office."

"But nothing about the father?"

"Not that I've found, not that anyone's mentioned."

"Right then."

Chris sat silently for a few minutes and then added, "Still, at least we know my parents didn't buy me. I suppose I should be thankful for small mercies."

"I'm so sorry, Chris."

"Why? That we live in a fucked up world? That Leyton couldn't manage to sell me because they're all a bunch of racist bastards?"

"Mmm, that."

"Well, puts a rather nice inverse spin on the old slave shit, anyway."

"Yeah, but I am sorry, 'cos it is shit."

"OK, I'll agree with that. I'm a very hard done by little boy." Chris shook his head, "Christ, Saz, let's not get too fucking PC about all this. The world's full of arseholes, it's not like that's news. Not to either of us. There's no anti-discrimination laws for dykes, remember. Not that anti-discrimination laws seem to be all that successful, mind you."

"Yeah, I know, but you're black and gay. And adopted."

"And my birth mother committed suicide."

"All of the above."

"Fuck, guess I win then, huh?"

"Yeah, sweetie, you win."

They sat together for half an hour, Chris staring into the middle distance, Saz waiting beside him. The most sensible thing to say was on the tip of her tongue but she didn't know how he would take it. Eventually she could contain herself no longer, "Chris, look, I really think—"

"I should speak to my mother?"

"Yeah."

"Yeah. I will. Soon. As soon as I feel sane about this anyway."

"Good."

"And maybe there's some organization too, right? Traces fathers?"

"Yeah. Probably. There's bound to be. I'll find out. OK?"

"Yeah. That'd be good. Thanks."

"Don't thank me, I feel like shit about this."

Chris looked up, confused, "Why?"

"Well, I started out looking for your mum and found Patrick's instead. You got nothing."

Chris shook his head, "Nah. Not nothing. You did find her. There was never any guarantee she'd be alive, I knew that. It's not that she's dead, not really. It's the circumstances of her death, the fact that she was driven to it. And that's why I need to speak to my mother too. I really fucking hope that she didn't know what went on to get the babies."

"Well, you did say your parents always offered to tell you what they knew about the adoption. They can't have known all of what was going on if that was the case."

"That's what I'm hoping too."

There was another silence and then Chris asked, "Did your friend Gary know where she'd been buried?"

"I found out before I came over. She's in Cornwall. I've got the address of the cemetery."

"Good. Thanks. We'll go down for the weekend. We could stay with Lillian, I suppose." Then Chris looked around as if he'd just woken up to the room, "Where's Marc?"

"Out in the garden being sensitive."

"Sweet."

"Very."

Saz left half an hour later. They decided to wait until Chris had spoken to his mother before they did anything else about attempting to find his father or any of his birth mother's family. Chris wasn't really sure that he needed to go that far distant anyway – it was the father he was more interested in.

Chris kissed Saz goodbye at the door.

"I am sorry, Chris."

"I know. Me too. But I do have a family; I probably should have spoken to my mother in the first place."

"You were looking after her, that's OK."

"And I have my new family too, right?"

Saz nodded, "Hell yeah, babe. We're the brand new holy family, the four of us. Jesus, Mary and Mary and Joseph and Joseph."

"I'll settle for two wise men."

"Is that all? You boys are slowing down in your old age."

Saz left them then, still more angry with Samuel Lees, unsure where to move next, but certain she wasn't heading straight home.

Out on the street she made two phone calls. The first was to enquire about Sukie – and the helpful nurse she'd met a few days before and spoken to every day since explained in very gentle tones that Sukie had died early that morning. She'd been trying to call Saz but hadn't wanted to leave a message with bad news.

The second call was to her home. She left a brief, exhausted message for Molly, "Moll, I told Chris about his mother, he's sort of OK, he's got Marc with him, but you might want to give them a call later. And, babe, I've just heard that Sukie died this morning. I can't fucking believe it. So you'll be delighted to know I've had enough. I'm going to speak to Helen or Jude tonight, see what they say and then go to the cops in the morning, tell them the lot. I'd rather run the risk of a burglary conviction than let it go on any longer. I can't tell you how much I'm hating all this. Telling Chris about his mother was the most fucking horrible thing I've ever had to do. I'll call you later. I love you."

Saz climbed into the first taxi she saw. It cost her less than ten pounds to get to Lees' house.

FORTY-FIVE

Saz rang the doorbell, assured herself that Lees wasn't there and then waited outside his mews house for fifteen minutes before making her move. It was late afternoon, the small courtyard with just six houses was quiet and warm. The short, squat houses were wide for mews buildings, each one painted a different pastel shade and loaded down with window boxes and hanging baskets which matched the colour of the house. An easy earner for the job-lot gardener, and no doubt a good five hundred quid per house on the service-charge accounts sent out by the freeholder. Very pretty though. And very private. The house diagonally opposite Lees' place was clearly empty for the summer. Early evening sunshine was pouring into the courtyard and yet all the front-facing curtains were tightly closed; either the occupants owned the most delicate furniture in the world or they thought that keeping their curtains closed for a couple of weeks might deter burglars. Saz discounted the possibility they might be vampires, and settled herself in the sunny far corner of their doorstep, partly hidden from the entrance to the mews by a watering trough full of purple geraniums. There she waited, open newspaper on her knee just in case anyone noticed her. Ten minutes later a young woman, her sharp suit only gently creased by the hot tube journey, came home from work swinging an evidently empty briefcase and let herself into the house next door to Lees'. Saz heard her call out as she closed the door behind her.

There was no audible reply. Five minutes later the male version arrived, equally sharp-suited, matching briefcase in slightly larger boys' version. He too called out when he entered the house, this time to her welcoming yell. Three quarters of an hour later Saz was still watching as they left hand in hand, City suits and briefcases discarded, both dressed down for the evening. She heard dozens of silver bangles tinkling on both the woman's wrists, coins and keys jangling in his pocket. What she did not hear, either when the woman first arrived home, or when they left the house together, was the high pitched whine of an alarm system setting into action.

She waited another ten minutes just in case either of them realized they had forgotten something and then sprang into action. The mews houses had been recently renovated. And while the old windows were now new, the replacements were wooden sashes, not incongruous aluminium. Wooden window surrounds are far more attractive and authentic than the modern offerings – more expensive too. And less safe. Saz attached herself to the sitting room window, placed her good shoulder beneath the lower one and pushed upwards with all her strength. She watched as the bolted catch slid up, caught on its other half and held firmly in place. She pushed again and noted with satisfaction that she was marginally stronger than the pine frame as the bolt began to pull away from the wood. She then squeezed her fingertips into the tiny space between the top window and the frame. This time she hung off the window, bounced up and down a few times and let her full weight pull the bolt downwards. Four more attempts up, another three down, two broken fingernails, and the bolted catch came away from the upper window, hanging onto its lower half by one bent copper screw.

Saz lifted the window and threw herself inside, slamming

it down behind her just as a taxi pulled into the mews courtyard. Standing back from the muslin-curtained windows, she watched it stop outside Lees' house and felt a rush of bitter disappointment as an old man eased himself out of the cab with some difficulty and paid the driver. The taxi drove off and, after an age of fumbling with keys, Saz heard through the adjoining wall the ritual of door open, alarm call, door slam and alarm switched off. She'd been right to assume Lees might feel the need for more careful security than his neighbours. She'd also obviously arrived an hour too late.

She took the next five minutes to rush through the young couple's house checking out the layout, assuming Lees' place would be its mirror image. Even now he was home there was a chance she might be able to get in somehow, possibly do so without him noticing, and although creeping around someone's house with them actually in it wasn't her favourite pastime, at least she wouldn't have to deal with the burglar alarm. Saz still wasn't even clear what she was hoping to find in Lees' house, what difference getting in might make. She also knew that with Sukie now dead, she was no longer prepared to wait. Not a lot had gone right that day but the view from the neighbours' back bedroom filled her with joy. Lees in his garden, throwing out crusts for birds. Lees reentering his house through what looked like French windows into the kitchen, exactly the same as his young neighbours. Lees leaving the doors open to let the soft evening light and air into his house. To let Saz into his house.

She waited in the neighbours' carefully tended garden for what felt like an age but was in reality only half an hour. First Lees pottered in the kitchen for a bit, put the kettle on, fished some biscuits from a tin. Then Saz watched as he took his tea and turned into the front room from the hall. He came back for the biscuits. Five minutes later he returned, evidently having forgotten that he took milk, carried the pint of milk from the fridge to the front room and back again, leaving it on the kitchen table, the fridge door standing wide open. Every step with the slow deliberation of age. Saz thought he was taking absent-minded professor a bit too far. Eventually there was quiet. No TV, no radio, no clinking of cup against saucer, no rustle of the evening paper. Saz assumed that now he worked from home, Lees must have an office in his house, more likely upstairs than down. She figured she would be able to get past the sitting room door and up the carpeted stairs silently enough, but she had to hope that Lees' favourite chair wasn't placed directly opposite the door. It wasn't.

She skated past the sitting room door, which was half shut anyway, holding her breath and praying that the renovations had eliminated any squeaky stairs. Unfortunately Saz's perfect silence went unrewarded; the top floor was a major disappointment. Two bedrooms completely empty but for a single bed and dressing table in each. Evidently Lees didn't keep his place ready for guests at all times. Nor did he either work or sleep upstairs. Saz was furious with herself for not guessing the stairs might be a little much at his age and painfully slowly went downstairs again. She waited for a moment outside the sitting room. There was still no sound. Almost no sound. Nothing but the regular rise and fall of faint, rasping breath. Samuel Lees was taking a nap.

After a minute or two Saz pushed the door open. The room was bright with evening sun, net-curtained windows facing the main courtyard. It might have been a lovely space, carefully furnished and newly decorated in muted tones, but for the fact that this room was obviously both Lees' office and his bedroom. Filing cabinets lined every wall,

piles of papers were scattered across the floor and an array
of medical equipment took up what room remained. Sun-
light filtered through the plastic veins of three different
drips and an oxygen tank and fell in a tangled shadow on
the sleeping old man.

Lees sat slumped in a smooth wooden chair, the incon-
gruity of his wizened frame marked against the sleek lines
of the modern furniture and the fat brightly-covered
cushions. He had covered himself with a blanket which had
slipped off to reveal thin legs encased in old cord trousers.
He had fallen asleep, cold cup of tea on the table beside
him and a narrow thread of dribble running from the corner
of his mouth down an unshaven chin, three-day-old grey
whiskers catching his spit. Saz was shocked to see how old
Lees seemed. Though he'd had difficulty getting out of the
cab, she hadn't seen his face clearly, and realized that she'd
somehow not yet matched his face with the body. She had
expected the strong middle-aged man Lillian described, or
perhaps the Marcus Welby reported by Molly – someone
more youthful and daring than his age might suggest. And
perhaps that had been Lees until recently. Molly's last article
on him had been published a few years ago. Saz remembered the awful speed with which age finally took hold of
her grandmother; it had seemed that she stayed stuck at
sixty forever until the day she suddenly turned eighty-five
and that was that. This man had been working full time up
until five years ago and he was already seventy-four then.
Maybe the late nights and weekends of research had finally
caught up with him. The problem was that Saz could feel
the beginnings of sympathy for the man – which wouldn't
be very useful at all.

She began to move around the room, quietly looking at
papers, opening cabinet drawers. Although he moved a
couple of times, even muttered something once, causing

Saz's heart to jump and then collapse back on itself in a major adrenalin rush, he never actually woke up. For the next hour Saz went from one pile to another, becoming increasingly disappointed. Not only were most of the papers irrelevant to her case, dealing with government research grants, textbook infertility cases, breakthroughs in embryo research, but they were also in a worse state than Patrick's father's office had been when she first walked in. Papers from 1978 were shuffled into doctorate files from 1953. Memos Lees had hand-scrawled and dated only last week were in a file marked "Confidential – 1959". While she found a couple of letters from Georgina's office, they were merely form references to accounts and matters outstanding, nothing with any juice. After a while the fruitlessness of her search became apparent and Saz became correspondingly less careful. Placing another useless file back on top of one of the cabinets, she turned just in time to watch it slide from the top of the pile, see gravity take it in one of those slow-motion moments from the filing cabinet to the floor, via the full cup of cold tea at Lees' sleeping side. The crash of splintering crockery and splashing liquid echoed through Saz's head for a ten-second eternity as the old man in front of her finally woke up.

"What on earth? What? What do you want?"

She didn't quite know where to start, "Ah – you must be Doctor Lees." The old man glared at her, his right hand held tight to the handle of a lethal-looking wooden stick. But he didn't speak.

Saz tried again, "Doctor Lees?"

This time he shook his head, frowned, glazed eyes slowly coming into focus. Once Lees had assured himself that he really didn't recognize her, realized that a stranger was in his room, he shifted himself with some difficulty, sat up straighter in his chair and, as forcefully as he could manage, asked her name.

"Saz Martin."

He didn't look very scary. Saz hardly felt the need for an alibi nor, irritated as she was with the waste of her afternoon, for further deception. "I'm here about Gerald Freeman. His son. The baby you sold him. And Sukie Planchet. Her baby too. Chris Marquand. Luke Godwin. I want you to tell me about them. All of them. They need to know."

At first he seemed to understand, started to speak. But if Saz had been hoping for either admission of guilt or even more information with which to convict, she was sadly disappointed. Lees muttered a few words, repeated the names she'd offered him, stumbled in the middle of the sentence and then looked at her, raised his stick to her face. He asked Saz her name. And when she had answered him, he asked her name again. And then again. And again.

FORTY-SIX

Saz was just about to laugh out loud at herself, at the huge effort she'd put into breaking in, all of which was now clearly pointless, when she realized how brilliant it was. She simply ignored the old man. He was clearly upset and irritated by her presence, but that was it. Whatever confusion had gripped him must be fleeting, as he'd seemed perfectly capable, if a little physically unsteady, getting out of the taxi. Saz took the opportunity of his disorientation to go through the room more thoroughly.

She left Lees sitting in his chair and started to look through his files as methodically as possible. At first the whimpering distress from the old man disturbed her – until she thought about Lillian's distress when she'd told her Patrick was alive, remembered how she felt having to tell Chris that his mother had committed suicide – and then she found she wasn't so concerned for the old man's unhappiness. And anyway, after another ten minutes, Lees fell asleep again.

Twenty minutes after that Saz found a file with Jonathan Godwin's name across the front. Lees' filing system was so chaotic that Saz didn't hold out much hope that it would contain any information especially pertinent to Luke, but she opened it anyway. On the top was a note from Leyton saying he'd sent on a copy of a letter for Lees' files. The letter was from Gerald Freeman addressed to Jonathan Godwin, care of Leyton. In the letter Freeman expressed his happiness at what he called his "now complete" family and added that last year he'd had the pleasure of attending the christening of another child, adopted by an old school friend – someone else he'd recommended to Leyton. He wished Godwin all the best with the joyful endeavour. Fortunately no one was around to see the sneer on Saz's face as she made the old school connection. She made a mental note to ask Chris where his father had been educated and put the letter aside. Next she uncovered a baby photo of tiny Chris, almost identical to the ones his mother had in her attic, along with a selection of release forms for Sara Fisher. There was also a sealed envelope bearing a man's name and a St Kitt's address.

Lees was starting to stir. Saz realized he might well wake up more lucid this time, so she grabbed her bag, stuffing the whole file into it. Then she heard keys in the front door. The sitting room led directly onto the hall and even now she could hear the door opening. The room itself held nowhere to hide and anyway, Saz concluded, breathing deeply to calm her fight or flight heart smashing itself against her ribs, there really wasn't much hiding to be done with an old man pointing his wooden stick at her and shouting "Martin! Martin!" Saz stood her ground and hoped for the best.

Georgina Leyton walked in, evidently concerned by the fuss her father was making. When she saw Saz, she took a step back. "What the fuck are you doing here?"

The language didn't exactly go with the perfect couture outfit, but Saz figured she had a point. Before she had a chance to answer, Georgina crossed the room to Lees. The old man was still shouting Saz's surname.

"It's all right Sam, I'm here now." Georgina fussed briefly with his blanket, offered him the oxygen which he refused, and slowly managed to hush him. Her presence seemed to remind him of where he was and he became calm again, apparently more sensible of what was going on.

Georgina turned back to Saz, "Well?"

Saz struggled to construct a coherent sentence and muttered, "Yeah, the back door, I . . . um . . ."

Georgina nodded, "Yes, you're right. Security here is shot to fuck. Can I fix you a drink?"

Saz frowned, "No. Thank you. Look, um . . . I know that Lees is your father."

"Well, that makes just the two of us for the moment. I doubt he knows it. Not the state he's in this evening, anyway. I assume it's your presence that's disturbed him so much?"

"I suppose so, but what . . .?"

Georgina poured herself a whisky. "But what has it got to do with you? Nothing at all. However, Doctor Lees has senile dementia, Ms Martin. It's not Alzheimers. Not quite as fashionable, unfortunately. Gets far less press attention, hardly one of the glossy charities. But the two look quite similar. Sometimes he makes sense, a lot of the time he doesn't. It's quite tedious actually, though more so for him I expect. On the rare occasion that he does make sense, Doctor Lees is a very clever man. However, as you can see, he's also not an especially well man. Too much hard work coupled with a life of drinking and smoking. It must be very depressing to know so much and be so stupid. My father is a salutary lesson to us all, I think."

"You think of him as your father?"

"He is."

"Yes, but Sukie . . .?"

"The Christian? Not sane enough to consider good parent material, I'm afraid. Adopting has always made perfect sense to me. If one person doesn't want a child – or in her case, can't cope with a child – why not give the child to someone who does? Didn't do any harm, not to my life."

"Well, no, but . . ."

"And it's got to be more pleasant than growing up in care, don't you think? It's not as if I was brought up by bad people. I think I've been extremely fortunate."

Saz stood in the middle of the room, looking from Lees to Georgina. "So I don't understand, if you were OK to know the truth, why weren't you honest with the other people once your father – Richard Leyton – had told you what really happened?"

"He didn't tell me the full story. He only told me I was adopted. I did a little digging around of my own, but I discovered the whole truth too late, just like everyone else. Richard Leyton knew he was ill; lung cancer tends to give something of a warning, he just didn't expect it to get him so quickly. There were several projects he still intended to tidy up. This particular little batch of secrets was one of them."

"But once you did know about the babies, when you knew what the mothers had been told, why weren't you honest then?"

"I talked to Luke some years ago, gave him his mother's name, and a little more. I gather the mother reunion wasn't especially fruitful, though I know he made better use of the information about his father's actual purchase of a baby. You spoke to Luke too, I believe? I did tell him I thought it was a little unwise to discuss his personal matters with a complete stranger, but what can you do? The man drinks too much, takes too many drugs. He's not always as sensible as he could be. Rather excessively rash sometimes." Then she added, almost as an afterthought, "Violent too."

Georgina crossed back to Lees and placed his shaking hand beneath the blanket, smoothed his messy hair, stared into his face. She shook her head, "Look at him. He's the one who needs protecting. I've known this man all my life.

He was my father's oldest friend. Perhaps I had a duty to tell the other adoptees their truths, but I believe I had a greater loyalty to him. Samuel Lees was one of the most amazing, inspired, passionate people I've ever known. The things he's done in the past ten, twenty years – the whole new lives he's made possible for people who thought they should give up hope."

"Yes, I know."

"This man's work has made a difference to a huge number of people. Even if he hadn't changed in the past couple of years, all this illness, even if I didn't have to parent him half the time, he's still the same man. Why would I betray that?"

"But it's other people's lives."

"You seem to think you have the right to involve yourself in other people's secrets."

"To tell them the truth."

"And truth's the most important thing, is it?"

"It is to me."

"Then you're being very naive. Most people never know half their family truths, no matter who gave birth to them, where they came from. The whole truth is not all it's cracked up to be."

"Your father sold seven babies."

"Five. I was a gift. Your friend Christopher was free."

"Oh, for fuck's sake." Saz could barely contain her anger, nor could she just leave it. She wanted to make Georgina understand. But even more than that, she wanted to force Georgina to agree with her. "Your father – birth father – used your adoptive father to sell other people's babies. To steal and then sell other people's babies. The money that you were brought up on came from those sales."

"Hardly. Leyton had plenty of money of his own. The fee was an added extra. In many ways I think it helped the adoptive parents to feel it was real. For many people things aren't quite authentic unless they actually pay for them."

Saz tried again, "Your fathers deprived those mothers of the babies they gave birth to. They lied to them and took away the children they wanted."

"Mine didn't. She wanted God to smite us down, although I gather she eventually managed to find forgiveness for her own sins. Very convenient, this born-again Christianity."

"Your mother got beaten senseless by someone mixed up in all this and she died in hospital this morning."

"Sukie Planchet died this morning, I know. But thank you anyway for breaking the news so gently."

"Shit, I'm sorry, I . . ."

"It doesn't matter. Really. Andrea Leyton was my mother. The woman who gave birth to me never wanted me. She asked my birth father to help her abort me."

"Even if she did, she did give birth to you."

Georgina smiled, "For goodness sake, you're incredibly emotive about it all, aren't you?"

"What do you mean?"

"I never knew her. Not really. She didn't matter. The delightful little birth-mother reunion is not the ideal scenario for everyone, you know."

"No, but . . ."

Georgina wandered around the room, absent-mindedly moving the odd ornament, her mind concentrated on explaining her position to Saz. "Listen, she didn't want me and she didn't grieve or suffer a broken heart when my father took me from her. No part of her ever played a mother to me."

"She never had a chance."

"She didn't want one."

Saz didn't know how to speak to her. It was as if Georgina

had simply decided to unhook from any attachment, real or imagined, she might have had with Sukie.

"Is that why you got someone to hurt her?"

Georgina laughed, "Ah, no. I didn't 'get' anyone to do anything. Nothing quite so crass. The woman was a nutter. After you went to see her, she called here. Samuel's number is in the book. He isn't hard to find. You found him after all. She started threatening him. Hellfire and brimstone mostly. She's done it on occasion over the years, but it never used to worry Sam before. He knew she wasn't especially sane. The problem is, he's not too comprehending any more either."

"What did she want?"

"Promised eternal damnation. Which is not new – he's been guaranteed that ever since he became involved in the fertility issue." She smiled at Saz, "Especially since he got into the dangerous field of promising families to those who cannot have them by more natural means."

Saz had no intention of having this discussion. She didn't know how much Georgina knew about her and Molly, but she certainly wasn't going to give away any more than necessary.

"And you think a religious fanatic's threat could harm him?"

"Last week, following your visit, she threatened to damage my father, to expose him. Now, to most people the rantings of a religious fanatic wouldn't mean a thing. However, to the far right and equally religious who've loathed my father's ideas for quite some time, a scandal from his past is just what they need to damage the work which is going on right now, the work he started."

"But that doesn't affect you directly."

"Not so. As I appear to have taken on both my adoptive father's work and my birth father's secrets, that woman opening her crazy mouth also was threatening to damage me. And not only me, but Luke as well." Saz's stomach lurched when she realized that Georgina was confirming her suspicions, "Luke?"

Georgina nodded, "He has his own reasons for caring that Samuel's story is kept quiet. Unlike you, I'm not interested in divulging truths from other people's lives. Anyway, I don't know Luke all that well, we've done a little business together. But he does seem to have a terrible temper on him, doesn't he?"

Saz stepped back towards the door, "You told him about Sukie so he'd shut her up?"

"No. You told him about Sukie."

Saz's throat was dry and she found herself protesting, "I didn't name her. I told him I'd spoken to my client's father's ex-mistress."

"That's right. And I told him who the client was. Then, once she'd started calling Sam, I merely mentioned to Luke that Sam had received a couple of threatening phone calls from the woman. What Luke did with the information was up to him."

Lees started muttering again and Georgina turned away to the table. "He probably wants a whisky. He quite likes a drink at this time of the evening. It's often when he perks up, sometimes even starts making sense. Are you sure you wouldn't like one?"

FORTY-SEVEN

Saz stood stock still, the open door behind her. In the two weeks since Molly had told her about the baby, she had managed maybe one good night's sleep. Her head was racing, heart fast-pumping with exhaustion and adrenalin-amplified fury. And Georgina's calm was incredibly infuriating. Quite clearly she believed that Saz had nothing to touch her. Unfortunately Saz thought she was probably right. She watched as the impeccably dressed woman fixed another drink for herself and her father, her thin body and piercing blue eyes forcefully reminding Saz of the battered woman now lying dead in a hospital morgue. Despite the huge array of nastiness Saz had been exposed to in the past, the idea that Georgina could possibly have known Luke would attack her birth mother had knocked her sideways.

Although it didn't surprise her quite as much as the heavy crystal glass that Lees threw from his chair, delivering a glancing blow to her right temple. "Interfering little madam!"

He was obviously not as frail as he had at first seemed. Nor quite as confused. Evidently his daughter was right when she said he was more himself in the evenings. Georgina stepped in to try to stop him hitting out further, but Saz wanted to hear.

"What could you know about wanting a child so badly that you would do anything at all to have one?"

"What?"

"I've studied this: our society values a man by the completeness of his family."

"And a woman too, actually."

"We live in a world that judges worth by the most basic ability to carry out a simple primal function."

"Yeah, well, I do know that. But the fact that our society has iniquitous values can't possibly justify your behaviour."

"What on earth could you know of it?"

Saz wanted to explain that she really did understand, could absolutely empathize with the parents who had adopted babies from him. But while she knew what he meant, she didn't really think that stealing other people's babies was such a fucking brilliant solution. She would have said exactly that, except that it was clear she'd already said too much. Lees was evidently not used to being argued with. He wrenched himself out of his seat and, before she had time to realize, his heavy stick came smashing towards her face. She ducked away from his aim and managed to avoid the full force of the great chunk of carved ebony knocking out her front teeth. She then found herself smacked forwards from behind by something altogether larger and stronger. Someone who had come in the door behind her, the door Georgina had apparently left open for the purpose.

Saz was winded by what felt like a boot to the kidneys. She struggled away from the source of the pain, half-blinded by the tears stinging in her eyes, retching from the force of the blow. Georgina was screaming at both Lees and whoever was beating Saz from behind. Lees was half up from his chair and shouting down at Saz crawling on the ground, trying to catch her breath. If Lees hadn't been entirely aware of what was going on when Saz first broke in, he was giving a very good impression of being all-there right now.

"Those girls could never have cared for the children they gave birth to. They were relieved. The babies were dead as

far as they were concerned. They didn't even have to feel
guilty about giving the child up. I made it better for them."

Saz tried to disagree. She really wanted to tell Lees he
was wrong, explain that probably those girls would rather
have been offered a choice, that it simply wasn't his right
to make those decisions for them anyway. She knelt up as
best she could, lower back throbbing with the effort. She
lifted her aching head to speak, but before she could get
more than three words out, she was kicked again from
behind, her head this time smacked with the full force of a
big body behind the boot. Then a hand came back from that
force to wrench her upwards by a fistful of hair.

As Saz turned, crying out against whoever was ripping
her hair from her head, the other hand smashing itself
against her body mutated into a thick fist slamming into her
stomach. She opened her eyes long enough to see Luke
Godwin's enraged face. She registered who it was that was
trying to hurt her so badly, and with that awareness came
the knowledge that Sukie had been in just such a position
just about a week earlier. Rather than scaring her, the
thought of Sukie's suffering infuriated Saz. Though a good
head shorter than Luke, she wheeled him round anyway,
dragging him with her from the hold he had on her hair.
The unexpected force pulling against him sent Luke
sprawling across the room and slammed him into one of
the heavy filing cabinets. Saz ripped Lees' stick from his
flailing hand and launched herself at Luke with it. She
managed to get in a couple of good smacks across his face,
ebony into cartilage and bone, one of which resulted in a
very satisfying crunch and a nasal yell from his bloodied
mouth, but she wasn't quite strong enough either to beat
back the tall man's own physical strength or to defend
herself from the blind fury that was fuelling it. Saz managed
to pull herself up so that she was standing over him, but as

she did so Luke kicked a heavy foot into her left knee,
sending her flying back into the three oxygen tanks against
the wall. From there, half pinned down by the heavy tank
that fell across her torso, Saz would have seen the horror
on Georgina's face, heard her screaming, if all of her own
senses had not been filled by the slow-motion sound and
vision of Luke scrabbling to his feet, lumbering across the
room to charge at her, the full force of his right boot into
the side of her head, her left eye, her nose. Though she
tried to push him away with increasingly battered hands,
his foot wouldn't stop: repeated mechanical crunch of his
fat boot against her head, neck, torso. Lees' old-man
shouting and Georgina's horrified screaming, constant
counterpoint anti-music to the other noise magnified inside
her head – sound of tearing skin, cracking bone. Eventually
Saz retired into her own darkness, nothing left with which
to fight back, animal-curled against the next thrust of abuse,
a beating following her around the room wherever she
managed to drag herself.

Burn scars stretched beyond breaking point, the soggy
thud of thick-bruised muscle, roar of spilt blood in her ears
and the torn sound of frail flesh louder almost than her
rasping breath. Almost. The beating kept coming in a relent-
less torrent and, bliss unconsciousness agonizingly distant,
the pain wouldn't stop either, even when Luke left her alone
for a second to get his breath. Hurt shuddering through her
in nauseous waves, from smashed head down to broken toe
and, achingly conscious still, back again. Half-grasped
words of Lees' ranting far-distant, same old subject in his
mouth, same old battle in his addled head. Georgina
screaming at both men to stop their noise, their violence.
As if the whole thing had taken no time at all and then
again as if it were never going to stop. As if the hurting and

the noise and the hammering blows were never going to
stop.

FORTY-EIGHT

Luke had been waiting in the hall while Georgina went into Lees' living room. They'd both heard Saz's voice inside the room, trying to make sense of what Lees was saying to her. Georgina had rightly guessed that Saz would go to see her father once she knew Sukie had died. Luke listened in the hallway to Saz's argument with Georgina and knew he believed Saz to be right. Knew that he thought the truth should have been told long ago, that he wished he had not had to benefit from his father's lying. That if anyone should pay, it ought to be Lees. Unfortunately, he also knew Georgina was completely safe. That was why she was still able to stay so calm about it all. The adoptions had been Richard Leyton's transactions and even though she now knew the truth, she could always claim the privilege of client confidentiality. He hated Leyton for that. For protecting his little girl even after his death, while the rest of them had to put up with all the shit.

Luke was not rational. There is no rationality in beating someone into unconsciousness. Or worse. He really wanted to beat shit out of Lees, his fist and foot aching to smack into the guts of the myth-man Georgina had told him all about. But Lees was no great genius. The bloke Luke saw when he crept into the room behind Saz was an old man, talking bollocks, ranting words and nothing. He wanted to smash out at Georgina, but she was so controlled – and controlling. Knew too much about him. So there was just

Saz left. And all this had been brought up by her, of course, so in many ways she was to blame. Mindless violence. Of course, it was only later that Luke put an order to his rage. In the moment of the fight, it was merely the sound of fist into flesh that mattered.

Saz lay crumpled at the bottom of the bed. It was a narrow single bed and the room was dark, dark because there were no windows. When the building had been converted this had been intended merely as an additional feature designed to give the place greater selling power. No attic, no basement, but one tiny room at the end of the hallway, perfect for conversion to a miniature office, ideal for a small child's playroom, or just useful for storage. Human storage. Saz lay where Luke put her. She had not moved for four hours.

When Saz did regain a semblance of consciousness she thought at first that she was dreaming. Nightmaring. There was no piece of her that didn't hurt. Hurt too small a word. Didn't screech – fingernails on blackboard, brakes too late – didn't scream out for attention, for help. And, as she very soon realized, no way of moving so as to minimize the extremity of pain. There was no place of comfort. Saz fell in and out of wakefulness some times for just seconds at a time, at others for much longer. Longer than she thought she could bear to be sensible of her own suffering. In those periods she knew she should try to stay awake, that she shouldn't let what was no doubt a fucking terrible concussion lapse into something worse, understood the rational medical reasons for staying conscious in the place of hurt. But she didn't really want to, the pain was too great. And anyway, Saz had no control over the alertness or otherwise of her mind. The otherwise of her mind that far preferred to drift off into the place of less pain than stay awake and allow her to remember again the savage beating that had

led her here. Saz had no idea what had led her here. Though
there was a sense that maybe this was what had happened
to Sukie, that maybe it was her turn now. She remembered
an argument with Georgina, her own insistence on the
necessity of complete truth. As Saz's battered lungs rasped
through pooled blood for stale air, the value of total honesty
seemed more than a little questionable.

But not to Luke. Some part of him desired understanding.
He explained what had happened. Explained though Saz
could only hear half of it – wanted to hear still less. Luke
knew his temper had long been a problem. Something he'd
inherited from his not-mother, something he kept honed
with copious quantities of whisky and coke, sharpened
further by a life of not enough sleep and too many money
worries. He'd been a little fucked when he turned up at
Lees' house. Georgina had told him about Sukie and it upset
him more than he cared to say. He had never intended to
hurt her so badly, he'd just believed Georgina when she told
him that Sukie was prepared to tell everything. And he had
too much to lose to allow her to do that. He hadn't meant
to go so far when he went to see Sukie, he just intended to
frighten her a little. But she would keep turning the other
cheek.

Saz slipped in and out of painful sleep, moments of agon-
izing consciousness laced with Luke's interminable story. It
was Georgina who first told Luke the truth about his adoption, had sought him out when Richard Leyton gave her the
truth about her own life, found him by going through
Leyton's papers and looking up the adopted children herself.
She already knew Patrick; he wasn't worth trying. She knew
about Saz's friend, Chris, and had guessed there would be
little potential there. But apparently Luke was ideal. His
situation back then was not happy. He was not especially
close to his adopted father, was an angry young man easily

persuaded of the cause of his unhappiness. Clearly lack of money was all that was keeping him back and, according to Georgina, lack of money was the easiest thing in the world to rectify. No, of course Jonathan Godwin had not wanted to put his money into his gay son's nightclubs and bars – it didn't suit his image at all. But then, when Luke had first asked his father for help, he'd had nothing to bargain with. Now he had Georgina behind him, and knowledge. Which was power to a potential blackmailer. Suddenly Jonathan Godwin was more than happy to back his son's enterprises. Saz should have been interested in his story, but something else was going on, something that required her more urgent attention than Luke's story of his unhappy life.

Something was wrong inside her body. Something more than the aching muscles and the rip in the re-torn muscles in her shoulder and the too-stretched burn scars. There was the broken nose, the probably fractured ribs, the eyes she knew she wouldn't have been able to see out of even if the room wasn't so dark. But Saz felt as if there was something else as well. Something she couldn't quite get to, something wrong inside, internal, organic. Her breath went in and out, gurgling and painful both ways, but then it didn't seem to really go anywhere. Like the oxygen wasn't getting through, getting to the right place. She tried to raise herself on one elbow to help herself breathe, but either her arm wouldn't work or her brain didn't know how to tell it to move. Her brain didn't know how to tell the rest of her to do anything. Air hung useless at the top of her lungs. Saz slipped from the dark room into a darker sleep.

When she awoke Luke had been out and returned with water and food. He ate a burger and offered her some. It wasn't merely that Saz wasn't hungry; the smell of the food made the bile rise in her swollen throat and threatened to choke her. She tried to speak to him, but her jaw wouldn't work and even opening her eyes for a moment was a second too long. She welcomed the water he held to her mouth, let it fall over her broken skin, hoping that the rehydration might wake her up, help her to stir herself. Mere water couldn't accomplish that much, but it did keep her awake enough to notice again the shooting pains high in her stomach, then down across her lower back. And the pain kept her from sleep long enough to hear the rest of Luke's story. He was drinking again now, whisky this time, cheap from a local off-licence. Saz wanted the dark liquid for herself, blessed numbness of drunken stupor. But Saz couldn't even reach out a hand, let alone ask for a drink. She was the perfect captive audience.

Luke was talking and Saz had no choice but to let the noise of his words wash over her.

"My mother just wasn't interested. Not shocked or horrified like your Patrick's mother. I told her what Georgina had told me, how Lees got the babies and she just said she'd believed him when he told her that the baby was stillborn. She'd wanted to believe. She didn't want the baby."

Luke finished the pint bottle and slumped back against the wall, "She said that if it turned out that Lees had been lying, then the lie had paid off. For all of us. Lees made his money, she got rid of an unwanted child, and I had a family who gave me everything. And fuck it, I realized she was right."

Luke saw that he was her son. His drive to make a success of his life and his business – they were also her passions. She had been fourteen, turfed out of home after the first, fumbling, no-fun fuck with the next-door neighbour resulted in a mess of pain and pregnancy. Extremely religious family, horrified by what they saw as her betrayal. Nowhere for her to go, but they packed her off anyway. Didn't want her dirty soul to infest the pure home any longer. A week on the streets, praying that cold and hunger might make her miscarry, and then she turned herself over to the authorities, turfed up at the hospital believing they had an obligation to look after her. They did. Lees did. She told Luke she remembered him as the kind man who promised her it would be fine now. And it was. She was fed and clothed and given a bed. It wasn't home, but then her own home had never been that comfortable or easy either. And it was quiet, she was left alone. Every time Lees came to see her, he reassured her, everything would be all right in the end. She wasn't to think about how she would cope with the baby, it would be taken care of. She was a child herself, she just needed to eat and sleep and rest. So she did.

Three months later there was the long and arduous labour. Girl body doing a woman's work. Then in the end the Caesarian anyway and the baby removed quickly, too small, not well, and she felt herself falling into anaesthetic sleep, drifting into the welcome ether kiss. The next day the nurse explained that Lees was coming to talk to her. The nurse was especially gentle that morning. Lees sat by her bed and held her hand and told her the baby had died. And she didn't know whether to laugh or to cry. Knew she was wicked to feel relief, but felt it anyway. She moved back home for a few years and worked out her time in the family that demanded payment for her transgression. Eventually she was old enough to move to London and found work in the City. Some years later she went to New York. She became a successful career woman, one for whom children and family were not a priority – work was all. She'd had lovers and partners and two husbands. But no children.

It was what she wanted. And then Luke had come along. He did not know her, she did not know him. She hadn't even known he existed until now. She didn't know how to be a mother, it wasn't in her nature. The truth was, it probably never had been. She could not be sorry, she simply was as she was. When Luke left, they shook hands. They did not meet again.

That night, Luke went home, drank most of a bottle of vodka, finished off half a gram of coke and smoked a few joints. Though he lay in bed thinking there might be tears, none came. At least not before sleep. He woke up the next morning cooler and calmer than he had been for years. She was right, his not-mother. She was so fucking right.

As he explained to Saz, "We didn't need each other. And it was kind of a relief. Because she didn't want me, she released me. She made it all so simple. I really was grateful to her for that, honestly. I got used to the idea that my birth mother wasn't interested, and used to my own decision to not be interested in her. And then I talked to Georgina and she explained about getting my father's money for the club. So in the end, I got everything I wanted. Until you turned up."

According to Luke, Saz turning up was a bit of a fucking shame. Saz heard some of the story, maybe most of the story, she couldn't really tell and she certainly didn't care. She was in no state to worry about Luke's wounded soul. She fell asleep eventually and when she woke again he was gone. She would have cried if she could – with both loneliness and despair at being alone and in so much pain – but her swollen eyes and the salt of the tears made it impossible. It was becoming harder and harder to breathe now, had been for the past few hours. Like trying to swim underwater and not knowing how to come up for breath, swimming in dark water where you don't know which way is up or down.

And there was the other thing, the something else that was wrong, something far inside, under skin and muscle and flesh – that was not going away, it was growing. Saz felt nothing and then everything. Knew that this was as close as she had ever been to the edge, and then knew nothing at all for another hour. Tripping in and out of consciousness, sometimes Luke was there, at other times she lay alone in the dark. Time was now less relevant than her ripped fingernails, though she had no idea how that had happened anyway, two broken nails that had now multiplied into all ten. No comprehension until a single lucid moment when she remembered scratching at herself, in dreamtime in a place where she had thought if she could just get into the lungs that were filling up, just drain herself of her own blood, then perhaps she would be allowed to come up for air. Some part of Saz knew what to do, an animal piece dragged up from cave days and generations of healing grandmothers and weeks of evenings devoted to *ER* and *Casualty*. Saz knew if she could just get in and let it out, let out the own self she was drowning in, then she'd be able to breathe again. But she couldn't get in, her hands couldn't break through her own flesh, didn't really want to, wouldn't do as they were told. And then Luke had been gone for a while and Saz couldn't even stay awake long enough to remember what it was she'd thought the last time consciousness had blessed her with the gift of pain and knowing.

Saz wondered if Molly was pissed off. Molly hated her being late. Molly would be worried. She'd be really fucked off. Saz shouldn't see so much of Carrie, it only ever ended in tears. She would be a better girlfriend from now on, she would stay at home and be in bed by midnight and be perfectly happy to do so. She wasn't going to worry Molly any more. She was going to be a good mother. Very good mothers. Saz kissed Molly, held her close and naked and smelt her girlfriend's skin, the warm somewhere between sweet and sour that was the smell of just Molly. Before the perfume and the makeup and the clean laundered clothes. Saz held Molly, they held each other, heart to heart – not comfortable, not naturally easy, but Molly insisted on it anyway. Saz's mouth opening for Molly's tongue, the kisses on her face, breasts, back, thighs. Saz fucking Molly, gently for the baby, not gently for the lover. Saz's arms aching for another five months of waiting.

Then Saz's body was awake and screaming out again. Last scream, real scream, first time out of her mouth with actual noise in so many hours and raw and angry and primal and fierce and no Molly to make it better and then Saz knew she was definitely doing this alone and Luke was very long gone and had no more stories to tell and then, because she was so lonely and because it all just hurt too much, Saz was very glad to fall back into the dark.

FORTY-NINE

Molly waited until ten that evening before she called Chris. He sat with her and the two of them waited another two hours before they called Carrie. The waiting was less to do with protecting Carrie's right to beauty sleep than with the fact that getting another person in meant they had accepted something was definitely wrong. As long as they hadn't spoken to Carrie there was still the chance that Saz might be out with her. Unlikely, unusual, but not completely impossible. Molly dialled her number a little after one in the morning. There was no reply at first, but she let the phone ring anyway, just in case. Called on and on three times. Three times past the nice BT lady telling her there was no reply. Molly knew there was no reply. She could hear for herself that there was no reply. But she had no one else to call. She knew there was a chance Carrie was simply refusing to answer her telephone. She was right.

Carrie knew nothing about where Saz might be. And at first all she felt was extreme fucking irritation that Molly was being so paranoid. Until she remembered that Saz had said something about going to visit Lees by herself. She told Molly not to worry, she was sure things would be fine, but the minute she got off the phone she called both Helen and Judith. The two women were generally far too straight for Carrie to have much time for, but she'd known Saz to call on them in times of crisis and this felt horribly like just such an occasion. Carrie figured that even if Saz only stayed missing for the next hour, Molly's concern was a good enough excuse. However, even if Helen and Judith were dykes, they were also police – too much fucking police for Carrie's liking. The phone calls were fast, the tone concerned and businesslike, but not especially chatty. As soon as she put the phone down from her second call to Judith, Carrie called Molly back to say she was on her way north. Eventually. She then untied the brunette, they dressed as quickly as possible – far faster than either of them had ever managed before – and ran down to Bar Rage. Luke wasn't there and Sharon reported, extremely pissed off, hadn't been there all fucking night.

By three in the morning they had all convened at Molly's flat. Marc had joined Chris, Patrick arrived half an hour after Molly's call, leaving Lillian at home with Katy and the children. Helen and Judith put aside their differences to be in the same room for the first time in six months. Carrie left the brunette with her straight friend at Bar Rage and came north the minute Sharon stopped spitting invective against her delinquent boss. Molly paced the room, took occasional sips from her refilled glass of wine, snapped at anyone who told her she ought to sit down and look after the baby, suggested they go fuck themselves.

Helen was furious with Molly for not contacting her sooner. Judith was even more furious with Helen for showing how angry she was. She too was bloody pissed off, but doing her best to stay calm in order to reassure Molly. Patrick wanted to storm Georgina's office, Lees' home, Georgina's home, Luke's home. Storm fucking anything, just get on with it. Get on with something rather than sitting around in the girls' house just talking and doing nothing. Marc told him to stop being such a fucking boy and sit down. Molly threw up, cried, drank half a cup of sweet tea, threw up again, stopped crying and spat out that she didn't care if Patrick was being a boy, if his attitude meant actually doing something, getting on with finding Saz, then it was infinitely preferable to sitting around and waiting and someone should bloody well do something because if they didn't then she certainly wasn't going to fucking well sit there and do nothing and didn't anyone have a suggestion? Carrie looked up from the coke wrap she was getting out of her wallet – it was late, they were all tired, and it was clear that even thinking about sleep was fucking ludicrous – and asked if anyone had a handy credit card. Three cards landed on the coffee table; neither Helen nor Judith even pretended to look away. Carrie chopped the lines fast and fat. They went down even quicker. Molly gave up on tea, finished the glass of white wine she'd been warming in her hand for the past hour, followed that with too much coffee too fast and, when the others had left, Chris and Marc stayed behind to hold her hand.

While Helen and Judith made important business calls from their respective cars the better not to worry Molly as they described, in technical terms, what they thought was going on – Carrie and Patrick decided to take matters into their own hands, Patrick driving across the northwest of the city and arriving at Lees' house twenty minutes before the police. Plenty of time for him to smash in the front window and pull Carrie into the house after him. Even in the dark they knew something was wrong. When Patrick finally found the light switch on the far wall, they discovered they had traipsed through an upturned room – and what looked like several pints of blood. Some from Luke's broken nose. Most, though they didn't know it yet, from Saz.

They ran through the small house in five minutes, Carrie screaming for Saz, Patrick slamming doors and smashing

anything in his way. It took them no time at all to confirm
that Saz was nowhere on the ground floor and it was only
Carrie's quick reactions that stopped Patrick from going
completely crazy when he opened the bedroom door at the
end of the hallway upstairs. In a dimly-lit room, with cool,
even temperature and an ioniser providing clean, fresh air,
Samuel Lees was safe from the mess downstairs, quiet in a
single bed against the wall, tucked up warm with medical
equipment at all four corners, watching over him as he slept
peacefully.

"Jesus Christ, it's him!"

Carrie grabbed him and hissed into his face, "Don't
fucking touch him, Patrick. Leave the man alone!"

"Why? Because he's old and I shouldn't hurt him?"

"No, you tosser, because he's lying in his own bed in
his own house that you've just broken into for no good
reason—"

"What?"

"Listen to me, for fuck's sake – no good reason that the
cops are going to believe. At least not until you've explained
the whole bloody story half a dozen times, to three different
moron policemen – and you've already made a mess of the
crime scene downstairs, charging through the bloody place
like an idiot. Having a go at him isn't going to help one little
bit."

Patrick relented, stepped back a pace, "It'll make me feel
better."

"We're not here to make you feel better. We're here to
find Saz. This isn't all about you, rich boy."

Carrie wondered for a moment if she'd pushed it too far
herself, saw Patrick's hand flinch at his side and was
relieved when he simply glared at her in the half-light, "And
what would you like me to do instead?"

"I'd like you to stop acting like a fucking idiot and get us both out of here before the cops arrive and we have to explain why we broke in. Saz obviously isn't here, we've been through the whole house, and I don't know about you, but I'd much rather get on with finding her than waste half the night explaining all this to the police."

"Fine. Whatever you say. So where are we going?"

"No fucking idea. I'll work that one out in the car. Now come on!"

Carrie ran off down the stairs and Patrick followed her, a last reluctant look at the old man, sleeping oblivious to Patrick's malice in his nice warm bed.

Carrie and Patrick left Lees' house and drove south down the Edgware Road, three police cars coming towards them from the opposite direction.

Patrick put his foot on the accelerator and muttered under his breath, "Too fucking late as usual."

Carrie didn't bother to comment; she didn't think it would help to point out that Patrick himself was one of the main reasons Saz hadn't spoken to the cops already. Fifteen minutes later they had been flashed by three speed cameras and were at Luke's apartment. Being a loft conversion it was harder to break in. Patrick had to wake several neighbours before one finally let them in, assuming him to be a jealous husband and not interested in protecting the dead-end relationship of a pisshead at four in the morning. Patrick smashed in the door to Luke's apartment and when they didn't find Saz there either, he broke up what he could anyway. Carrie couldn't be bothered stopping him this time.

Molly sat on her sofa, her head on Chris's shoulder, eyes on the phone, willing it to ring. An hour later she watched the sun rise over the Heath. Marc made still more weak coffee and Molly stroked the small swelling of her stomach, wondering at what age you explain the word missing to a child – and then hating herself for even thinking like that. When first Patrick and Carrie, and then both Judith and Helen, called in just after seven with no news of any sort – neither good nor bad – Molly prayed. Though she didn't know who to.

Eventually Molly realized she had to lie down. She wanted to get away from the place of most tension, away from the phone that rang constantly but with no good news. She went into their bedroom, thinking that maybe she would stretch out on their bed, where at least the feeling of Saz was close. Five minutes later she was just dozing off when she sat up in shock, having remembered where Saz might be. She recalled a conversation after Saz had met Luke in the garden behind his bar. Molly hadn't been especially interested, had been much more concerned with the possibility of reinvigorating their sex life that evening. But she had listened to Saz's description of the bar garden; it sounded nice. And so did the designer flats Luke had pointed out behind the tall back wall, the highest ones overlooking his beautiful bit of green. And he'd told Saz she could have a look around if she wanted. The estate agent was a mate. He had a spare key.

London was well and truly awake now, the rush-hour journey agonizingly slow for Molly and Chris. They'd left Marc to make all the right phone calls, to get people to the new flats as soon as possible. But Molly wasn't able to sit at home and wait anymore. She knew that if Saz was there – and if she was hurt – then she'd be taken to the nearest hospital anyway, so they might as well head over the bridge.

They arrived just as Saz was being stretchered out of the building. Molly trying unsuccessfully to switch her brain from lover-mode into doctor-state, unable to look at the bloody mess of her girlfriend and translate the sight into the medical terms that might have allowed her a chance to cope. Molly wasn't going to get a chance to cope.

FIFTY

Lees was old and ill and lived on. As did the adoptees and the fertility clinics he founded. There were some happy mother-and-baby reunions, some not. At the clinics there were some successful assisted pregnancies, some not. Lees' name was dropped from the letterhead of the clinic where Molly, Saz and Chris had conceived.

Georgina's house was found to be quiet, tidy, and empty. A thorough search of her safe, drawers and cupboards revealed that she didn't keep any important personal effects – keys, money, cards, passport – at home. Nor, it was later discovered, at the office. Perhaps she liked to keep them with her at all times. Maybe she felt safer that way.

Georgina liked Geneva. She didn't like playing little wife very much, especially not second little wife, and Switzerland was somewhat land-locked for her ocean-loving tastes, but it was better than nothing. Luke may have believed her when she said she was covered by client privilege, but she hadn't been entirely certain herself. She thought she might as well stay out of the way until it was all tidied up.

Luke was found late the following night at a pub in Margate, beating shit out of the barman who refused to serve him – too pissed long before he even walked in. Three hours later, when they had managed to sober him up enough to make sense of his jumbled words, he explained that he had not left Saz at the flats to hide her, but simply because he didn't know what else to do and by the time he'd come to his senses, Georgina had already gone and he didn't know who else to ask for advice.

For a long time afterwards he thought he still heard Saz screaming for him to stop. Heard Saz and Sukie screaming for him to stop.

In going through Saz's bag for evidence, the police found the letter for Chris's father. Chris was allowed to take a copy for himself. But he held off finding out about the blood family until he knew about this one.

For two days Molly and Chris sat either side of Saz's bed, Patrick and Carrie pacing the corridor, Saz's mother and sister sitting silent by the window. And Saz's mother couldn't even begin to cry.

When Saz opened her eyes in the early hours of Friday morning, Molly was sleeping, her head in Chris's lap, everyone else asleep or dozing in the waiting room.

Chris was on his feet in an instant, "Molly, she's awake, quick!"

Molly held Saz's hand, her eyelids fluttering, "Babe? Saz?"

Carrie ran out to get a doctor. Chris waited until Saz actually focused on Molly and then left to tell the others, "I'll get her Mum, OK? I'm just outside, all right? I'm right here. If you need me."

Molly nodded, her only attention on Saz, "Babe? Can you hear me?"

Saz's swollen mouth opened a little, her dry throat rough and sore, "Yeah . . . Christ . . . what the fuck . . .?"

"Doesn't matter, hon. It's OK now, you're all OK now. You're going to be fine now."

Molly was lying, but then she was a doctor. She was allowed to. Saz winced, trying to focus on her girlfriend.

"Ouch."

"Yeah, very ouch."

"Baby OK?"

Molly smiled, "The baby's fine. You're the idiot who ended up here."

"Sorry."

"I know. Listen, Saz, you did good. They found Chris's letter in your bag. The one for his father. He might even have other relations now, aunts and uncles for the baby."

Saz tried to speak, but caught her breath suddenly as a sharp stab of pain ran through her, "Good ... baby's going to need family."

Molly nodded, held her hand more gently, stroked Saz's bruised forehead, "Don't talk. You don't need to talk. You just need to rest. You have to be careful now, most of you is broken somewhere."

From Molly's point of view – her job giving her an all too clear understanding of Saz's precarious condition – it was a gentle understatement. But her next request wasn't, she held Saz as close as she dared, "You really can't do this any more, Saz. I mean it. Not any more. You understand?"

Saz would have nodded, but her displaced vertebrae, fractured collarbone made it impossible, tried to answer her agreement but she couldn't get enough breath to reply.

Molly could hear Chris returning with other staff, with Saz's family.

She repeated herself, more urgently this time, "You hear me, Saz? You're not going to do this any more."

Saz opened her mouth a fraction, breathed in pain, spoke her whispered assent in a rasping shudder, "OK. No more."

Molly picked up Saz's thin hand, careful of the drip, and held it against her belly. Though she knew it was probably too soon to feel anything, Molly thought that maybe she imagined some tiny movement. The baby settling between its mothers.

When Molly looked back at her girlfriend, Saz's eyes were closed.